Seeking
Tranquility

Also Available by Amy Schisler

Novels
A Place to Call Home
Picture Me
Whispering Vines and *The Good Wine*
Summer's Squall
The Devil's Fortune

Chincoteague Island Trilogy
Island of Miracles
Island of Promise
Island of Hope

Buffalo River Series
Desert Fire, Mountain Rain
Under the Summer Moon

Children's Books
Crabbing With Granddad
The Greatest Gift

Spiritual Books
Stations of the Cross Meditations for Moms (with Anne Kennedy, Susan Anthony, Chandi Owen, and Wendy Clark)
A Devotional Alphabet

Seeking Tranquility

By Amy Schisler

ISBN-13: 979-8-9852232-1-7

Published by:
Chesapeake Sunrise Publishing
Amy Schisler
Bozman, MD
2022

To the saints, heroes, and everyday people who make sacrifices for the ones they love. May they know the true worth of their endeavors.

The Moon is distant from the Sea,
And yet, with Amber Hands –
She leads Him – docile as a Boy –
Along appointed Sands –

Emily Dickinson

Local Waterman Rescued by Coast Guard

Chincoteague saw its first boating accident of the season yesterday morning when John Herriot fell off his boat while trying to untangle a trotline from around the anchor. While positioning the boat for his next haul, Herriot became distracted and ran over the line. Herriot was bending over the stern in concentration when another boat went by, creating a tremendous wake that swept Herriot overboard. Commander Aaron Kelly was patrolling the water and saw Herriot attempting to get back on his boat. Kelly assisted Herriot. Neither man was hurt in the incident. Police are looking into the matter as a case of reckless driving, but so far, no suspects have been identified.

The Chincoteague Herald, May 10

Chapter One

Christy handed the police officer a bag containing a Pony Pork doughnut, a glaze-covered creation baked with brown sugar and bacon. Personally, Christy thought the mere idea of that combination was revolting, but it was a popular choice among the male clientele.

"Have a great day, ladies." Nick, a regular at the Sugar and Sand Donut Shop, tipped his hat as he walked out.

"He's really cute," Christy said in a matter-of-fact tone, watching the twenty-something in the crisp, blue Chincoteague Island Police uniform smile and wave at a couple passing by.

"And taken," Diane said. She nudged Christy out of the way and placed a tray of fresh doughnuts on the counter.

"Story of my life," Christy said with a smile and pulled out a sheet of wax paper from the box to transfer the doughnuts to the display case.

"What are you, twenty-three? You've got plenty of time." Diane smiled at the next customer and took their order.

Christy bit back a sarcastic retort that she was twenty-four and had zero time in her busy days for men, or anything else, and finished unloading the tray of hot, fresh pastries. She could feel her hips expanding just from inhaling their mouth-watering aroma. Cinnamon, blueberry, chocolate, and lemon scents escaped from the case in a mixed wave as she closed the door and hefted the large tray back to the kitchen. When she returned, after making a stop in the staff bathroom, adjusting her ponytail, and washing her hands, a lull had fallen over the Sugar and Sand.

"What a story, huh?" Diane asked, wiping down a table.

"About the boater?" Christy asked. "Does stuff like that happen a lot around here?"

"Not usually with locals, more often with tourists who rent boats without any knowledge of how to use them. Just wait until summer. All kinds of crazy things happen once the island is crammed with people."

"At least it keeps things interesting," Christy remarked dryly. Though she liked the island well enough—it was pretty, and the people were nice—she missed the fast-paced life in and around D.C.

"Any plans for the weekend?" Diane asked, moving to another table.

"Besides working?" Christy took a deep breath and blew it up, sending a stray hair flapping in front of her eyes. "All I ever do is work."

"Things picking up at the store?" Diane walked behind the counter, tossed the rag into the basket under the sink, and rinsed her hands.

"Yeah. It's getting crazy. I must have made two dozen shirts on Saturday afternoon, and it's only mid-May. That giant iron thingy scares me to death."

Diane laughed. "Custom shirts are the most popular item sold here on the island other than toy ponies."

"And doughnuts," Christy said.

"And doughnuts." Diane nodded and straightened the napkins, coffee stirrers, and smoothie straws on the counter as she talked.

"Are you going to keep both jobs through the summer?" Diane glanced toward the door once the straightening was finished, and Christy wondered if she was avoiding her gaze. She knew that it was hard on Diane if Christy had to run out before everything was tidied and ready for the next business day, but Diane was willing to work with her—so far.

"Unfortunately, I have to. I don't really have a choice." Christy bit her lip and looked down at her hands. "Now that I'm Molly's guardian, I've got to support us both. I'm going to make sure she has a good childhood and then goes to college. She's so smart, and she has the ability to make more of her life than I have."

Diane turned toward Christy and tilted her head, giving her a sympathetic smile. "You're smart, too, and you're still young. Don't count yourself out yet. Your ship will come in someday."

"Hmph. You mean the Titanic? It already sank." Christy crossed her arms and leaned back on the counter. Behind her were an array of blenders used to make healthy, and not-so-healthy, smoothies. She wasn't this pessimistic by nature, but today was one of those days. She felt the stress of their situation riding her like one of those mermaids with a whole ship perched on her back, taking the brunt of the wind and waves. And the ship that Christy carried on her back was in distress.

Diane gently laid her hand on the young woman's arm. "Honey, you've got a big, happy life out there waiting for you. Anybody who'd do what you've done deserves only the best in life, and the good Lord is going to see that you're rewarded for it."

Christy sighed and shrugged. "I didn't really have a choice, did I? Molly's my half-sister, and I'm all she's got with Mom and Fred gone." She looked up and blinked the tears away. Even after two years, the reality of their deaths still stung. She supposed it always would.

"I know it doesn't seem fair, but somewhere in this mess, God has a plan for you. Molly's lucky to have you, and your mom's watching over the both of you."

The bell chimed, and both women looked up at the opening door.

"Good morning, Paul. How are things on the island today?" Diane asked, giving Christy a chance to turn away and wipe her eyes.

"Quiet, just the way I like it." Paul took off his police cap and pointed to the coffee pot. "Could you make it a double, please? Stacey's the best assistant the department's ever had, but her coffee is like drinking brown water."

"Why don't you just tell her that she needs to add more grounds to the pot?" Diane asked, pouring a large cup of steaming coffee.

Paul shook his head. "I have. She says it's the maker and keeps saying we ought to get one of those fancy pod things."

"No!" Diane gasped, her hand over her heart. "Not one of those 'fancy pod things'!"

Paul smiled. "Laugh all you want. There's a reason half the town comes here for their coffee, with or without a doughnut. Everyone else has switched over to those machines, and the fine art of brewing a good cup of joe is dying faster than those machines can spit into the cup."

"Well, you don't have to worry about me switching over to a Keurig or any other fancy kind of coffee maker. I'm a little too old-fashioned for that."

Christy rolled her eyes, wishing they did have a Keurig so that she didn't have to clean out the giant, metal coffee maker every day. She hated that chore.

As usual, Paul tried to pay Diane, and Diane shooed him away. When the door closed behind him, Christy said, "You give half your inventory away to the local police and firefighters. Oh, and the Coast Guard, too."

Diane lifted her shoulders and let them fall. "They deserve it. It's the least I can do. Their jobs aren't easy, especially this time of year and running through the fall. They make a lot of sacrifices in the line of duty." She turned to Christy. "And we take care of our own around here. You remember that."

Christy nodded. It was a nice sentiment, but she had to rely on herself. Nobody else was going to pay the bills or buy the groceries or make sure Molly was taken care of. Christy was on her own for all that.

Diane locked the door and sat down on one of the stools by the counter. She brushed the short hair off her forehead and let out a long breath. She was more than ready to retire, but then what?

She tilted her head to the right and let it grow heavy, feeling the tension as the left side of her neck stretched and pulled, then she slowly tilted to the left and stretched the other side. Her lower back ached, her feet were swollen, and summer was still a few weeks away.

To say that she loved her shop was an understatement, but this had been her life for over thirty years. Her grandmother taught her to make doughnuts as a little girl, and she began experimenting with different toppings and flavors almost from the start. By the time she was in her early twenties, she was running a pastry shop in downtown Philadelphia, adding her own creations to the menu whenever the owner would allow. The doughnuts became the hit of the neighborhood, and they could hardly keep them in stock. When the owner wanted to buy the recipes from her and sell them as his own, she'd consulted an attorney. A few months later, with a nice fat check in her purse, she left the Keystone State and headed south to the Eastern Shore of Virginia where she had vacationed as a child. She bought a house and the shop and had been there ever since.

All these years later, Diane had many friends, a nice house that overlooked the Assateague Channel, a good relationship with God, and the desire to close up shop and spend the next twenty to thirty years lying on the beach, watching the wild ponies kick up sand.

She didn't regret not getting married. The right man had never come along. She did regret, though, never having children or grandchildren, someone to leave the shop and all her recipes to, someone to spoil on birthdays and Christmas, someone who would love her the way she had loved her own grandparents.

She thought that was probably why she'd hired Christy on the spot. The poor girl just looked like she needed someone to love her. When Diane found out that there was a younger sister, no parents, and no other family around, she knew she had to help. It was her Christian duty, after all. Yet it had become much more than that. In just a couple short months, Diane truly had grown to care for those girls. She watched Christy work her fingers to the bone, mixing, baking, cleaning, and waiting on customers only to leave when the shop closed at two in the afternoon and run down the street to work until five in the evening at a t-shirt and souvenir shop. Then she'd go home, cook dinner, make sure her sister was ready for the next day of school, and do it all again the following day.

Christy wanted no handouts, no free doughnuts or extra pay. She worked for a little more than minimum wage and some meager tips, but she was a hard worker. Diane learned that Christy quit college just before her senior year to care for her orphaned sister. The two had all but run out of the money Christy had saved to finish school, and what money they had inherited from her stepfather, Christy was determined, would only be used for Molly's college education. Diane didn't know how much that was, but she assumed Molly would make it through school without any loans. It was the here and now that was the problem.

Because Christy was so set on not touching her stepfather's money, she had to sell their house, pay off the mortgage, and move into the tiny two-bedroom cottage Molly's dad had bought for the rocket launches he sometimes attended at the Wallops Island Flight Center. With the NASA test facility just off-island, several of the scientists and other personnel lived in or rented houses on Chincoteague.

Diane stood and stretched, her back cracking all the way up her spine. She wished there was some way she could help Christy without the girl being able to object. There had to be something she could do.

"Marge? Molly?" Christy set her backpack on a chair by the back door and walked through the house. The silence was eerie, and she stifled a shiver that threatened to slither down her back. She called again at the bottom of the stairs, put her hands on her hips, and looked around, compressing her lips into a tight frown. She walked to the front of the house, opened the seldom-used door, and stepped out onto the porch. Christy always parked on the side of the house and used the back door, something she got from her grandmother who said front doors were only for salesmen and strangers.

A trio of young boys, about Molly's age, rode by on their bikes, and the two women across the street leaned into each other's yards. Christy often wondered if their whispered chats were about her and Molly, but she felt guilty at the thought. They'd never been anything but kind to her.

She craned her neck to peer down the street on one side and then the other. She reached into her back pocket and retrieved her phone. The screen was blank, no missed called or messages. Where could they be?

Just as she was contemplating calling Marge's house or the police station, she spotted Molly and the older woman heading toward the house from the park across the way. Molly was too old for swings and sandboxes. What had they been doing?

She furrowed her brow and squinted, able to make out something shiny in Molly's hand, long and tubular... Oh! She was carrying her telescope. Christy smacked herself on the side of her head. Of course. There was a rocket launch this afternoon that Molly had been talking about nonstop, along with everyone else on the island. How could she forget? She must be delirious from lack of sleep. She stifled a yawn and forced a smile as Molly and Marge approached the front yard.

"Christy, you should have seen it." Molly's words came in a fast jumble of excitement. "It was just like when we used to watch with Dad. We saw the whole rocket go up, and we could see the fire propulsion even after the rocket was out of site. It's just a test rocket, but still, it was so cool. It wasn't one that Dad worked on, but it made me think of him. And we still have the comet passing by tonight. It will be visible just after sunset, remember? Can we still go? Can we try to see it?"

Christy felt out of breath just listening to the barrage of words. "Slow down, Squirt, I can hardly keep up with you."

"That child knows more about the sky and stars and rockets than any adult I've ever known. You really should see if there's some kind of summer program she can do at Wallops Island." Marge smiled and shook her head. "Though she could probably teach those rocket scientists a thing or two." Marge flinched, realizing all she had just said. "I'm sorry, I…"

"It's fine," Christy assured her. "Molly's just like her dad. I know he'd be really proud of her."

Marge looked down at the ten-year-old, short for her age but making up for it in spunk and brains. "He sure would be. Anyway, you should look up their programs. Molly would love that."

"You know, you shouldn't talk about a person like they're not present. I'm standing right here, and I am the subject of the discussion. And for the record, I might be interested in a camp at Wallops if there's one that can teach me more about astrophysics. The book I got from the school library is quite rudimentary." Molly frowned, shook her head, and walked past Christy into the house.

"I'm sorry," Christy said. "She can be a bit pretentious sometimes."

"Not at all. I was being rude talking about her like that. Sometimes I forget that her mind is much more advanced than mine is."

Christy smiled. "Thanks for staying late and for taking her to the park. I'm still trying to figure out what to do once school is out and the Windjammer starts staying open later."

Marge waved her hand in the air as if shooing away a fly. "Don't worry about it. I'm having the time of my life helping you and Molly. It sure beats sitting in that stuffy old newspaper office all day. Best thing I ever did was sell that to the Kelly girl. She has a whole crew working there now."

"Kelly? Isn't that the name of the Coast Guard officer who saved the waterman?"

"Sure is," Marge said, puffing out her chest with pride. "My doing, that one. Kate came here with nothing, no money, no job, no local family, running from an abusive ex. And she had a baby on the way! I hired her right away. She was covering the local events for me when she met Aaron. He's an islander who got lucky and was given command of the Coast Guard station here in his hometown. Now, Kate's a real islander, too."

Marge smiled sympathetically at Christy and patted her arm. "Don't worry, sweetie. Diane and I think of you as a full-fledged islander, too. We watch out for each other here," Marge parroted Diane's words. Christy wondered if that was the island slogan, something they ran in the real estate ads—*move here, and we'll watch out for one another.*

"Well, as much as I appreciate your help and am glad that you're enjoying your time with Molly, I can't take up your whole day and your evenings and weekends once school ends. I promise, I'll figure something out."

Marge reached out and took hold of Christy's hand, looking her in the eye.

"What did I just say? You're one of us now. Don't worry yourself about what you'll do come summer. We'll all figure it out."

Maybe it was the island slogan, and maybe one day Christy would believe it applied to her. For now, she had a hard time believing that anybody in this world looked out for anyone other than themselves. That was the most important lesson she'd learned in the past two years— look out for number one.

The moon hung low in the sky outside Christy's window. She was exhausted, but sleep eluded her. She and Molly had returned to the park, with its big open sky, so that Molly could see the comet. Christy was certain it would be a bust, but sure enough, they were able to see it even without the telescope.

As they peered up at the sky, Christy saw flashes of other times they'd sat on a big blanket under the stars— Mom, Fred, Molly, and herself. Though she never had any real interest in stars or planets, Fred had made it seem so interesting and exciting. He told them the names of every star in the sky and talked about the space shuttles and rockets that visited nearby planets and moons. He was working with a team that was devising a rocket to go all the way around Jupiter when he was killed. The team member who spoke at the funeral said that NASA had lost one of its best and brightest, and she believed him.

Christy inhaled a deep breath and let it out. Marge was right about getting Molly into some kind of space camp, but how would they ever afford it?

She bit her lips and wondered... Could there be a scholarship program? Or something for kids of NASA scientists? Would Molly still qualify?

She dug deep into her brain and came up with the name of the man who'd said such kind words about Fred. Maybe she could find a way to get in touch with him and ask him if he knew what she should do. It couldn't hurt.

With that plan loosely formed in her mind, Christy closed her eyes and drifted off to sleep. In her dreams, she joined her mother, Fred, and Molly under the stars, and all was right in this world and beyond.

"Yes, I'll hold. Thank you." Christy sighed as she listened to the elevator music drifting through the phone line. She glanced nervously inside, but things were still calm in the doughnut shop.

"Christy? Christy McLane? Is that you?"

She smiled at the familiar voice. "Hi Mr. Patterson. It's me. I hope you're doing well."

"I'm great, thanks. And it's Sam. How are you? How's Molly?"

"We're great. Hanging in there. Anyway, it's Molly I'm calling about. She's really interested in space, like Fred was." Her words caught in her throat, and she swallowed before continuing. "In fact, we moved to Fred's place on Chincoteague, and I've learned that Wallops runs some really good camps over the summer…" She paused, trying to blindly gauge his reaction.

"They do. I've worked with them before. I'm sure there's a website you can go to for more information."

She was quick to jump in, and she hoped he didn't misunderstand what she was asking for. "Yes, I've been there, but…" She took a deep breath. "It's been tough lately. I never knew how expensive it was to live in the D.C. area. Even selling the house didn't help because there was the mortgage to pay. Fred had insurance. Mom's wasn't much more than what I needed for the funeral, but his gave us a little bit of a cushion. Having this house helped. It gave us a place to come and get settled, but money is tight, and I'm wondering if NASA offers any scholarships for things like this, for children of employees, or for..." She couldn't bring herself to say, "orphans of employees."

There was silence for a moment, and Christy worried that he thought she was asking for a handout, which was just what she was afraid of. Before she could figure out what to say next, she heard him take a breath.

"I think there might be," he said, and she felt relief wash through her.

"Really? That would be wonderful. Just send me the link or the paperwork, whatever you need. I'll get it in right away. I know summer is almost here."

"I think I have all the information I need. Let me look into this, and I'll call back if I need anything from you. Is this a good number?"

"It is, and thank you, Mr. Patterson. Thank you so much."

"Sam. And I'm happy to help. Fred was one of my closest friends." He paused. "I should have reached out to you to make sure you girls were okay. I'm sorry."

"Don't worry about us. We're doing just fine. I've made some friends." *If you count Marge and Diane*, she thought. "And Molly is doing really well in school. We're happy here."

Well, happy wasn't really the right word but for now, this was what they had, and she wasn't going to wallow in self-pity. Well, not more than she already did when she started thinking about her lost adulthood anyway.

"I'm glad, Christy. I'm really glad. Listen, I've got to run, but I'll get back to you once things are set, okay?"

"Sure, no problem. Thanks again, Sam." She forced out the name though it didn't feel right calling Fred's colleague by his first name. "I'll talk to you soon."

They said goodbye, and Christy went back into the doughnut shop with a smile on her face. With Molly enrolled in a camp for the summer, maybe things wouldn't be so crazy for her.

She frowned.

There might be the issue of getting her there, but she'd worry about that once everything was in place. This was going to be good for them both. She could feel it.

"You look happy," Diane said as Christy washed her hands at the sink in the back of the kitchen.

"I think I just found a way to be able to send Molly to a summer camp at Wallops."

Diane raised her brow in surprise. "Really? I didn't know you were looking into that."

Christy nodded and pulled a paper towel from the roll. She faced Diane.

"Marge suggested it. I knew it was a great idea right away. I should have thought of it myself. The only thing I didn't know was how to pay for it. I probably could have taken it from Molly's account since this is technically education, in a roundabout way, but the cost of college seems to be rising by the day." Christy looked worried, and Diane felt her heart tug.

"You know I would have helped you with that," she began, but Christy raised a hand in the air.

"Nope. I would not ask you to do that."

"I would have offered."

Christy shook her head. "I know, and I thank you. I called someone Fred worked with and asked about scholarships, and he said he knew of one he was going to look into. As soon as I hear back, I'm going to sign her up."

Diane smiled. "Oh, that's wonderful. Good for you for doing that." She felt almost like a proud mother even though she had nothing to do with Christy's ingenuity. "Molly's going to love it."

"I hope so. I hope they can keep up with her. I told Marge, Molly will probably be running the camp by the end of the summer." Christy laughed, but Diane wondered if Christy might be right. There was a chance Molly might actually be bored at a camp for kids. Christy continued, "At least I won't have to find someone to watch her all day for the entire summer."

"You know she can always come here and hang out." Even as she said the words, Diane knew that was an awful idea. Molly should be with kids her own age, enjoying her summer break, doing childhood things. And so should Christy.

"Thanks. You've been so good to us. I really appreciate it."

For the first time Diane saw a glimmer of hope in Christy's eyes. "It's my pleasure. Now..." She looked around the shop. "I think we've sold all we're going to for today. Why don't you take a couple hours off before you're due at the Windjammer."

"Thanks, but I couldn't do that. I haven't mopped or wiped down the counters—"

Diane took Christy by the elbow and led her to the front door. "I insist. It's a beautiful day, and you never take any time for yourself."

"But I haven't clocked out," Christy protested. "And my purse."

"Hold on." Diane ran to the back of the store and grabbed the purse from the hook. She returned to the front and handed it to Christy.

"Done. Go, find a place to relax and enjoy a couple hours of solitude."

She practically pushed Christy out the door before heading back to the kitchen. She glanced at the timeclock on the wall but didn't punch Christy's card. Diane had already decided that the afternoon was on her.

Christy started walking toward the Windjammer. She might as well get in a couple extra hours. She needed to get on the owner's good side. He wasn't local, and he wasn't friendly or understanding. When he found out she had a child at home, he didn't ask questions but looked at her like she was trash.

"Don't think you can have off every time your kid gets sick," he said. "You shoulda thought of that before you got yourself in that boat."

She didn't bother correcting his assumption that she had been a teenage mom. What good would it have done? He'd made up his mind about her already.

She tried looking for another job, but waitressing was out because of the late hours it would require, and most of the other places were operating on limited staff since it was the off-season. Now that summer was approaching, she could probably find something else, but why rock the boat at this point? Her schedule seemed to work for her and Molly, and she could always reassess after they'd been here for a while longer, and she'd gotten to know the other businesses and owners.

Except, there was no time to get to know anyone or anything. She worked from six in the morning until two in the afternoon for Diane, and then worked at the Windjammer until it closed at six in the evening. Soon, it would start staying open later, and she'd have to rely on Marge or pay a babysitter. Thank goodness Diane had suggested Christy talk to her friend, the retired newspaper owner, and the two had hit it off. Molly loved Marge, and the feeling seemed to be mutual.

Christy stopped before going into the t-shirt shop and looked up and down the street. Instead of working early, maybe Christy could take the time to check out some of the other shops. She might get lucky and actually find something better than working for Vince, pressing designs onto cheap shirts.

For the next two hours, Christy wandered through the galleries, boutique shops, and the bookstore. She made small talk with the people in the shops and got some great book suggestions at SunDial Books, if only she had time to read. How she missed reading...

She splurged on a bracelet with moon and star charms that she would put away for Molly's birthday next month. When it was time for her to go to work, she didn't have any new job prospects, but she felt good. For the first time in a long time, she felt like normal twenty-four-year-old.

Camp Openings at Wallops

Wallops Island Flight Center still has limited openings in its Space Adventure Camps this summer. Camp includes meals, extra-curricular and social activities, evening events, day trips, course equipment, and supplies. The co-ed camp combines fun and learning, providing kids with the opportunities to build and launch model rockets, code and build robots, and fly drones. Campers will participate in collaborative and hands-on projects designed to develop strengths and build new skills while working with experts and going behind the scenes at the aerospace facility. For dates and more details, see the Wallops Island Space Camp website.

Chincoteague Herald, May 20

Chapter Two

"I'm not sure I understand," Christy told Mrs. Daniels, Molly's fourth grade teacher. "She's already the youngest child in the class. How could this be good for her?"

Christy had gone to school with a girl who was a year younger than the rest of the students, and she had never fit in. She was teased and bullied and ended up transferring to some school where nobody knew her age or circumstance.

"I know that this is highly unusual, and that Molly has only been with us for a few months, but Mr. Urbansky and I feel very strongly that this is the right move for Molly."

"But what about everything she will miss in the fifth grade?" Christy tried to think back fourteen years, but all she could remember from that year was learning about sex education. Was there really anything all that important that happened in fifth grade?

"She would have to do some work over the summer, but for the most part, she would just pick up on everything next year without a problem. She's years beyond her peers as it is. She'd just need to learn some new math skills, but honestly, she could probably teach the subject."

"But sixth grade is middle school. She's ten. Is she really ready to be thrown to the sharks?" Christy vividly remembered middle school, and her memories were not pretty.

"Well, yes, that is of some concern. She's awfully small, and the high schoolers are going to seem like giants—"

"High schoolers? You said sixth grade. You can't be thinking of moving her all the way into high school!" Christy felt sick. What was Mrs. Daniels thinking? She wanted to stand up and bolt from the room and might have if the teacher hadn't gently laid her hand on Christy's arm.

"I'm sorry. I assumed you knew. Our middle and high schools are combined."

"You want her to go to school with high schoolers? She would be lost in a sea of bigger kids. Kids who drive and drink and have sex and—"

"Whoa," Mrs. Daniels said. "Let's slow down a bit. There are fewer than three-hundred kids in the school, and almost half are middle schoolers. The school itself is small. She would not be lost. Furthermore, while there are issues there just like in any other school, these are good kids, top-notch students who go on to good colleges and military academies. Molly would fit right in."

"She fits right in where she is," Christy insisted.

Mrs. Daniels sat back. "Do you really believe that? How often does Molly talk about her friends?"

Christy pressed her lips together and thought about it. "Well, she talks about her classes, science and math mostly, and what she's learning." *Actually, what she already knows and has to patiently sit through while everyone else learns it*, Christy thought. "And she talks about her friend, um…" She tried to come up with a name or two but drew a blank.

Shaking her head, Mrs. Daniels breathed in and out through her nose. "She doesn't have any. I hate to say it, but she doesn't have a single friend. She eats lunch alone every day, usually reading a book, and she never engages with any of the kids at recess. She either reads or does homework. She gravitates toward any and all adults who enter the room. The volunteers love her because she's such a big help, but the other children are intimidated by her. Have you paid attention to the way she talks?"

"What do you mean?" They'd moved to the island from Central Maryland, not far from NASA, and she didn't think they had any kind of accent.

"She doesn't talk like a ten-year-old. She converses like an adult. The kids don't…" She inhaled and thought for a moment. "They aren't able to communicate with her. She's years ahead of them. To be honest, Christy, sixth grade probably isn't advanced enough for Molly."

Christy sat back against the hard, wooden chair and stared at the teacher. She felt like she'd had the wind knocked out of her, but she couldn't disagree. She knew that Molly was academically superior to her peers, but to move her up a grade? She needed to talk to her mother. She needed to talk to Fred. She didn't know what to think or say or do. How was she supposed to process this? How was she supposed to make the right decision when, to her, Molly was just her little sister?

Mrs. Daniels patted her hand. "I know it's a lot to take in. Why don't you take a few days to think it over? Talk to Molly. I'm sure Mr. Urbansky would be happy to talk to you, too. I bet we could arrange for you to visit the school, take a tour, sit in on one of Molly's potential classes."

Christy just nodded. Her mind was in a fog. She stood quietly, thanked Mrs. Daniels, and promised to get back to her. The drive to the Windjammer was a blur, as was the rest of the afternoon.

The morning sun shone through the kitchen window, and the heavenly smell of freshly baked doughnuts filled the air. Diane once thought she'd tire of the smell, but it never got old.

"Have you heard anything about the camp scholarship?" she asked Christy as they filled the case with freshly baked doughnuts. The young woman had been lost in thought ever since she arrived.

"Yes and no. I got a call from Mr. Patterson saying I would be receiving some paperwork in the mail." Christy shrugged. "Nothing yet."

"Oh, you know how the mail is these days. It'll be here today or tomorrow. Or next week." She made a face trying to get Christy to smile, but she didn't seem to notice. "Is there something bothering you, Christy?"

Eyes, fraught with weariness, blinked once then twice, and Christy pressed her lips together until they turned white. "Can I ask you a question?"

"Of course, you can. I've always told you that I'm here if you need anything or want to talk." Diane closed the case and motioned with her head. "Come on. Coffee time." She picked up two mugs and filled them with hot coffee, then topped them both off with a bit of French vanilla cream. It was the only way she drank her coffee, unless it was a pleasant evening with friends and there was alcohol on hand. She'd gotten Christy hooked on the cream as well.

They took a seat at the counter, and Diane checked the time on the coffee-and-doughnut-decorated clock on the wall. They had everything ready for opening with fifteen minutes to spare. She waited patiently while Christy blew on her coffee a few times then took a sip. She put the mug back down and looked outside toward the street. Diane was tempted to ask her again if anything was bothering her, but the answer to that was obvious.

After a very deep inhale, Christy spoke, never taking her eyes from the window. She slowly repeated the conversation with Molly's teacher, the worry on her face becoming more evident as she spoke. The poor child looked ten years older than she was. When she finished, Diane took a long drink and sat back, trying to come up with the best advice. Never having had any children of her own, solutions to these types of problems sometimes came easily to her as they often do when you've no skin in the game. But other times, she had to draw on the bits and pieces of intellect she'd gleaned from years of watching other families tackle issues.

Much as Christy did, Diane took a deep breath and blew it out before asking, "What does Molly think?"

Christy's eyes widened in surprise. "I... I haven't asked her."

It was Diane's turn to be surprised. "Why not? She's the one who's going to have to live with the decision."

Christy shook her head. "She's a child. She can't possibly know the ramifications of her decision."

"Based on what her teacher said, and on what you know as her sister and in loco parentis, do you really think she'd make a decision through the same thought process as a normal child?"

Christy's face reddened as she snapped, "She *is* a normal child."

Diane felt the sting as if she'd been slapped and reproached herself for her careless use of words. "Yes, of course she is." Then she rethought the carelessness. "And she's not."

The percolating coffee machine seemed as loud as a train whistle as the two women sat staring at each other. Finally, Christy's features softened, and she slowly shook her head.

"I know," she said with a sigh. "She's not really normal. At ten, I was still coloring and reading Nancy

Drew. Molly makes rockets out of straws and paper towel rolls and reads Scientific American." She looked down at her hands. "I get it. I get what her teacher is saying. Up until recently, it never occurred to me that the conversations Molly and I have are not the kinds of things a normal ten-year-old talks about—dwarf stars and the theory of gravitational pull and the possibility of life on one of Jupiter's moons. Those types of topics were frequently discussed at the dinner table, so of course, Molly would know about those things and talk about them. But yesterday, the whole time I was hanging up shirts and folding swim trunks at the store, I kept thinking about the things I did at her age, and I realized Molly isn't at all like other kids, and it's not just because her father introduced her to all this stuff." She threw up her hands as though they held and released all the things her stepfather had taught them. "She *knows* what she's talking about. She *gets* it. She's years beyond other kids her age or even older ones."

Diane sat quietly and listened, letting Christy give more examples of Molly's advanced intellect. She nodded and made the proper noises when necessary but let Christy unburden everything in her poor, young heart, including her own "incognizance"—a word that made Diane smile under the circumstances—as to how to make the right decision.

With empty mugs, a ticking clock, and a room full of verbosities hanging in the air as if a cartoonist had exhausted his supply of word balloons, Diane knew there was no more time to dwell on the conversation. Besides, to her ears, the answer was obvious.

"I think you already know what you have to do, Christy. It's time to talk to Molly and see if she's in agreement."

"And what if she's not? What if this scares her to death?"

Diane thought about the precocious little girl and smiled.

"If she truly doesn't want to move up, or if it frightens her, then you can discuss with the school the possibility of waiting another year. But do you really think that will happen?" She stood and walked toward the door.

Christy stood, too, and picked up the mugs. "Is this what it feels like to wonder if you're about to make a decision that will alter the entire course of your child's life?"

Diane laughed as she unlocked the door. "You're asking the wrong woman, but in my humble opinion, as they say, Molly can handle whatever course her life takes."

In a folder tucked under her arm, Christy carried an enrollment form, a health form, and the letter she'd received from NASA letting her know that Molly had been awarded enough money to cover all three camps being offered that summer. She could have mailed the papers, but she wanted to be sure they got into the proper hands. She had to beg Dr. Swann's receptionist to squeeze Molly in for a physical and didn't want to lose that precious form in the mail. Besides, she was anxious to visit the facility ahead of time and quell any sadness that might overcome her at the thought that Fred wouldn't be there.

Taking a deep breath, Christy headed toward the building, reminding herself how proud Fred would be of Molly. The child was not only ecstatic about camp, she had no reservations at all about moving up in school and seemed relieved that she was being given the chance to attend middle school. Molly was also relieved that somebody finally recognized her situation and had the wherewithal to do something about it.

Christy smiled, thinking about Molly, and turned down a corridor that led her to the correct office. She handed over the contents of the folder, and the woman behind the desk kindly smiled at her and reached out a hand.

"Well, you're Molly's mother. I've been looking forward to meeting you. I'm Linda."

Christy felt a slight twinge in her stomach as she shook Linda's hand. "Um, I'm Christy, Molly's sister. And her legal guardian. Our parents were… They're deceased." She gestured toward the papers. "My guardian status is laid out in here."

The woman sucked in a quick breath, and her mouth formed that O-shape that people tend to make when they're at a loss for words.

"I'm so sorry. I just meant, I, well, I guess that explains it. It's just not normal for us to receive a check that covers the cost of all three camps and then some."

"Excuse me? 'And then some'?"

"Well, the check covers the camps and any expenses Molly might incur, and included with the check were these." She reached behind her and picked up a backpack and handed it to Christy.

The backpack was brand new with the tags still attached. Inside were a water bottle, a baseball cap, and a t-shirt, all with the NASA logo. There was also a bottle of sunscreen and a box of bug repellent wipes. Christy closed the bag and looked up, unable to close her mouth.

"These all came with the scholarship?"

Linda's brow creased behind her glasses, and her perfectly defined, red lips pursed. "Scholarship?"

"The one that paid for camp? It included all of this?"

Linda was clearly confused, but her features softened into a smile as she nodded. "Of course, yes, all of this was included. We're really excited to have Molly join us."

"Christy? Christy McLane?"

Christy looked up at a familiar face—grey hair, wire glasses, and a kind smile. It took her a moment before a name clicked in her head. She smiled broadly as she went to him.

"Dr. Johnson. It's so good to see you again." She reached out her hand but he opened his arms, and she naturally fell into them, remembering his kindness at the funeral and how attentive he always was to her and Molly when they visited here with Fred, which they had each time a rocket was launched.

The older man released her and grinned ear to ear. "I was elated to hear from Sam that Molly was going to attend our camps. I had no idea that you had relocated to the area."

Christy's heart ached for just a moment as she recalled why they had moved. "We had to sell the house in Rockville, so we moved into Fred's cottage on the island." She forced a smile. "We love it here, though, and Molly is doing really well in school." *To say the least*, she thought.

"How wonderful. That means you two can stop in and visit and attend our programs. That is, if you're interested."

"I think we would be, Dr. Johnson. Thank you."

"I see you've met Linda. You probably remember Jane. She just retired, and Linda is doing a splendid job taking on Jane's role of keeping this place running smoothly."

Christy smiled, and then she realized that Dr. Johnson wasn't alone. Behind him stood a young man, who seemed to appear out of nowhere, with dark curly hair and bright blue eyes hidden behind thick glasses, which he nervously pushed up on his nose. She looked at him and smiled.

"Hi," she said.

"Oh!" Dr. Johnson jumped as though he'd forgotten the man was behind him. "Christy, this is Jared Stevenson. He's just beginning the summer here with us.

He'll be helping with some of the camp programs, so you may see him from time to time."

Christy reached out her hand. "Hi, I'm Christy McLane. My adopted father, Fred, worked here occasionally."

The man's eyes suddenly lit up, the bulb in his head switching on with realization. "Fred McLane? As in Dr. Frederick McLane, the man behind the Jupiter Papers?" His eyes were wide with awe. "I've read them at least six times. He was brilliant." Christy flinched at the word *was*. Perhaps realizing he said something wrong, his face turned red, and he looked down at his shoes.

"Yeah, I suppose so. Fred was great. My biological father passed away when I was three, and Fred married my mother and adopted me. My sister, Molly, is theirs." It always felt funny to admit that, the fact that Molly was 'theirs' while she wasn't. Though she rarely called Fred her father, he truly was in every sense of the word.

Sensing her discomfort, or perhaps just wanting to move things along, Dr. Johnson looked past her. "Linda, is everything in order for Molly to attend camp?"

"Yes, Dr. Johnson. The, um, scholarship has been applied, and I gave Ms. McLane the other items."

Dr. Johnson looked down at the backpack that Christy clutched. "Wonderful. I look forward to seeing you and Molly around this summer. If either of you needs anything, anything at all, don't hesitate to contact me." He reached into his pocket and took out a gold case from which he extracted a business card. He handed

Christy the card. "I mean that. Anything you need, you just call or email me."

She glanced at the card.

Dr. Simon Johnson, Ph.D., Planetary Sciences, Astronomy, and Astrophysics

She felt her fingers tighten around the card with the familiar accolades behind the name, then she felt a twinge of pride. Perhaps Molly's name would someday be on a card like this. Her fingers relaxed, and she looked up at Dr. Johnson and smiled.

"Thank you. Molly is so excited about camp. We'll be counting the days until summer."

She said her goodbyes and went out to her car, placing the backpack on the seat beside her. There was something strange about the scholarship and all that it included, but she wasn't going to question it. Whatever had been arranged was for Molly's benefit, and for that, Christy was eternally grateful.

"These are all for me?" Molly's eyes were wide as she emptied the contents of the backpack, one by one, onto the kitchen table.

"All for you, Squirt. I think you're an official NASA camper now."

"This is so incredible! I can't believe I'm going to a camp at NASA."

"Well, technically, you're going to a camp at a flight facility operated by NASA. I mean, it's not exactly the same."

"You're wrong," Molly said, her eyes wide and blinking like an owl's. "It's NASA's premier location for conducting research using suborbital vehicles. They've launched more than sixteen-thousand rockets into space, and they track low-orbiting spacecraft. The facility conducts about fifty missions a year, and..." She elongated the word and paused dramatically. "It has even sent supplies to the International Space Station." She nodded her head as though to punctuate the importance of her words.

"Wow, I'm impressed," Christy said, and she meant it.

"They do impressive stuff," Molly said, tugging off her shirt and pulling the NASA tee on instead.

"Not with the rockets, with you. I'm impressed by you. How do you know all that?"

Molly cocked her head to the side and blinked several times, giving Christy a look Molly had perfected to show how underestimated she felt she was. "I read. Duh. And I followed Dad's work. He was a genius, you know."

"You don't say," Christy mused, knowing the apple didn't fall far from the tree.

"You know, he could have worked at Cape Canaveral or the Johnson Space Center if he'd wanted to, but Dad liked it here. And at Goddard. He said the other places were too big and fussy." She wrinkled her nose as she opened the step stool and climbed up to the sink to fill her water bottle.

"Molly, I haven't washed that yet." Christy reached for the bottle, but Molly nudged her away, finished filling it, and twisted on the cap.

"It doesn't need washing. It's healthier to introduce the body to a variety of germs before adulthood." She hopped down and gathered her things. "Call me when dinner's ready. I have to get started on my math homework. Mrs. Daniels wants to see how much I can do before the school year ends. I looked at it on the bus ride, though, and it's nothing like the stuff I watched Dad do. I should have it all finished within a week at most. I'm hoping to skip sixth grade math and move right into algebra. That way I can start trigonometry by ninth grade. I wonder if the school has an astronomy class…" Her voice trailed off as her bedroom door closed.

Christy leaned against the kitchen counter and released a stream of air. Her little sister was quickly outgrowing her.

Great White Makes Late Return

OCEARCH reported that Mary Lee, a popular Great White Shark, has made a late return to the coastal waters off Assateague. Tagged with a transmitter on September 17, 2012, Mary Lee is a favorite of shark watchers, and her return creates a frenzy of enthusiastic fans trying to catch a glimpse of the Great White. Named after the mother of OCEARCH expedition leader, Chris Fischer, Mary Lee typically finds her way to the area in early May and is usually far from these waters by the time swim season begins. The shark's return sent warning signals of various kinds to everyone on the island. Why was she so late in returning to the area? How long will she stay? Are there other sharks with her? Is it safe to go into the water? Scientists and Beachgoers alike can't help but marvel while at the same time, remain wary of what this means for the summer.

The Chincoteague Herald, May 28

Chapter Three

"Well?" Diane asked when Christy appeared in the kitchen mid-morning on Monday. "How did the tour go?"

"Good. Molly liked the school. The principal was nice, shocked when Molly told her that she'd done almost a year's worth of math in one weekend." Christy smiled but shook her head. "She's pretty amazing, and I know this is the right thing for her academically, but socially? I'm so scared I'm making a mistake." As she talked, Christy hung her purse on the hook and clocked in. "What do I do if she's miserable?"

"It sounds to me like she was miserable where she was, or at least, making the best of a bad situation that didn't help her get ahead or feel comfortable."

Christy reached for her apron and put it over her t-shirt. "I know. It's just that…"

"You're all she has, and you know that every decision you make will impact her future."

Christy blew out of puffed cheeks. "Gee, thanks. That's exactly it."

Diane checked on the doughnuts in the oven. She had an order from the Ladies Auxiliary of the American Legion for two dozen of her secret recipe cinnamon apple cake doughnuts. She closed the oven and faced her young employee. "You're doing just fine. And if I've gotten to know Molly at all, I know that she will let you know if you aren't."

Christy smiled. "You're right. She has no problem telling me when I'm wrong."

The bell on the front door jingled. "I'll go out," Christy said.

"Yell if you need me," Diane called, reaching for a potholder to pull the trays from the oven. She heard a male's voice and the sound of surprise in Christy's cheerful response. Setting the pan on the cooling rack, she peeked into the storeroom.

"Yes, please. Assorted would be great."

The young man pushed his glasses up onto the bridge of his nose and looked around the shop.

"How do you like it here so far?" Christy asked as she added doughnuts to a box.

"I don't know yet. This is actually my first trip onto the island. I've only been here for a week."

"Where are you staying?"

They clearly knew each other, which Diane found interesting. Christy didn't seem to know anyone except the few people she worked with and Molly's teacher.

"They've got a few cottages on-site for interns. I share one with another guy. He's from Lancaster. In Pennsylvania."

Christy's hand stopped mid-air, and she smiled at the man. "Yes, I know where Lancaster is."

"Oh, sorry." His face reddened as he pushed up his glasses again. A nervous habit, then, rather than a poor fit. "I didn't know if you were from this area."

Christy resumed packing the box. "From the Western side of the Chesapeake Bay originally, but yeah, the Mid-Atlantic area. What about you? Where are you from?"

"A few different places. I've lived in Massachusetts for a while now, college and grad school." He looked away, seemingly embarrassed, and Diane wondered why.

"Boston?" Christy asked as she closed the pastry case.

The man shook his head. "Cambridge." He looked away again, and Christy's mouth hung open for a moment before she closed it.

"Oh," she said before tucking the wax paper neatly into the box. "The big H. Fred went there, too."

"Yeah, I know. He was one of the reasons I applied. I always hoped maybe he'd do a guest professor gig there or something."

Christy smiled. "Actually, he would have liked that. He was a fantastic teacher as far as Molly was concerned. Wait until you meet her. She's going to blow you away."

Diane watched as Christy walked to the cash register and rang up the order. The man—he really was quite cute with that curly hair, those big, blue eyes, and his adorable shyness—reached into his pocket and produced a credit card.

"Can I use this? It belongs to NASA."

"No problem. Any coffee? We really do make the best around."

"We've got one of those Keurig things, but thanks."

Diane smiled at that.

"But maybe…"

Christy looked up.

"Maybe I could get one to go. Since you said it's the best."

He gave what almost passed for a smile, his cheeks flooding with color, and Diane's own heart pitter-pattered. Yes, he really was adorable. And just about Christy's age…

"Okay," Christy said. "Let me get that."

"Um, can we go ahead and run these through first? I don't want to charge the coffee on this card."

Christy stopped and nodded. "Oh, yeah, sure. That makes sense."

"Thanks."

The young man watched Christy's hands gracefully run the card, but when she looked up to hand him his receipt, he quickly looked away and took it with a nervous but polite motion.

"Cream or sugar in your coffee?"

"No, thanks."

When Christy stepped away to make his coffee, his eyes followed her every movement, from picking up his to-go cup, to filling the cup from the spout, to carefully sealing the lid. Only, Diane realized, his eyes weren't on her hands but on the hair that streamed down from her ponytail and the bit of her face that he could see when she turned to reach for the lid. As she turned around, he blushed again and looked directly at the cup she was carrying rather than her face.

It was a beautiful dance they orchestrated as Christy made the coffee, glided to the register, and finished the sale while his eyes followed her back and forth behind the counter as though mesmerized by the sway of a honeybee in flight. She was completely unaware of the effect she had on him, and Diane smiled at his attempt to keep it that way.

The bell jingled, and both Diane and the young man startled.

"Good morning, ladies," Nick called, tipping his hat as he walked across the room.

"I've got Nick. You go ahead and finish here," Diane said, scooting behind Christy.

Once Nick was out the door and the next three customers who followed in on his heels were taken care of, Diane looked at Christy.

"Did you know that young man?"

Christy wrinkled her brow in confusion. "Dean? From next door?"

Diane shook her head. "No, the first one. With the curly hair and glasses."

Christy's face relaxed, and she shook her head. "Not really. His name's Jake or Jed, or... Jared! It's Jared. I met him the other day when I dropped off Molly's camp papers. He's an intern at Wallops."

"He seems nice."

Christy wrinkled her nose. "I guess so. Quiet. Smart, too. He went to Harvard. Or goes there, maybe. I'm not sure." She grabbed a dishcloth and began wiping down the counter.

Diane acted as though she hadn't overheard the small bits of conversation they had. "Oh? Another rocket scientist in the making?"

Christy shrugged. "I guess so. He's a fan of Fred's."

"Fred had fans?" Diane didn't know that was a thing—to be a fan of a little-known rocket scientist.

"I guess. He said he read one of Fred's papers. That's all he said though. Except he just told me that he went to Harvard because Fred went there." She made a face somewhere between dismay and bewilderment. "Is that weird? I mean in a stalker kind of way?"

Diane shook her head. "I don't think so. I always wanted to learn to cook at the Cordon Bleu because Julia Child went there."

"Hmm…"

"Anyway, he seemed nice. From the split second I saw him anyway." She cast a sidelong glance at Christy who seemed lost in thought. "Do you think so?"

"Huh? What? Sorry, I was thinking about stalkers. What did you ask?" She smiled but looked like her mind was elsewhere.

"Nothing, dear. It wasn't important," Diane said as the bell rang again.

The rest of the month flew by faster than the hummingbirds in Diane's feeders in front of the doughnut shop. Before Christy could process the movement of time, the island was packed with people, and the Sugar and Sand and the Windjammer were busier than beehives on a spring day. June was almost over, and camp was beginning. Packs of boys and girls from ages five to fifteen gathered at the drop-off location inside the facility to be checked in by a dozen or so men and women around Christy's age. While they waited to be checked in, Christy gazed around the room and felt self-conscious in her Sugar and Sand t-shirt next to all the NASA Staff logos.

"Hey," said a familiar voice, and she turned and met the blue eyes that sparkled behind Jared's glasses. She gave him a wry smile.

"Hey. There are a lot of kids here."

He looked around. "Yeah. These are popular camps."

"I never went to camp. I always wanted to go to a sleepaway camp, but until Mom married Fred, well, it just wasn't possible." She felt herself blush. It wasn't that they were poor or anything, but there wasn't much extra for things like camp.

"Me neither. We moved too much."

"Which group will you be working with?"

"I'll be helping a little with the Space Camp. It's a lot more advanced than the eco-camps and more aligned with my field of interest."

"I was surprised that they offer eco-camps that are marine biology-based." She watched a couple boys roughhouse as their workout gear-clad mothers chatted, water bottles in hand.

"Well, we are on a series of islands off the Chesapeake. There's a lot of research here focused on marsh plants, marine animals, and sand erosion, stuff like that."

"Here, as in at the lab?" She squinted through her sunglasses, confused by the coastal-based research.

"Yeah, I mean, a lot of what we do centers around marine life." Jared pushed his glasses back and looked past her as he talked. She'd noticed this about him. He didn't look people in the eye, not her anyway. He seemed tremendously shy. And a man of few words, except in the case of science apparently.

"NASA has satellites that were created to monitor the oceans. They record seasonal changes in the ocean surface, phytoplankton content, sea-to-ice ratios, rainfall, sunlight in the sea, surface temperatures, and stuff like that. It helps predict cataclysmic events like floods and droughts and climate cycles like El Niño."

"Wow," Christy said. "I guess I never realized that."

Jared shrugged, still not looking directly at her, focusing instead on the top of her head or shoulder, never her face. "Most people probably don't, and Dr. McLane wasn't involved in any of that. I'm not either, though I do work with and research the moon's influence on the tides."

"Molly's more interested in space flight than weather research." She shuffled ahead in line, and he stayed beside her. "And she likes to do things, like make rockets and stuff, not just observe."

He nodded. "She should be able to create and launch rockets, learn about why we explore space, do some science experiments, stuff like that. It really depends upon the age group. The older kids get to do coding and build robotics."

She looked down at Molly, who had her nose stuck in a book about interplanetary space travel. Biting her lip, she leaned toward Jared and spoke quietly.

"I'm pretty nervous about all this. Molly is a little, well, different. I'm not sure the stuff for her age group will hold her attention."

"Is attention an issue? Is she on medication?"

At first, Christy was surprised by his question, but as she looked around at the rambunctious boys and skipping girls, she understood.

"Um, no. That's not quite it." She looked up at Jared—he was several inches taller than she was, quite tall in fact—and waited for him to make real eye contact with her. "Let's just say that she could probably explain your Harvard textbooks to you."

His eyes narrowed, but she nodded, a serious look glued on her face. He bent down to look at the book Molly was reading and quickly straightened, his eyes wide in surprise. "Oh! I see. Um, how about I keep an eye on her for the first couple days and see how she does.

If she's bored, maybe we can bump her up into a group that would interest her."

"Is that allowed?" She wasn't quite sure what he had in mind, but the more she watched the other kids, the more certain she was that Molly wouldn't fit in here either. "I mean, she's pretty advanced. I know she's among the younger kids in the space camp, but she's skipping to sixth grade in the fall, and there's some talk about putting her into high school math and science."

"Give me a day or two, then we'll talk. Okay?"

"Last name, please?"

Christy looked at the teenager behind the table. "McLane, Molly." She looked back at Jared. "Thanks. I appreciate it. I don't want her bored, and I really don't want her disappointed."

"Molly's all set," the girl said. "Molly? Are you ready to have some fun at camp?"

Molly stopped reading her book and looked across the table. "I'm curious. Will this camp allow us to dig into the concept of interplanetary travel and patched-conic approximation? My dad was working on a satellite that would circle Jupiter when he died, and I'd like to go a step or two farther and see if we can slingshot human beings around the planet."

The girl's jaw dropped, and Jared burst into laughter. Molly was stone-faced as she waited for a response. Christy was both horrified and nearing panic.

"Don't worry," Jared said. "I'll figure something out." He looked at the girl whose mouth was still a welcoming exploration site for large insects. "Jill, I think

Molly and I will go see Dr. Johnson and have a talk with him about camp." He reached out his hand. "Come on, Molly. Let's see which group would be the most interesting one for you." He looked back at Christy and mouthed, *I've got this*, giving her a thumbs up.

Christy watched them walk away then turned to Jill. "Sorry about that. She's, uh, a little precocious for her age?" She shrugged, and Jill nodded, stunned into silence.

Diane laughed so hard she thought she might break a rib. Or two. "Oh my gosh! What did you do?"

"What could I do? I apologized and then left as quickly as I could!" Christy downed her cup of coffee. "I wish this was something stronger, to tell the truth. I'm a bundle of nerves. I've spent all morning waiting for my phone to ring so they can tell me to pick her up and never take her back."

Diane looked at the clock. "It's been a couple hours since you dropped her off. No news is good news. Besides, Jared sounds like a gem. I'm sure he has it under control." Diane watched Christy for any sign that the girl recognized that Jared was gold waiting to be tested by fire, but nothing flickered.

"I hope so. I'm just really nervous."

"Molly will be fine. She's adaptable."

By the time the morning rush slowed down, and the lunch crowd had come and gone, there were still no calls from camp. Diane could see the worry slowly draining from Christy's body. She smiled more genuinely and walked a little less hunched over, the world no longer so heavy on her shoulders.

Diane looked up, sad to see the time ticking by on the clock. The longer Christy worked for her, the more time Diane wanted to spend with her. For the first time in many years, she felt like she had a family of her own.

"Looks like you need to head to the Windjammer."

Christy's face fell. "Yeah, I guess so. I really hate it there. If you hear of anything better, please let me know."

"You know I will," Diane promised. In fact, she'd been trying to figure out that 'something better' for a few weeks now. She hoped to find it soon. "Now, go clock out and scoot. You don't want to be late."

"I sure don't. I feel like I'm always on thin ice there as it is." She took off her apron and headed toward the back but stopped and turned back to Diane. "Hey, I'm going to do a special dinner this weekend for Molly's birthday since I'm off Sunday afternoon. Want to join us?"

Diane felt her heart swell. "I'd love to. I wouldn't miss celebrating little Miss Molly for anything in the world."

Christy beamed. "Thanks, Diane. See you tomorrow."

Diane waited for Christy to leave for the t-shirt shop before locking the front door. She was glad it was only Monday. She'd need the whole week to decide what kind of present to get an eleven-year-old girl with the brain of a forty-year-old Einstein.

Jared was bewildered, which didn't happen often. "Can you repeat that?"

"The payload. What's its mission? When you know that, plus how much it weighs, you can determine the mechanics of the rest of the rocket."

"Who did you say this kid is?" Avi stood up and squinted at Molly as she inspected the various parts of the rocket that littered the workspace.

"She's supposed to be in the camp for middle schoolers but she's, uh, kind of beyond that. We tried the high school group, but that wasn't quite right either," Jared said.

"So, communication, weather monitoring, spying, planetary exploration, or observation?" Molly asked.

"Experimentation," Chloe answered. "We're basically sending a science experiment into space."

"What experiment?" Molly took a seat and looked at the student scientist with interest.

Chloe grinned and pulled up a seat next to Molly. "Zero-pressure balloons. Do you know what they are?"

Molly nodded enthusiastically. "They have air ducts on them that allow gas to escape. They demonstrate the way pressure is released as the rocket rises into space."

"Good job," Chloe said, raising her hand for a high-five. "I like this girl, Jar. She reminds me of me."

Jared smiled and nodded. "Yeah, I can see that."

Molly beamed. "What else?"

"What else do you want to know?" Avi asked.

"Everything!" Molly squealed.

The group laughed, and Molly seemed delighted by the attention.

"I was going to show Molly how to build a Cubesat. I've gotten the clearance for mine, and I thought it would be right up her alley. Her group is building model rockets, but Molly's done that a lot and was hoping for something a little more advanced," Jared told them.

"I don't know," Chloe said, looking at Molly. "Building model rockets is pretty cool."

"But I don't want to build models," Molly said. "I'm more interested in building interplanetary rockets that can reach the outer planets."

Chloe and Avi exchanged looks. Chloe pursed her lips and nodded. "Yeah, Cubesats sound good."

"What's going on in here?" They turned to see Dr. Johnson smiling at them from the doorway. "Molly, what are you doing in here? Jared, didn't we agree that she should be with the high school camp?"

Molly giggled like the ten-year-old she was. "They're building model rockets. Like I haven't done that a thousand times already." She rolled her eyes, and Dr. Johnson frowned. He looked at Jared.

"Explain, please."

"I'm sorry. I know I should have checked with you, but you were in a meeting. I was thinking, maybe Molly could do part camp and part more advanced stuff. She'd enjoy the coding week and possibly the robotics, but the rocket stuff seemed so... I don't know. Below her?"

"That's not your call to make, Jared." He motioned for Jared to follow him into the hall. Jared felt his face redden. He pushed up his glasses and faced his supervisor.

"Dr. Johnson, I really am sorry. It's just that she's every bit as smart as Dr. McLane, and she's only ten. To put her in a group that isn't going to benefit her would be to slow down her progress and will lead to frustration, maybe even acting out."

Dr. Johnson gave him a long stare. "Are we still talking about Molly?"

Jared blinked a couple times before answering. "Yes." He glanced away and then back. "And no."

"We give it two days, then reassess. And you call Christy and explain what we're doing. Now. She should have been notified hours ago. Ask Linda if we need a special form for this. And follow the same rules that apply in camp—no taking her anywhere alone, no closing doors when you're in an enclosed space, no letting her go any place without a buddy." He scrunched his face. "I mean, if she needs to use the bathroom or anything, Chloe goes with her. Is all that understood?"

"Yes, sir, I get it. No problem. And thanks, Dr. Johnson. I really appreciate it. I know what it's like for Molly, to an extent anyway. Chloe and Avi know even better than I do."

"Don't thank me yet, Jared. We're going to take this one day at a time. This program is important to our facility and to all the people involved, including the campers. If something goes wrong—"

"Dr. Johnson," Molly spoke up from the doorway.

"Yes, Molly?"

"Do we have to launch the Cubesat here, or can we take it home for Christy to see? I know she misses Daddy, too, and this might make her feel like we're all together watching one of his rockets go up."

Silence engulfed the room. Jared locked eyes with Dr. Johnson.

Dr. Johnson nodded and stooped down. "Here's the deal, Molly. I'm not sure how long you will be working with Jared on the Cubesat. We need to check with your sister and see how you do today and tomorrow. I'm not making any promises about this arrangement you and Jared have going." He looked up at Jared with a glare. "If anything goes wrong, you're out of here, doctorate or not. Just remember that."

"Yes, Sir." Jared felt sweat begin to pool under his arms and at the base of his back. He'd really messed up this time. He looked down at Molly and wondered what he'd been thinking.

Molly looked from Dr. Johnson to Jared and back to the doctor again. She blinked and said in a small voice, "I hope I didn't get Jared in trouble."

"I hope Jared isn't getting himself in trouble."

"Dr. Johnson. I know that being here this summer is really important to Jared. If it was me, working and studying here would be a dream come true. I also know that people my age aren't usually allowed to do this kind of thing. NASA spends lots of time and money on developing satellites here, and I can't do anything to mess that up or get Jared or you into trouble. I promise I'll be good."

Dr. Johnson smiled at Molly. "Thank you, Molly." He stood back up and looked at Jared, still glaring. "See me at the end of the day."

Jared swallowed as he watched Dr. Johnson walk away. He'd screwed up and wondered now if he'd gotten in over his head. He should have spoken to her sister about the possible change of plans. Better yet, he should have taken her back to the high school camp and left her there.

Then again... He pictured his younger sisters, Emily aged fourteen and Missy aged seventeen. If one of them was in Molly's shoes, this is exactly what he would do for them.

"And Chloe and Avi are so cool, and if I'm allowed to help Jared with his Cubesat, you might be able to come watch when it goes off..." Molly prattled on while she set the table and Christy cooked a chicken and rice dish on the stovetop. She enjoyed the sound of her sister's chatter, especially when she sounded like a normal almost-eleven-year-old. Well, except for all the talk about satellite launches and payloads. Still, her conversation with Jared bothered her. If this didn't work, would Molly be crushed at having to go back with the other kids? Would Jared's future at the facility be ruined? Well, Christy wasn't sure she cared about that. If this situation was harmful to Molly in any way, she'd find a way to press charges against this Jared guy. He might seem well-intentioned, but who knows. Christy suddenly felt very uneasy about letting her sister hang around with this intern. She didn't know anything about him.

Christy put the skillet on the table and stuck a large serving spoon into the rice. "Okay, Squirt, stop talking long enough to eat some dinner."

Silence ensued for a few minutes as they began to eat, but it didn't last.

"Do you think Jared's cute? Chloe says I'm lucky to be working so close to him all summer because he's cute."

Christy's fork stopped halfway to her mouth. "Chloe does know that you're ten, right?"

"Yeah, but I'm the only other girl in the group, so there's that."

"There's that," Christy muttered. Her misgivings were growing by the second.

"So, do you?"

"Do I what?" She took a drink of lemonade.

"Think he's cute?"

"I don't know. I don't know the guy."

"What does that have to do with anything? I don't know Zac Efron, but duh!"

"I base cuteness on more than looks," Christy said matter-of-factly.

"He has really blue eyes. You don't notice them as much with the glasses on, but when he takes off his glasses to rub his eyes, they really pop."

They really pop?

"Molly, you don't have a crush on Jared, do you?" If so, Christy was putting a stop this whole thing. She felt sick and wondered what the heck was going on with this man.

Molly scrunched her face. "Ew. He's old. If I'm going to have a crush, I'm at least going to pick one of high school guys in the camp. He'd be closer to my age even if not my intellect."

Christy resisted rolling her eyes and looked sternly at Molly. "Let's get this straight right now. No crushes. No dating. No boyfriend-girlfriend thing going on. No getting rides home from camp or school from anyone. No being alone with this Jared guy or any other guy. No going anywhere there alone. No…"

"Okay, okay, I get it. Sheesh. Learn like I'm sixteen, live like I'm eleven. Oh joy."

"Hey," Christy pointed her fork at Molly. "I can yank you out of the camp, get you a babysitter, and switch you back to sixth grade at any point this summer or even next year. If this doesn't work, or if you do anything, anything at all, to make me think this satellite thing or moving up a grade is a bad idea, that's it. You're back to kid camp at the YMCA and staying in elementary school. You got it?"

Molly picked up her plate, fork, and glass and walked to the sink. She reached over the lip to put them in the basin and headed toward her room. "Yeah, yeah, yeah. I got it." She stopped and turned back to look at Christy. "But just remember, missy, after I graduate from Harvard at the age of eighteen, you're going back to school on my dime, and I get to make the rules."

Christy gave her sister a stern gaze, her stomach in knots. "Deal, Squirt. Now, go get a shower before the movie, and lay out your clothes and stuff for tomorrow. Marge is picking you up at eight a.m. sharp."

Molly gave a mock salute and skipped down the hallway.

Christy put her elbow on the table and covered her face with her hand. "I'm in big trouble," she said to herself. "Big trouble."

After Molly was in bed, Christy did a little research of her own. There were no convicted criminals named Jared Stevenson, not that she could find anyway. There was one mention of him on the Harvard website as having received a fellowship to pursue his doctorate with NASA. No photograph, though, so she hoped this guy was really Jared Stevenson and not a pedophile who kidnapped him and stole his identity. She knew that was reaching, but still… What bothered her the most was that Jared had no social media presence at all. What twenty-something in the Twenty-First Century had no Facebook, no Twitter, not even a LinkedIn profile? Who was this man, and why the interest in her sister?

Increase in Drug Use Reported

Local police are warning of an increase in drug arrests and hospitalizations this summer. Though drug crime is not typically a problem here on the island, local police have seen a rise in drug offenses in the past month. Three arrests have been made for use of narcotics, and four homes have been broken into resulting in the theft of prescription medications. Police warn that the uptick in narcotics that is plaguing the rest of the country may be making its way to Chincoteague. A strain of heroin never seen before in this area has been detected in several patients, and officials worry that a deadly strain is being peddled on local streets. Please report any suspicious activity to the Chincoteague Police Department.

The Chincoteague Herald, June 10

Chapter Four

"I've got that," Dr. Johnson said, holding the back door open for Christy. She maneuvered through the door and placed the cake on the picnic table. Molly and Chloe were playing cornhole against Jared and Avi while Diane watched and cheered for the girls. Marge was digging candles out of a little box to put on the cake.

Christy looked around at the odd group. What a strange list of invitees for an eleventh birthday party—two women in their sixties, a sixty-something-year-old man, and three NASA students in their twenties. She let Molly decide who she wanted, and this was her enclave of choice. What would their parents have said? The only good thing about it was that she'd get to spend a little time with Jared and judge him for herself.

"Are you ready, Christy?"

Christy looked at Marge who gestured toward the cake. Eleven candles were embedded in the white icing. Instead of flowers, blue and red rockets decorated the frosted field around yellow lettering that spelled, "Happy Birthday, Molly!"

"Sure, let's light it up."

They called everyone over and sang *Happy Birthday*, then Marge helped Christy serve the lemon cake and Funfetti ice cream, Molly's favorites. After the cake, the cornhole games continued, and somehow Christy found herself taking Molly's place while Molly and Dr. Johnson put together the bottle rocket he had given her. In addition to the rocket and the bracelet from Christy, Molly got a NASA sweatshirt from Chloe, a book on space flight from Avi, tickets to the Lockheed Martin IMAX Theater at the Air and Space Museum from Jared—including one for Christy which put her mind slightly at ease as far as that went—and a brand-new ten-speed bike from Marge and Diane to take Molly anywhere she wanted to go on the island, within reason.

Though there was some joking about science things that went over Christy's head, she was relieved to find that Chloe, Avi, and Jared seemed to be normal twenty-somethings. Well, normal for geniuses working toward degrees in aerospace science. Based on what Molly said, Christy was sure that Chloe would be swooning all over Jared, but she treated both boys like brothers, which was unfortunate for Avi, who couldn't take his eyes off her.

Jared was relaxed around his colleagues, and Christy found out more about him. He was older than Chloe and Avi. They were both graduate students doing summer internships—both were only twenty, prodigies like Molly. Jared, contrary to her assumption that he was an intern, was a Ph.D. student working at the center while writing his dissertation on something that had to do with the makeup of the seas on the moon. She didn't know if that made her feel better or more suspicious. His mother was a store manager, and his father was a high school English teacher somewhere in the Midwest. He came about his lifelong interest in space the same way many children discover a fleeting interest in the planets—after a visit to the Smithsonian's Air and Space Museum, hence the IMAX tickets. It appeared his interest wasn't fleeting.

Though he wore glasses that he pushed back constantly, even when they were perfectly perched on his nose, Jared was not the typical stereotype of a science nerd. Watching him run around the yard with Molly, Christy noticed that he was quite athletic with long limbs that were strong and steady in their movements. He laughed freely and easily when he was relaxed and having fun. He seemed to like being with the others, just not her, she decided. He was nice enough to Christy, but he acted like he'd rather shoot bamboo up his fingernails than face her. She couldn't figure out if it was because he didn't consider her to be as smart or educated as the rest of them, or if it was because he couldn't be trusted.

Jared told them he had two younger sisters, and he seemed perfectly at ease joking with Molly and bantering back and forth with her, but he barely looked at Christy. She tried to engage him in small talk, but she only garnered those few bits of information about his family. The most words he'd said to her so far were about NASA the day she dropped off Molly for camp. And while Chloe and Avi truly were nice to her, Christy began to feel very uncomfortable around Jared. Was it the situation with Molly or her lower IQ?

Though she knew she was smart, Christy couldn't compete with their intellect, nor their knowledge of things she would never master and, honestly, didn't care to. As the day went on, she felt more self-conscious than ever and slowly withdrew herself from the partygoers except to keep a close eye on how Jared acted with Molly, which she had to admit was just how she imagined a big brother would act.

She cleaned the dishes, packed cake for everyone to take home, and busied herself in the kitchen while everyone else enjoyed themselves outside. Marge and Diane offered to do all the cleanup so that she could join in the festivities, but she convinced them that they always did things for her and that today, she wanted them to sit and have fun. She peeked out the window now and then but felt little incentive to join in as Dr. Johnson and Jared helped Molly adjust her new bike. At least she trusted Dr. Johnson to keep his eye on Jared and the situation.

Around dusk, when Christy had run out of things to do and wondered if everyone was going to leave soon, the kitchen door opened, and Jared looked around, his eyes finally falling on Christy. He quickly looked away.

"Um, Molly asked me to see if you have stuff for s'mores. Something about it being a birthday tradition to kick off the summer?" He flicked his gaze her way and then looked down at the linoleum.

"Oh!" Christy had completely forgotten. "Yeah, I've got everything. I'll throw it all together and be out in a minute."

Jared stepped inside and let the door close behind him. "I can help," he offered. For the first time that day, he lifted his eyes to meet hers directly, and she felt the stir of nerves in her belly. She really didn't want to be alone with him.

"Uh, sure. The graham crackers and marshmallows are in the little pantry there." She gestured to his left. "I always keep the chocolate in the fridge." He nodded, keeping his eyes on hers, and she suddenly felt even more uncomfortable. "The roasting forks are in the cabinet above the fridge. I'll need my stepstool."

She started looking around, her mind going blank even though she always kept the stool neatly tucked beside the back door next to where he was standing. Without saying a word, Jared walked to the fridge and reached up, opened the cabinet, and looked to Christy for help.

"On the right, you should feel the handles."

He ran his hand along the bottom of the cabinet and withdrew four roasting forks one at a time, handing each to her.

"They're setting up the wood in the fire pit. Do you have a lighter?"

"Oh, yes! Of course. It's…" Why was she so nervous? She could barely think straight. She wasn't sure how she felt about him, and it didn't help to have him standing there watching her, the blue eyes that never looked her in the face now following her every move. She moved toward a drawer and dropped one of the forks. They both bent to pick it up, and their hands brushed. She jerked away as though she was too near a flame. Jared, seeming to sense her unease, picked it up and gently took the others from her.

"Let me take these out. Do you have a tray you can throw the rest of the stuff on and follow me?"

"Sure. I'll just grab the one I used for the burgers. I already washed it, so it's clean. I mean, there's no bacteria or anything on it. I mean…" She wanted to kick herself. She grabbed the tray from the drying rack where it had already sat long enough to dry, and hastily grabbed the items from the refrigerator and pantry.

"Lighter?" Jared asked.

Christy huffed out a breath and gritted her teeth, willing the blush to stop crawling up her face. He must think she was an absolute moron. They probably all did. She just wanted him to leave so that she could breathe again. She didn't like the way he made her feel at all.

She opened a drawer and grabbed the long green lighter, adding it to the tray. Jared opened the door for her and ushered her out. She kept her attention on opening the crackers, marshmallows, and chocolate while the others lit the fire. The rest of the group continued to talk and laugh, the adults included, while Christy sat in her chair and watched the flickering flames. Her gaze flickered as well, from time to time casting quick glances between Molly, Chloe, Avi, and Jared.

Was this the way it was going to be then? Molly was going to make lots of friends, all of them close to Christy's age, while Christy worked around the clock and had only two retirees for companionship? No matter how advanced Molly was, she was only a kid and would need to count on Christy for a long time to come. Christy was supposed to protect her from guys like... She stopped herself as she watched them laughing and talking together. Was Jared all that bad? He didn't seem to be, plus she'd had a chance to talk to Dr. Johnson earlier, and he sang Jared's praises. Still, she couldn't dismiss the discomfort she felt around him.

Christy looked back at Molly. Soon, she would grow up, go to college, move away, maybe to Florida or Houston, and Christy would...what? It would be too late to go back to school by then. Everyone her age would be married and well into their family lives and careers by then. She'd be left alone. She supposed this was why people got cats.

She wrinkled her nose, not a cat person.

"You okay?" Diane leaned in, looking concerned.

"Yeah," Christy managed a smile. "Tired, but look at her." She gestured at Molly, a huge grin on her face with a string of sugary marshmallow trailing from her lips. "She's so happy. She's just... one of them."

"One of what?"

"One of the ones who've got it all together, who know what they want in life, who have the brains and the means to make it happen. All sunny skies and laughter and a full life ahead of them."

"Is that really what you think? That they all have everything, and you have nothing?"

Christy opened her mouth then closed it. She took a breath. "I didn't say that. They just..."

"Are enjoying themselves. Not letting their cares weigh them down. Being young people. It's not about their brains or their bank accounts or what degrees they have or will have. It's about choosing happiness."

Christy turned to Diane. "You make it sound so easy."

"Nothing is easy. Do you really think it's easy for Molly, being the way she is? Think of how she must feel on a daily basis. That's how all of them probably grew up feeling. I bet it was hard for them to make friends, to figure out what to do with the talents God gave them. Nobody has it all figured out from birth. Heck, I'm sixty, and I still don't have it all figured out."

Christy looked back at the others. She noticed that Jared was watching her with interest. When their eyes locked, he didn't look away, making her insides squirm. Darn, she wished she knew if she could trust him.

His mouth turned up slightly in a small smile before he looked down at the empty roasting fork in his hand. Christy felt that unease in her gut again. He leaned down and said something to Molly, who looked over at Christy.

Without a word, Molly reached into the bag of marshmallows and held one up. She took the roasting fork from Jared and pushed the marshmallow onto it, then held it in the flames. Christy watched the puff of sugar and gelatin as Molly turned it around and around, until the whole thing was perfectly browned. Jared held open a prepared graham cracker, and Molly slid the marshmallow on top the chocolate while Jared sandwiched the s'more together. Molly set the fork down and took the treat from Jared. She walked over and handed it to Christy, then leaned down and gave her a tight hug.

"This is the best day of my whole life," Molly whispered into her ear. "Thank you."

Christy whispered back, "You're welcome, Squirt."

Was it sweet or creepy that Jared had helped Molly make her sister a s'more? There must be a way to find out more about him even if it meant spending more time with the Fantastic Four.

Christy looked at the text on her phone and frowned.

"You working or taking a break to look at your phone?"

She quickly shoved the phone into her back pocket, avoiding Vince's eyes. "Sorry. I'm working."

She picked up a pair of swim trunks that had been thrown on top of the pile and hastily folded them, placing them back in the stack in the correct size order.

"You got a better place to be?" Vince asked, sliding up next to her, too close for comfort as always.

"No, Sir. I'm happy to be here." She kept her eyes on the pile of clothes, straightening things that needed no straightening.

"Cause I got a lot of kids who'd kill for this job." He placed his hand on the small of her back, and she fought the urge to jerk away while stifling a cold chill. "You want this job, right?"

She'd been waiting for this moment ever since Vince was hired as the manager—'hired' being a loose interpretation of his showing up one day and telling her that his uncle said he could run the shop while he was 'lying low.' Christy didn't show any curiosity as to what he'd done to require being banished to a small barrier island in the Mid-Atlantic though she was certain he wanted her to ask.

Vince was from Elizabeth, New Jersey, a fact he was proud to tell anyone who would listen. So much for lying low. He had a thick accent and a tattooed body under his white t-shirt that went perfectly with his shaved head. His accent and the way he spoke reminded her of the harmless Joe Jr., Sandra Bullock's neighbor in the movie, *While You Were Sleeping*, which she and her mom considered one of the greatest Christmas movies of all time long before Hallmark cornered the market on holiday rom coms. Only, Joe Jr.'s advances toward Lucy were cute if completely futile, while Vince's were totally creepy. When he 'leaned,' she wanted to run.

Christy side-stepped out of his reach and moved around the display table, concentrating on the swimwear on the other side.

"You hear me, Chrissy?"

"It's Christy," she said in a low voice through gritted teeth. She looked up at him with an unfriendly gaze. "I heard you, and yes, I want this job."

He smiled, a row of bridged teeth visible on the upper left side of his grin, and she wondered if they'd been knocked out in a fight. "Good. Then you'll go out with me tomorrow night so we can discuss a raise. Seven o'clock?"

She thought of the text she'd just received and previously had mixed feelings about answering, but now...

"Sorry, I have plans." She turned and walked toward the shirts hanging on the wall as though to check that they were properly ordered. She felt a tight squeeze on her upper arm as her body was yanked backward and forced to turn.

"Don't walk away from me when I'm talkin' to you. I said, we're goin' out. We have things to discuss. It's a *business* meeting." He grinned, but his eyes were as cold as ice.

"I told you, I have plans." She looked at her arm, already seeing discoloration appearing under his firm grip. He slid his hand down to her forearm and twisted it, pulling it behind her back until she felt a shot of pain. He pulled her arm so far and twisted it so hard, she thought he might break it. "Let go of me," she demanded, though her mind raced with fear.

"You might wanna rethink that answer," he said before quickly releasing her arm when the front door swung open. Three teenaged boys entered the store, laughing and shoving each other the way young boys do.

Christy made a hasty retreat to the other side of the store, her breath coming in short rasps as she rotated her shoulder and rubbed her arm. She swallowed the bile that had begun to rise in her throat and blinked back tears. While Vince kept a wary eye on the boys, she busied herself with the souvenir mugs, picture frames, and cheap glass ponies that lined the shelves.

The store was busy for the rest of the afternoon. The second the clock read six, Christy punched out and fled. She sucked in the evening air as she made her way to her car, seething mad but also sadly resigned to the fact that she had to return to the store the following afternoon.

She hurried to her little blue Ford EcoSport, a gift from her mother and Fred when she got into college, and unlocked the car, sliding inside and slamming the door. Sitting in the driver's seat, doors locked, she pulled her phone from her pocket and typed a reply to Chloe. She'd never bowled in her life, but she suddenly had a desire to learn how, if only to give her an excuse to steer clear of Vince De Carolis. Of course, if Jared was there, she might be able to get a better feel for him and his intentions for Molly.

Avi's thirteen-year-old sister was on the island, along with his parents, enjoying a weekend of sun and sand away from New York. Though the girl was a bit older than Molly, Avi insisted that the two would hit it off. He seemed to recognize, probably from experience, that Molly needed friends close to her age but had little luck finding any, and he was certain that Anya would be a good match for her wit. He was right. The two girls bonded instantly.

Christy watched them chatting over root beer floats while she waited her turn to bowl. She was glad Molly was hanging out with someone close to her age, even if Christy wasn't having near as much fun as her sister.

"Want some pizza?" Jared sat down across from her at the round table and slid a cardboard box of pizza between them.

"Um, no thanks. I'm not really hungry," she replied, though her stomach growled in protest, and she hoped he didn't hear it.

"Are you sure? I can't eat the whole thing, and Avi and Chloe got their own." He wrinkled his nose. "They both seem to think anchovies are the greatest topping ever discovered."

Christy's look matched his, and she shook her head. "Ick. I never could stand the smell of them."

"Same." He pushed the box toward her. "Come on. It's pepperoni. I'm betting you're a pepperoni kind of girl."

She wanted to resist, not ready to trust him, but her mouth had started to water as soon as he opened the box and the smell of cheese, tomato, and garlic hit her nostrils. At the word pepperoni, her saliva took on a life of its own.

"Maybe just one, if you don't mind. I didn't bring any extra cash."

"Who cares about that? Just eat. I'm not asking for money. It's already paid for."

An image of Vince flashed into her mind, and she pushed it away, not wanting to consider what he would be asking for over their 'business dinner.' He'd only brought it up once when they were working that afternoon, but she'd avoided him as best she could after that, and since it was Friday, the store was busy. She was grateful for small miracles.

"So, Molly's doing great. Thanks for letting her stay on this week. She was a big help with the Cubesat. I'll miss her help when she's at camp in July, but I know she's looking forward to learning how to code."

Christy helped a string of cheese into her mouth and chewed her bite before taking a long drink of root beer to wash it down. "She enjoys working with you. She says she's helping you with your research, too. Is that true?"

Christy wasn't crazy about Molly working so closely with Jared, but so far, everything seemed to be going smoothly. She'd talked to Dr. Johnson earlier in the week, and he also seemed pleased with the way things were working out. She supposed that was a good thing.

Jared laughed and nodded. "Believe it or not, she is. I'm doing research on the moon's craters, and she's really good at helping me talk through my hypotheses." He glanced over at Molly and Anya. "Who'd have thought I'd have an eleven-year-old assistant?"

"You can let her go whenever you want, you know. You don't have to babysit her all summer. If she likes the next camp, you're free to tell her she has to attend the others."

Jared cocked his head to the right and peered at her. "Do you want me to send her to camp? I mean, I will, but I think she'd be happier doing research. Honestly, she really is good at it. Unless you're not comfortable with her working with me. I get that. I have sisters, and I'm not sure I'd like it if they were spending all summer doing research for someone more than fifteen years older than them. I totally understand if you want to end this."

"Well…" Christy looked at her sister who was waving her hands around in the air as she told a story that had Anya in stitches. She smiled and turned back to Jared. "I mean, she's a kid. And you're a… man." Sitting across from him made his age—twenty-eight, according to Molly—all too real, and she felt that uncomfortable stir in her stomach again. She still hadn't been able to learn anything else about him, but Dr. Johnson seemed to be happy with the situation, having admitted to her that he had also been unsure about it at the start.

Christy looked down to find that she was pulling apart the crust on her pizza. She sat the piece down on the paper plate in front of her.

Jared's face turned serious. "Are you worried about…? About me? I'd never—"

She immediately thought about Vince and shook her head. She no longer got the same vibe from Jared that she got from Vince, but there was something about Jared that still made her uneasy, like he was keeping secrets. Why didn't he ever talk about his family or his childhood?

"No, not that. Well, kind of, yes. I mean I don't really know you and, well, don't you think she should be with other kids her age?" She bit her lip, all the fears she'd held onto for the past two years, especially for the past two weeks, fighting to spill out.

"Can I be honest?"

"Hey, you two, break's over. Are you playing or eating?"

They looked over at Avi who was gesturing to the screen where the scores were entered.

Christy wiped her hands on a napkin as she stood. What was he going to say? Was he going to confess to being a serial child molester? She didn't think so. In fact, despite his lack of sharing his life story, he was kind of starting to grow on her though she couldn't say exactly why.

"Coming," she called to Avi. "Sorry, can we continue this?"

Jared shrugged. "Sure."

He wore a frown. Christy felt bad for cutting him off, and she did want to know what he thought. "Seriously, I really do want to hear what you have to say. It's important to me, for Molly's sake."

She gave him a quick smile and hurried over to pick up the ball they'd suggested she use. She didn't think he was as creepy as she feared, but she was uncomfortable talking to him one-on-one. He was not only older and smarter, he had a worldly sense about him that made her feel even more inadequate. Or was it still mistrust? She wasn't sure what her gut was trying to tell her. She just couldn't make up her mind, liking him one minute, then questioning everything about him the next.

Lining up her body like they'd shown her, Christy took a few steps and raised her arm back, then shot her arm forward, releasing the ball. She expected it to roll right into the gutter as it had on each of her previous attempts, but she watched in amazement as it continued down the center and hit the middle pin. It didn't have the force it needed to knock down more than the center pins, but she squealed in delight as though she'd sent all ten flying.

"All right!" Chloe yelled. "Before the night is over, you'll be racking up the strikes!" Chloe high-fived Christy as the ball reappeared from the chute.

Jared was behind her, leaning his face close to hers, and she felt her stomach do a little spin. "You can't hit them all, but you might get lucky and slingshot one over to knock down one or the other on the other side. Try this."

He leaned down and placed one hand on her arm and the other on her side, not far from where Vince had laid his hand the day before. This time, though, she did not recoil from the touch. She let Jared walk with her, guiding her down the slippery lane, and allowed him to maneuver her arm into a release while Avi shouted, "Hey, you're not supposed to help the other team."

They stood and watched as the ball struck the three pins on the right, knocking them down and sending one pin over to the left where it caused the last two pins to bobble before one fell and rolled out of site.

"Yeah!" Jared yelled, pumping his fist into the air.

Christy just stood in amazement, watching the bar drop down and sweep all the pins into the abyss behind the lane.

Chloe squealed in delight. "I knew it! You're a natural! You just needed to get the feel of it."

As the double meaning of Chloe's words entered her mind, Christy felt herself blushing. She looked toward Jared but didn't make eye contact. "Thanks," she said in a rushed breath. She saw him push back his glasses and nod. Her mind was a jumble of thoughts.

"Sure. Chloe's right. You're a natural."

"You're up, Jared," Avi said, and Jared hastily moved to pick up his ball.

For the first time that night, his aim was way off, and his ball hit the gutter only halfway down the lane. He looked at Avi and shrugged, pushing his glasses up again.

For the rest of the night, Christy avoided looking at Jared, unsure of what she was feeling. They had little to nothing in common, and she still knew so little about who he really was. She felt like a small fish in a big pond being circled by a hungry shark.

Later, as they walked through the parking lot, Christy quietly asked, "Hey, what were you going to say earlier? About Molly?"

For a moment, Jared wrinkled his brow in confusion, but then his expression softened, and he nodded.

"Let Molly find her own way. Let her make her own friends and find her own path in life. Everyone deserves the chance to have a past and a future. Let Molly decide hers."

Christy stared at Jared as Molly told Avi and Chloe goodbye. She slowly nodded, thanked him for his advice and the pizza, then told them all goodbye.

As the sisters rode their bikes back to the house, Christy couldn't help but think that perhaps Jared's advice stemmed from something in his own experience.

Employment Opportunities on the Island

The Chamber of Commerce announces the following job openings:

Accomack Public School System is hiring substitute teachers for the upcoming year. Teaching experience is not required.

MJ's Steak and Seafood is hiring waitstaff and bussers. Check Facebook for more info.

Island Explorer is hiring Nature Tour Guides and Kayak Guides. Hours are flexible, and jobs run through the rest of the summer and into the fall. Must be energetic, hardworking, honest, trustworthy, and have good communication skills. Boating and kayak skills a must. Call the number below.

The Chincoteague Herald, June 15

Chapter Five

"Something's bothering you and has been for a couple days." Diane looked at Christy and waited for an answer. She had tried to give Christy the time and space she needed to come clean, but she hadn't said anything. Christy was typically quiet, but not like she had been since arriving at work on Friday morning. Diane had given her two days to open up to her and was tired of waiting.

Christy put down the frosting knife and sighed. "It's that obvious?"

"Afraid so. What's going on? Is everything okay with Molly?"

"Yeah, she's fine." Christy smiled. "Believe it or not, she's actually helping Jared do research for his dissertation."

"I'm not surprised at all," Diane said, sculpting a doughnut with pink icing. "So, if Molly's fine, then…?"

Christy picked up another doughnut and took her time smoothing a layer of chocolate on it then topping it with crushed peanuts.

"Well, there are a couple things actually. I'm not sure how I feel about Jared." Diane's brow shot up with interest.

"Not like that!" Christy adamantly shook her head, though Diane wasn't sure what 'that' meant. "I mean, Molly really likes him and he seems nice enough, but I can't find out anything about him. He has no social media and says very little about his family or his childhood. He says he has two sisters, both in their teens, and they don't have social media either. It's just weird, don't you think? Like, I can't figure out who he really is."

Diane frowned. "He hasn't done or said anything to Molly that concerns you, has he?"

"No, but don't you think it's strange that someone his age doesn't mind having a kid hang around him all day? I mean, don't you think it's kind of creepy?"

Diane wasn't sure what to think, but she knew who to talk to about it.

"Hmm... let me think about this and see what I can come up with. What else is bothering you?"

"I need another job. Fast. Like, yesterday. I can't stand working at Windjammer."

Diane eyed her carefully, noticing how Christy concentrated on the doughnut and didn't look up as she spoke. "What happened?" she demanded, no longer tolerating this beating around the bush.

"I just can't do it anymore. I hate it." Christy put down the doughnut she was working on and finally faced Diane. Tears were in her eyes. "Vince is a creep. I need to get out of there."

"What did he do?" Diane made sure her tone left no doubt that she expected an honest answer.

"He hasn't exactly done anything, not really, but he…" She looked away as color filled her cheeks. "He wants to discuss a raise." Christy looked back, her eyes meeting Diane's, and the meaning in them was clear.

"That jerk. I oughta call Paul—"

Christy grabbed her arm. "No, don't. He didn't do anything. I just need to get out of there. I mean, he might try something." She bit her lips. "Yeah, I think he's going to try something, and maybe that's why Jared is creeping me out. There's just something about both of them… Anyway, I need to get out of there."

Diane nodded and made up her mind. "Look, I didn't want to say anything before I was sure it was happening, but Delores told me that she's thinking of retiring."

"Delores?"

"The librarian at the elementary school," Diane clarified. "She's worried that they won't find a replacement. You'd be great."

"But don't you need a degree for that? Like a master's degree? I don't even have my bachelor's."

"I know, and that's an issue, but how close are you? A semester? Two?"

"Two. A whole year." Christy shook her head. "And there's no way I can go back and get one any time soon."

"What if there was?"

Christy looked at Diane, her mouth hanging open just a bit. "How?" she asked, sounding unsure.

"Well, when Marge's daughter wanted to get her degree but had three little ones at home, she went online. She signed on while the kids were asleep, and the professors were very understanding that she had children and a home and were willing to work with her when she needed extra time or—"

"No, I'm not doing that. First, I can hardly keep my eyes open during the day as it is. Second, even online classes cost money. Third, I need a job now, not after another year of school."

Diane had already put a lot of thought into this and had made some inquiries. "I talked to Mr. Urbansky yesterday afternoon."

"You what?" Christy shot her a look of indignation. "About me? What the—"

"Now, Christy, calm down. I was only inquiring about the possibility of how someone could work her way into a possible position if one were to become available. I asked what would need to be done if that person needed a little more education."

She could tell that Christy was getting ready to lose it but at the same time, was interested in the answers, so Diane plowed ahead.

"He said that something might be able to be worked out if the person came on as a teacher's aide. There's a program that helps students pay for school if they sign a contract promising to stay at the school and teach for four years."

Christy nodded, and Diane took that as a sign to continue.

"If you took the online classes and finished your undergraduate degree, they would then pay for a couple classes a year of a graduate program, and there are plenty of library schools offering online degrees."

Christy frowned. "But aren't schools cutting librarians from their budgets these days?"

"I'm sure that some are, but the school library program here is alive and thriving."

"I don't know."

Diane wiped her hands on her apron and went around the table. She took Christy by the arms, and Christy winced, pulling her left arm away.

Diane saw the look on her face and gently reached for her forearm. She pulled the short sleeve up and sucked in a breath at the sight of the dark blue bruises on her upper arm, the exact size and shape of a man's fingers. She looked at Christy's face and saw shame in her eyes.

"Vince?" Diane asked, her blood beginning to boil.

Christy pressed her lips together and nodded.

"And you don't want me to call Paul?"

Christy vigorously shook her head. "Please, don't. I just want to get out of there."

Diane swallowed. "I'm calling Mr. Urbansky this morning. We're going to get you into that school immediately."

"But it's summer. They can't possibly have any reason to hire me now."

"Then we'll come up with one. You're not going back to that place even if I have to pay you to cut my grass." Diane put up her hand. "Don't argue with me. We're going to figure this out. Today."

Diane was as angry as a fly trapped in a windowpane. She spent the rest of the day and all evening thinking about Christy and that lech she worked for. Worked, in the past tense. Diane went with her as soon as they closed the shop and stood by while Christy told Vince she was quitting, effective immediately.

He tried to give her a hard time and even threatened to withhold her last paycheck, but Diane stepped in. "Do I need to get the police involved?" she asked. "I know exactly how many hours Christy puts in here, and I also know what kind of business you're operating on our family-friendly island."

Vince's eyes widened, and he stood up straighter, his face flushing bright red. "What's that supposed to mean, lady?" He flexed his fingers as though he might ball them into a fist and punch her.

Diane held her position and turned her features to stone. "You heard me. I know what you said to Christy and how you tried to get her to perform after-hours work for you."

She saw something pass across his features, relief maybe? Then he squared his shoulders and pointed at Christy.

"Get outta here and take your grandmother with you."

They hurried from the store and didn't look back.

The man gave Diane the creeps. He was just as slimy as she'd pictured him. There was something else, too, that bothered her, but she couldn't put her finger on it. She was certain she'd never seen him before, but something about him was so familiar. She supposed she must have seen him around town.

Diane smiled when her phone began to buzz, and all thoughts of Vince and the Windjammer vanished as she answered in a sweet voice.

"Hello, Simon, how was your day?"

They talked for an hour, and Diane felt like a teenager.

It wasn't until they hung up that she realized she'd forgotten to talk to him about Christy, and she really wanted his advice. Oh well. She'd have to talk to him about it tomorrow.

The bell jingled over the front door, and Christy looked up at the smiling face of Dr. Johnson. She stood quickly, causing the chair she'd been sitting in to wobble.

"Dr. Johnson, hi. I didn't expect to see you here. Is Molly—"

Dr. Johnson held up his hand and laughed. "Good afternoon, Christy. Don't worry. Everything is fine at Wallops. Your sister has taken the place by storm, and everyone there is enamored with her."

Christy relaxed and smiled. 'That's good. I was afraid she would be getting in the way by now."

"Oh, not at all. In fact, there's a specialized program we offer that I think she should apply for. Normally, it's for juniors and seniors in high school, but..." He gave her a knowing look.

"But Molly doesn't exactly do normal."

He nodded. "I wouldn't ordinarily be in favor of such a move. It's risky to put someone her age in with middle or high schoolers, but given what I've seen this summer, well, I think she handles it beautifully. She'd have to apply, but I'm sure she'd get in."

"I'll talk to her about it. Thanks."

"Christy," he began. "Has anyone ever talked to you about Molly being a true child prodigy?"

He motioned to the table where she had been filling sugar shakers, and they both took a seat.

"Well, like I mentioned to you at her party, she's being moved up a grade in the fall. She'll be in sixth grade at the combined school. Honestly, I wasn't in favor of it at first, but after I talked to Diane and then to Molly, I felt like we should give it a try."

"Yes, I've been thinking about it ever since you told me. Do you know if she will be doing sixth grade work?"

"As far as I know, though she has talked about moving up a little farther in math."

Dr. Johnson nodded. "That's a start." He hesitated, and Christy waited, sensing he had much more to say. "However, I'm not sure that even that will be beneficial. Molly is... how do I put this? Special doesn't seem to cover it." He pursed his lips and his eyebrows knitted together in one curvy line across his forehead. "Exceptional," he said, seeming satisfied. "Molly is exceptional. She needs more than the average middle school can give her, no matter how good the school is."

"I don't understand." Christy felt a wave of turmoil in her gut not unlike the waves on Assateague Beach just before a storm.

"Molly needs more of an advanced education. She's going to top out in school and be bored, perhaps even regress academically but especially emotionally, if her needs aren't properly met." He took a deep breath. "You see, with a true child prodigy, the demand for learning can never be satisfied. There is a constant need to learn more, to advance beyond current understanding, and it's very difficult for a teacher or parent to keep up with the child's intellectual pace. Frustration can set in if the adults in the child's life aren't able to satisfy this need for learning.

"Even trickier to navigate than all this is how to allow the child to be a child. When pushed, they often find that they can't handle life emotionally or psychologically. In my experience, and I have a lot, it's better to let the child go at his or her own pace. Give them options and let them choose. For example, would you like to continue in sixth grade or move up to ninth? Would you like to do sixth grade English and tenth grade math? Would you like to begin college at twelve or fifteen? Or wait until you're older?"

He stopped speaking and looked at Christy, perhaps sensing she was overwhelmed, because she was. At the same time, though, Jared's words came back to her about letting Molly make her own decisions.

"I think what Simon is trying to say," Diane said, walking in from the kitchen, "is that you and Molly need to have a serious talk before fall, perhaps in the company of a specialist in this area."

For moment, Christy couldn't figure out who Simon was, but then it clicked. She turned back to him. "I don't even know where to begin."

Dr. Simon Johnson nodded. "I'm sorry if I caught you off guard. I'm sure that none of this comes as a surprise, yet at the same time, a total surprise."

"That's a good way to put it," Christy agreed. A thought struck her, and she asked, "Who was it? The child you had to learn all this for?"

"My daughter, Elena." A sad look passed over his face, and Christy worried that Elena had been one of the ones who couldn't handle it.

"Is she…?" Christy didn't know what she wanted to ask. Somehow, the answer felt too big for her to hear.

His face turned to amusement, and he beamed with pride. "She's wonderful. She lives on the other side of the country. I don't see her as often as I'd like, but she's doing well. She's one of the top medical researchers in the world, but none of her work paid off in the way she'd most hoped." He made a noise somewhere between a laugh and a cry. "Her mother died of pancreatic cancer. No cure. It was sudden yet felt like a lifetime. Elena blamed herself for so long, thinking she hadn't done enough to find a cure."

"Oh, Simon," Diane said, laying her hand on his arm in an intimate way that surprised Christy. "I'm so sorry. I didn't know."

He smiled warily. "It's not the kind of thing you bring up at a child's birthday party or over dinner on a first date," He chuckled, smiling at Diane.

Christy felt a jolt in her chest. What was going on here, and why hadn't anyone told her? She studied the way they were looking at each other. That must have been some first date…

"Anyway," Dr. Johnson said abruptly. "Can I make a recommendation?"

"Um, sure," Christy said, not sure of how else to answer.

"Talk to the school. Include the principal and guidance counselor. Bring in an outside person if need be. Have them test Molly. A few prodigies excel at everything, but most have very specialized interests and skills—high level math, various sciences or medicine, languages, etcetera. You want to know where Molly falls in her ability not just to learn but to understand and retain information. Once that's done, ask them if Molly can create her own schedule and workload, even if it's just in certain areas. We know she has a high capacity for math and space science, but maybe she's deficient, at her level of deficiency anyway, in language learning or memory skills. You need to know what her strengths and weaknesses are. Let her dictate her own education for a year, then see where she falls. They may want to test her again after that to see if she's at the right level or needs to accelerate. But to be honest, she'll know without being tested, and she'll let you know."

Diane stood to help a couple who had come into the shop while they'd been speaking.

"You said that regular school might not be enough for her," Christy said. "Does that mean she should go away to a different school? Do we need to move again?" The thought made her heart ache, not because she longed to stay on the island but because she dreaded the upheaval and the costs of relocating.

"Not necessarily. If the school is willing to work with her, and if they have teachers willing and able to monitor her progress, she can succeed by her own power."

"If we do this, if we go to school and get Molly on some kind of specialized learning plan, will you go with me? Will you talk to them? Please?" She heard the pleading in her own voice and wished that Fred was here. The thought made her stop and sit up straighter. "Do you think Fred knew? Did he see this in Molly?"

Dr. Johnson nodded. "I think he did. Think back to the discussions you had around the dinner table, the books he gave her to read, the way he taught her. I had some very interesting conversations with Molly last week, and I wouldn't be surprised if Fred was planning on doing exactly what we've just talked about."

Christy sat back, dozens of flashbacks scrolling through her mind—the talks around the dinner table that centered on space and rockets, the nights they spent under the stars observing the night sky, all the books Fred bought for Molly that she devoured, the special outings the two of them took to museums, lectures, and other things that normal kids never would have had an interest in. Fred was teaching Molly to get used to advanced thinking, to attend lectures, to talk to adults about science and math on an adult level.

"I think you're right. I don't know why I never saw it before."

The shop was busy, but Diane was able to follow most of the conversation. She rejoined them just as Christy wondered aloud why she had never noticed Molly's situation before.

"Well, you were away at school for three years, right?" Diane said, sitting down at the table. "Those would have been the years when Molly was really beginning to show her potential. Is that right, Simon?"

He nodded. "Yes, though she probably spoke early and read voraciously even as a very small child."

Christy nodded. "Yes, that's correct. Even I knew she was talking and reading very early and had an understanding of things far beyond what was normal."

"So, back to your request. Yes, I will go with you to the school. I have lots of data to back up what I've told you, and I have experience as a parent and as a supervisor and mentor. You call and make the appointment, and I'll make sure it fits into my schedule."

Christy frowned and turned to Diane. "I've been thinking, and I'm not sure about the job at the school, especially with Molly making this big change. It might be too much at once."

"What job?" Simon asked.

Diane turned to him and explained the situation with Vince as delicately as she could, but Simon's face turned red and his jaw tightened. His anger receded as she told him that Christy had already quit working for Vince.

"If it's money you need to finish school, that's not a problem."

"Oh no," Christy protested. "You're already doing enough to help us. I'm not going to take your money."

"A loan then. You keep working for Diane but take the classes you need to graduate. I'll pay your school expenses and anything Molly accrues for advanced studies, and—"

"That's not necessary. At least as far as Molly's concerned. She has money for her education. Fred saw to that. It's the everyday things that we're struggling with." She looked away, obviously embarrassed by their situation, but Simon handled it beautifully.

"Dig into that account to pay your expenses. Set up a budget for yourself. I can help you create one based on your financial situation and expenses, if you want me to. I can guarantee you Molly won't need that money to pay for college. That brain of hers is going to see to that. Figure out what you need to live on for the next year plus six months to get yourself a job and secure benefits.

You do have benefits now, right? Insurance? Molly is entitled to that."

"Yes, Gloria in Human Resources was very helpful in getting all that set up. Molly has good insurance until she's eighteen and receives a nice monthly payment from the account Fred set up, but it's Molly's, not mine. It goes straight into her savings account along with the rest of the money for her future."

"What about you?"

"I tried staying on Mom and Fred's insurance, but I couldn't keep the same policy." Christy shrugged, raising her hands, palms up. "It was too expensive to have my own."

"Weren't you Fred's daughter, too? By adoption, I mean?"

"Yes, but I didn't think—"

"You mean you didn't ask." Dr. Johnson frowned. "Call Gloria. Get yourself insured. You're all Molly has. If something happens to you, what is she going to do?"

"That never occurred to me," she said, and her face turned red. She let out a long breath. "I've been so careless. There's so much I don't know."

"Not anymore. You have questions? You just ask. Either one of us." He motioned to Diane. "If we don't know the answers, we'll get them. In the meantime," he looked down at his watch. "I have to get back to work, and you have some research to do."

"Research?"

"On colleges. Get that figured out and start applying."

"Today," Diane said firmly before turning her attention to Dr. Johnson. "Thank you. I'll help Christy follow through on everything, and she will give you a call."

Dr. Johnson smiled at Diane and said, "And I'll give you a call."

Christy looked away, trying to hide the smile, but Diane saw it and knew what she was thinking.

"Thanks, Dr. Johnson. For everything." Christy said before leaving the two of them alone in the front of the shop.

"Thank you, Simon, for coming by to talk to Christy and for all your help. They're really special girls."

"I agree," Simon said. "And they're lucky they have someone so special looking out for them. I'll call you later," he promised.

Diane watched him leave then practically floated back to the kitchen where Christy waited with a knowing grin on her face.

Carnival Open, Fireworks Ready!

The Annual Chincoteague Volunteer Fireman's Carnival
is officially underway. Rides, games, and food for all ages
are available at the fairgrounds every Friday and Saturday
night through the end of July, culminating with the
Annual Pony Penning during the last week of the
carnival. Enjoy live entertainment on the fairgrounds
stage or try your luck at bingo. All proceeds benefit the
Chincoteague Volunteer Fire Company. The Old-
Fashioned Fireworks Display, celebrating the birth of
our nation, will be held on the carnival grounds July 4 at
10 p.m. The fireworks are sponsored by the
Chincoteague Volunteer Fire Company, the Town of
Chincoteague, and the Chincoteague Chamber of
Commerce.

Chincoteague Herald, June 15

Chapter Six

"I'm going to start taking high school math and science in the fall," Molly proudly told Jared on Wednesday morning.

"Oh really?" He stopped reading and looked toward the doorway. "What classes?"

Molly bounded into the room and sat in the empty chair near the desk. Jared turned to give her his full attention.

Molly talked nonstop for twenty minutes about the meeting she, Christy, and Dr. Johnson had with the school the prior afternoon. She told him that it took some persuading, but Dr. Johnson convinced everyone that Molly was capable of doing the work. Molly was obviously exhilarated by the prospects of her higher learning.

Jared smiled and felt genuinely proud of Molly and slightly proud of himself for pointing out to Dr. Johnson that Molly was more than just a bright little girl. Jared was no prodigy. He just liked space science and wanted to learn all he could about it. He thought he might want to teach others about it, too, but he wasn't sure if he

wanted to teach or write or both. Working for NASA
was also a possibility, one that Dr. Johnson had brought
up on numerous occasions, but Jared always thought of
himself as more of an academic than a nuts-and-bolts
kind of guy. He liked studying science but was happy to
let someone else do the hard work. He wondered in
which direction Molly would go—mechanics or
academics. And once she was in college or out working
somewhere, what would Christy do? Would she follow
Molly or finally lead her own life? From what he'd
learned from Molly, her sister had given up all her own
hopes and dreams to make sure Molly was taken care of.
He greatly admired that but wondered whether Christy
regretted her decision.

"So, anyway," Molly said, and Jared realized he had
zoned out again—a habit he'd been trying to curtail his
entire life. "What are you working on today?"

She hopped down from the chair and stood next to
Jared, standing on tiptoe to lean over him and look at
the book he was reading. Papers littered the desk,
covered with his thoughts and questions. He'd never
been a neat and tidy worker.

"Research on Tranquility."

"There's going to be a full moon tomorrow night.
Christy and I are going to the beach to get a good look
at Tranquility. Want to come?"

"Um…" Of course, he wanted to join them. There
was no other place he wanted to be, but Christy didn't
seem to like having him around. She was always so
nervous and rarely met his eye, like she thought he was

a serial killer, or worse, a pedophile. Then again, he often avoided eye contact with everyone, and he did pay a lot of attention to her younger sister, so maybe that was on him. He should find a way to get her to trust him.

"Come on. It'll be fun. You can tell Christy all about your research. She likes hearing about that kind of stuff." Molly had a point, and he wanted to spend time with Christy. Maybe that would push her toward trusting him.

Jared smiled. "Oh, really? Does she? Or does she just listen because you like to talk?" He often teased her about her interminable chatter, and she was good-natured about it. He was surprised that she was so talkative. He'd done a fair amount of research on prodigies in the past couple weeks, and it seemed that most of them were quiet and very shy. Not Molly. Although he wondered if she acted differently around kids her own age, and he thought it would be interesting to observe her in a different setting. He couldn't help but notice that there were no kids her age at the birthday party, but when he mentioned it to Chloe and Avi, prodigies themselves, they acted as though they hadn't even given it a thought.

"I'll tell you what. You see if Christy is okay with me being there. If she is, then maybe I'll go."

"How about if you all come? That way, she won't think I'm trying to set you two up or anything."

Smart kid, he thought, although the thought of her setting them up wasn't an unpleasant one. Then again, he couldn't get that close to her. He just needed to earn her trust.

"If Christy says it's okay, and if the others say yes, then sure. I'll be there. For now, you need to get back to coding camp, and I need to get back to my research, okay? I have a lot to do, and I'm running out of time. The Fourth of July is a few days away and summer will fly by after that."

"Why are you here?" Molly suddenly asked, and Jared sat back and looked at her with both surprise and interest.

"What do you mean?"

"Why. Are. You. Here?" She asked the question as though he was a five-year-old.

"I'm doing research for my doctorate."

"Why here? Aren't there other, better places to do that? Like at the Smithsonian or the Ames Research Center in California or the University of Stuttgart where the German SOFIA Institute is? They're all doing major research on the moon." She laughed. "Well, not *on* the moon."

Jared rolled his eyes. "Funny, kid. Ha-ha."

"I'm serious. Why here?"

Jared sat back and looked at her. Dr. Johnson had asked him the same thing when he applied to do his research at Wallops. He gave Molly the same practiced excuse he'd given to his now-boss.

He didn't have the means to travel to Stuttgart and live there for several months, nor could he afford to live in Southern California. He knew he'd have access to the same information here and could work in a quiet place that had little foot traffic and few distractions. It was also a good place to work on a Cubesat that would aid him in his research if he could get the approval and funding to send it to the moon, which he had been granted. With similar projects already in the works at Wallops, Jared's particular focus on the Sea of Tranquility gave him a leg up in being allowed to do his research there. He also promised to help with the camps and assist Dr. Johnson with his own research project on gravity waves.

Those penetrating green eyes stared him down for several moments, and Jared felt uneasy, like this child savant could read his mind as easily as she could read the highly advanced book on his desk. After giving him an unfathomable look, she blinked and nodded.

"Makes sense," she said as though she needed to let the information go through some kind of internal data processing before she could accept the validity of his excuses. "Well, I'm outta here. I have to check on Chloe and see if she's having any luck with her part of the rocket, and lunch time will end soon. She and Avi are having a disagreement about some of the calculation. I think I've got them figured out."

Jared shook his head. He was certain she'd have the problem solved in half the time it would have taken Chloe to explain everything to her.

He turned back to his research and thought about her question. Why was he here?

It had been two months since he'd arrived. He'd done a lot of research, worked on the Cubesat and was waiting to get closer to the launch date before completing the final steps, and he had helped Dr.

Johnson with some of his gravity wave research. Jared's research was coming along nicely, and he hoped that the Cubesat would help him prove, or get closer to proving, his hypothesis.

He didn't know what he would do once he had his PhD, but he knew he never wanted to stop learning about space, and he hoped that being here all summer would help him discover his purpose. He was a firm believer that God had a purpose for him but had no idea what that purpose was. Why had his life taken such a drastic turn when he was so young, and how had that turn of events brought him to where he was today? Were they even connected at all?

Yes, of that he was certain. Jared didn't believe in coincidences. He and his mother had their entire lives ripped away from them for a reason. He became interested in space for a reason. He was at Wallops for a reason. He met and was now watching over Molly for a reason. He would have to be patient while God revealed to him what that reason was.

"All set," Jared said, moving away from the telescope he had propped up in the sand. "In case anyone wants to get an even better view than with the naked eye."

He sat on the opposite side of the blanket from Christy, and she felt both relieved and disappointed. Like everything else about this summer, she felt completely conflicted about Jared. She only understood half of the conversations they all had, and that was thanks to Fred and their family discussions, but everyone still treated her like she was part of the group. She didn't engage but nodded or hummed in acquiescence when they asked if she agreed. They didn't seem to notice that she was lost half the time, or they were too nice to say anything.

"When's Anya coming back?" Molly asked Avi.

"Tomorrow. They're spending the holiday and all next week here. You two will have plenty of time together. In fact," he turned to Christy. "Mom asked if Molly could skip going to Wallops a few days next week. They're going to do some exploring and thought Molly might like to join them."

Christy looked at Molly, whose eyes glowed with excitement.

"Oh, please, Christy, please. I really want to explore with Anya. We haven't done any exploring since we got here. And I really like Anya. She…" Molly looked down at her hands, then raised just her eyes and looked at her sister. She spoke quietly. "She likes me."

Christy's heart broke. It was the first time Molly had ever said anything like that, and Christy saw how important it was to her to have a friend close to her age.

"Of course, Molly. Avi, she can spend all the time with your family they will allow. But I warn you…" She looked at Molly and gave her a wicked grin. "They might get tired of having this squirt around too much!"

"You love having me around!" Molly tried to act indignant, but her grin broke through.

"You're right, Squirt. I sure do." Christy grabbed Molly and rolled her onto the ground, finding all her ticklish places.

Molly giggled but begged her sister to stop, and Christy obliged. She sat back and looked up to catch Jared smiling broadly at her. She felt her face turn red and looked away. She pointed to the sky as dusk settled in.

"So, when's the best time to see Tranquility?"

"Once the darkness sets in," Jared answered.

"And what's so special about it?" Christy asked, genuinely interested. "I mean, what's your dissertation about?"

Everyone turned to him. From what she could tell, only Molly had been privileged to glimpse small parts of his research, and everyone seemed curious.

Jared laid back on the blanket and remained quiet, staring up at the round, grey object in the sky. After several moments, he spoke, not to Christy, but in a way that seemed as though he spoke directly to the moon.

"In photographs, when color is processed and extracted, the Sea of Tranquility has a bluish tint, unlike any other place we can see on the moon. Scientists believe this is due to the high metal content in the basaltic soil. In addition, there's no mass concentration, or gravitational high, in the center of the Sea." He turned then to Christy. "It's not really a sea, which you probably know, but early observers of the moon thought it was because of the way it looks from earth. It's actually a large plain most likely formed by volcanic eruptions as evidenced by the basalt that forms the plain." He turned back to the sky.

"Anyway, as I was saying, there's no gravitational high there, which is strange. My theory is that the two are related—the lack of gravity and the high metal content, maybe something to do with magnetism, but lithium would be even better. I'm hoping my Cubesat will send me back some pictures that can help identify, through digital processing, the types of metals that are present in the basalt. If there's lithium present, we've found a whole new source that will impact the future of things like cell phones, electric cars, computers, whatever uses lithium batteries. So far, we only know what's in the rocks brought back by Apollo 11. Unfortunately, the photographs taken by Ranger 8 and Surveyor 5 didn't yield anything conclusive."

While Jared spoke, Christy couldn't help but think of Fred. Their enthusiasm was so similar, as was their love of space and things space related. No wonder Molly liked him so much.

Christy reclined and looked at the moon, trying to follow what Jared was saying. As she listened, she found that she had a new appreciation for the moon and wondered what knowledge humans could possess from that lifeless satellite orbiting the Earth. Was Jared right that it might contain the key to running our electronics? She stared at the Sea.

"If you were to go to the moon, would the Sea look blue like in the photographs?" she asked.

"I'm not sure," Jared admitted. "There's not much light on the moon. In fact, the back of the moon gets no sun at all, so we don't even know what's back there."

"So, the dark side of the moon really is mysterious, like the song in Mulan says."

Christy felt eyes on her, and she looked up to see everyone staring at her. "What?"

"Nothing," Chloe said. "It's just kind of cute that your knowledge of the moon comes from a song in a Disney movie."

Christy felt stupid, even betrayed, by people she thought were becoming friends, and she held back tears as she stared up at the moon. Molly scooted over to her sister and laid her head down on Christy's chest. "I get it," she said, almost in a whisper. "I feel like that, too, when other kids don't get me."

Suddenly, Christy's eyes filled with tears. She pushed Molly away, aware that her little sister was only trying to help but unable to accept her pity. She stood and walked off toward the high waves that crashed onto the beach. She hugged her arms tightly to her chest as tears streamed down her face.

"I'll go," Jared said, getting up from the blanket and pushing his glasses up on his nose as he quickly followed Christy toward the surf.

When he caught up to her, her cheeks glistened in the moonlight, and he felt a sudden urge to reach down and dry her tears. Instead, he matched her steps, walking swiftly beside her, almost at a run.

"Hey," he said, trying to sound casual. He didn't really know how he should sound. Even at his age, this was uncharted territory for him.

Christy kept walking, not acknowledging that he was there.

"I'm sorry. I mean, for what Chloe said. I'm sure she didn't mean it the way it sounded."

"You mean, like I'm stupid? Like you all are solving the problems of the universe while I sit home and watch Disney movies?"

"Nobody thinks you're stupid or that you sit home and watch Disney movies. Though I'd be okay with that, to be honest. The watching Disney movies part." He'd hoped she would smile, but she kept looking straight ahead, the same downtrodden look on her face.

"Christy, look." He was beginning to get winded. "Christy!" He practically shouted. "Please, I'm not used to walking this fast in the sand."

She cut her gaze at him, gave him a scathing look, but slowed down. A little.

"Thank you," he said. "I haven't been very good about exercising this summer, and sand isn't the easiest track to run on."

"Same," she said. "And I haven't been watching many movies either." She stopped and faced him. "I work all the time. Or I did. Now I'm working and filling out paperwork. And when I'm not doing that, I'm cooking and cleaning and grocery shopping and worrying about Molly. I meet with teachers and now a psychologist and Dr. Johnson, and anyone else who I need to talk to or take Molly to, so that I can make sure she grows up well-adjusted and able to handle high school classes and possibly college before she's even through puberty. All this…" She gestured wildly at the beach and pointed in the direction from which they came. "It's make-believe! It's me trying to be normal, trying to give Molly some normalcy in her young, screwed up life. I don't have the luxury of sitting around writing about the moon, not to mention watching movies."

She looked away, and he saw her wipe the tears from her face as new ones replaced the ones she tried to erase.

He felt his heart constrict. He thought his life was rough, but it was nothing compared to hers. Or was it? There was some common ground.

"I'm sorry about your parents. I guess that really derailed things for you."

She snorted. "You could say that."

Her tear-stained face glowed in the bright light that reflected from the moon, giving her an other-worldly look that he thought was appropriate given their circumstances.

"I was adopted by my stepfather, too."

He felt her stiffen and wondered if this revelation had the desired effect.

"You were?" She shifted slightly and glanced at him before looking back out at the ocean.

"Yeah, when I was seven. He's the only dad I've ever known." But not the only dad he knew of. He shook away the thought.

Christy's voice shook when she spoke. "I was four when my dad died. He was really young and in perfect health, but I guess that didn't matter."

"My father..." He looked over her head at the cresting waves and thought for just a second about the magic spell the moon cast on them, causing them to crest higher and stronger when it was full. He swallowed and stared at the white peaks, zoning out... and then he remembered she was waiting for him to speak. "My father left us, and then we moved as far away as we could get from him."

She turned to him, her eyes wide in disbelief. "You did? He just left?"

He took a deep breath. "I think so. I mean, there are a lot of things I don't know, and my mother won't tell me."

And there were things he was forbidden to share. It had been hammered into his head since he was a small child. He was never to talk about his early years, most of which he didn't remember, or tell anyone that his real name was Giovanni, not Jared. Sometimes he was surprised he remembered that, but one's name is hard to forget.

"Honestly, I don't really remember most of it." He knew his mother had been told to stick to as much of the truth as she could because that made it easier to lie, so he did the same. "I remember a lot of police being involved. Maybe Mom called them, or a neighbor. I don't really know, and Mom doesn't talk about it."

"Wow, and I thought my past was messed up."

She had stopped crying, which was his goal, and she was looking at him, which she almost never did, so two points for him. Maybe he could gain her trust after all.

"Do you want to tell me about it? I mean, I only know bits and pieces from Molly, but that's not really your story, is it?" He gently prodded, hoping she would open up to him. He couldn't figure out why she acted the way she did around him, around all of them. Well, part of it might have to do with his relationship with Molly, but did she really think they all thought she was stupid? Clearly, she was not. Perhaps knowing some of her background would help him get the whole picture. Besides, he needed to stop talking about his own past before he said something he'd regret.

Christy looked down at her toes nervously digging little trenches in the sand, and Jared patiently waited. Finally, she took a deep breath and exhaled before looking down the beach toward the others. They'd walked some distance, but Jared could see the threesome as they gazed through the telescope, pointing out things in the darkening sky.

"Maybe we should just head back," Christy said.

Jared wanted to touch her, to put his arm around her, but he hesitated. He wasn't a very touchy-feely kind of person, and he got the feeling she wasn't either.

"We can head back, but I'd still like to hear about your mom and your life before Dr. McLane—I mean Fred."

He saw her smile a little, but she shook her head. "It's not very interesting."

"Can I be the judge of that?"

She finally looked up, her eyes staring into his for the second time since they'd stopped. "You really want to hear it?" she asked, her voice still a little shaky, and her eyes full of doubt.

"I do. If you want to tell me." And he did. He realized that he was dying to know her story, and he had the strangest feeling that this was why he was here—that this had something to do with finding his own purpose.

White foam reached their bare feet, and Christy squealed and jumped out of the way, stumbling in the sand. Jared caught her arm, and her head whipped up, her eyes wide, but she didn't pull away. He felt his heart drop from his chest into a part of his abdomen he didn't know existed. He turned and looked toward the grassy outcrops that lined the top of that stretch of beach but thought the sand was a better place to sit. He let go of her arm, pulled his sweatshirt over his head, and walked up closer to the grass. Christy stood by the water as he spread the shirt on the sand far from the reach of the waves.

"Come on." He gestured toward his sweatshirt and sat beside it on the beach. "Tell me. The others are fine without us for a few more minutes."

Christy took one more look down the beach before walking over and settling down on his shirt. Then she slowly began to talk.

"I was thirteen when Mom met Fred at the school where she worked. She was a history teacher, and Fred was a friend of one of the science teachers. He made some kind of presentation to his friend's class. When he was leaving, he bumped into Mom—literally."

Christy smiled, remembering how her mother loved telling the story. "Fred walked out of the classroom and closed the door behind him, and Mom was walking down the hall. Fred turned to head out, and he bumped right into Mom, sending a whole armful of tests she had just copied into the air. They were all collated, but the stapler on the fancy copier was broken, so she was taking them back to her classroom to staple them. They flew all over the hallway. She was giving tests to three different classes on three different periods in history on the same day, so all the tests were different, and they were completely mixed up. Fred felt terrible, so he offered to go to her classroom and help sort them. By the end of her planning period, he'd asked her out, and…" She turned toward Jared with a smile. "The rest, as they say, is history. No pun intended."

Jared laughed. "Dr. McLane must have felt like an absolute idiot!"

Christy laughed, too. "He did! He acted like he hated it when Mom told the story, and she told it to everyone, but it was so obvious that he loved hearing it. He said it was love at first sight."

Christy inhaled the salt air deeply through her nose and sent it out in a long stream of breath through her parted lips. "I miss them," she said quietly, fighting back more tears.

"What happened to your biological father? If you don't mind me asking."

She found that she didn't mind at all.

"He died of a massive aneurysm. He was thirty-one." She looked at Jared and shook her head. "Can you imagine? He thought he had his whole life ahead of him, then one day, he was just sitting at his desk—he worked for an insurance firm—and he slumped over and never woke up. I don't remember much about him." She tried to conjure his face. "I have a couple pictures, but I never feel like I'm actually seeing him, the real him. Just posed shots with fake smiles."

"Did you like Dr. McLane when you first met him?"

She nodded enthusiastically. "I loved him as much as Mom did. He was so nice and attentive to us both. Mom told him about me on that very first day and let him know that everything in her life revolved around me. From the beginning, he agreed one hundred percent, and we did everything together. I wasn't a little kid by then, though, and I was pretty quick to let them know that they could go on real dates without me. They did, but most of what they planned included me, and we kind of became an instant family."

Jared's head bobbed. "Yeah, I know what you mean. My dad was like that, too. From what I've learned, you and I were lucky. I don't think that's how it usually goes."

"I'm sure you're right." She looked down and picked up a handful of sand, letting it run through her fingers.

"How did you feel about Molly coming along?"

"It happened pretty fast. They married about nine months after they met. The following year, Mom was pregnant. Molly was born a couple months after my fifteenth birthday." Christy kept playing with the sand as she thought about that day. Her friends thought it was weird that her mother was having a baby, but Christy had been so excited.

"I know that most kids would probably resent going from being an only child to a big sister at fifteen, but I adored Molly from the start. I'd never seen my mother truly happy, and suddenly we had a perfect family of four. A few days after they brought Molly home, Fred asked me if he could adopt me. I was on top of the world."

"I was eleven. Some of the other guys teased me, but I was pretty excited. I loved Missy from the start, too, and then Emily came along. It was pretty great." He smiled, and Christy found that she liked the way he smiled when he was relaxed.

She looked across the beach to the waves and remembered that summer after Molly was born when they came here for the first time. It was the first time she'd ever gone on a real family vacation, and it was perfect.

"How come you call him Fred?" Jared asked.

Christy rubbed her hands together, loosening the bits of sand that clung to her fingers, and thought about his question for a moment. She'd often wondered that herself.

"I don't really know, to be honest. He said I could call him whatever I wanted, and to me, he was totally my dad. But I'd only ever called him Fred. It felt weird to call him anything else. When Molly and I talk about him, then and now, he's Dad. But when I think about him, I think of him as Fred, the man who saved our lives." She looked at Jared and smiled.

He held her gaze, and she understood what Molly meant about his blue eyes popping behind his glasses. Without thinking about it, she reached up and gently slid them off his face.

Jared gave her a shy smile. "You realize I'm practically blind without those."

"Sorry," she said, blushing at what she had just done. "Molly said… Never mind." She handed his glasses back and watched as he put them back on, pushing them up with his finger.

"Molly said what?"

She looked away and shook her head. "Nothing. Just the ramblings of a kid."

"The view is much better this way," he said quietly, and she felt his gaze on her.

Christy tilted her head and looked at him. "Huh?"

"Never mind," he repeated her words and looked toward the water. "I guess we should get back."

The evening had turned into night, though not a dark night. The full moon glowed in the sky, and light danced on the water.

Jared stood and reached for Christy's hand. She hesitated but let him help her up. She pulled his shirt up with her and handed it to him.

"Thanks. For the shirt and the talk."

She suddenly remembered what had sent her running down the beach and was embarrassed. "I'm sorry about my behavior earlier." She looked away.

"You were hurt. I'm the one who should apologize. I'm sorry we hurt you."

"It wasn't you. It wasn't even Chloe. I mean, I hate that she said that, but..." She started walking back, and he walked by her side.

"What?"

She just shook her head. How could she possibly express how she felt when she was around him, around all of them? Even Molly.

Jared stopped walking and loosely took hold of the sleeve of her sweatshirt. "What?"

"I'm just not like you."

"Not like me?" Confusion showed in the creasing of his features.

"Not like any of you. I didn't even get to finish college. I'm not a genius or anything. I don't understand half of what you all talk about. I hang out with you guys because of Molly and because, well, because I don't have any friends here. I know you're all nice to me because of my sister, and I appreciate it, but I know I'm not like you." She willed herself not to start crying again. What was wrong with her? Why was she so emotional these days?

"I'm not either," Jared said.

Christy looked at him, trying to read his expression. "What do you mean, you're not either?"

"I'm not a genius. I mean, yeah, I admit that I'm smart and have a natural understanding of science, even on complex levels, but I can't read a lick of Shakespeare, much to my father's disappointment. I can tell the name of every moon in our solar system, but I can't remember the lyrics to songs."

"But you went to Harvard."

"So? Lots of people go to Harvard."

"But…"

"But nothing. I'm good at tests, so I got good grades and made the cut, but I'm not like Molly or even Avi. What about Fred? Was he a genius?"

Christy thought about it. "Well, I don't think he was technically a genius, not like Molly is."

"And you felt comfortable with him, right?"

She saw his point and nodded.

"Then stop worrying about how you fit in with us, with me. I'd like to think that you hang out with us because you like us, not for Molly's sake."

She thought there was a note of sadness in his voice, and she felt compelled to… She reached up and lightly brushed her fingers against his jaw line. She felt him tense under her touch, but she kept her hand on his face.

"I'm sorry. I shouldn't have said that. I do like you. I mean, I like all of you."

His hand found hers and gently took it from his face, but he held onto it, looking down at her with a striking intensity in his eyes. "I like you, too," he said in a husky voice.

He let go of her hand and turned, walking toward the group, and she felt a flutter like a flock of birds taking wing in her stomach.

Misty's Descendant Born to Angel's Stormy Drizzle

On June 30, 2022, Angel's Stormy Drizzle, the sixth-generation descendant of Misty of Chincoteague, gave birth to Misty's Moonlight. The foal, born on the night of the full moon, is the great-great-great-great grandson of the world-famous Misty of Chincoteague, immortalized in the 1947 book by Marguerite Henry. The Beebe Ranch will be open for visitors beginning on July 20 to kick off Pony Penning Week and will remain open Wednesday through Saturday for the rest of the season.

Chincoteague Herald, July 2

Chapter Seven

"So, what are you doing this evening?" Christy asked. She bent down with the dustpan and swept up doughnut crumbs and sand.

"Not much. Making dinner. Enjoying a bottle of wine, watching the fireworks from the back deck." Diane's voice was casual, but her face glowed as she removed her apron.

"Alone?" Christy asked in a teasing voice.

"Maybe. Maybe not."

"Perhaps a certain scientist will be joining you?" Christy hung the broom on a hook behind the kitchen door and gave Diane a pointed look.

"Maybe..." she said again, this time with a devilish grin on her face.

Christy rushed over and took her hand. "You are making your special sea bass with mango salsa, aren't you? On a bed of wild rice and kale?"

Diane laughed. "And what if I am?"

"Ha! I knew it! No wonder you've been dancing around here all day with your feet barely touching the ground."

Diane rolled her eyes but then shot a look at Christy. "And you? I noticed a bit of a spring in your step."

Christy felt the heat spread across her cheeks. "I might be going out for dinner and then fireworks on the beach."

"With Molly?" Diane asked, though Christy had already told her that Molly was watching the fireworks from Anya's condo with its perfect view of the water.

"With Jared," Christy said with a shrug. "Just a casual evening."

"Ha!" Diane said mockingly. "And I knew it! You've been holding out on me."

"Not really," Christy said. "We all—Molly and her cohorts—watched the moon rise the other night. I guess that's what you'd call it." She purposely didn't mention the other things that happened that evening. "Anyway, Jared and I had a nice talk, and the next day, he texted me and asked if I wanted to go out tonight." She started packing the few unsold doughnuts and pastries into bags for the food bank.

"I knew this would happen," Diane said with a smile as she emptied the coffee pot. "That day he came in to buy doughnuts to take to work, he couldn't keep his eyes off you."

"What? No way. He wouldn't even look at me."

"He wouldn't make eye contact with you, but he never stopped looking *at* you."

Christy felt her insides curl up into a tight ball. "Really?" she asked in a small voice. She still wasn't sure where this was going, if it was going anywhere, but she liked the idea that Jared had noticed her before she was 'Molly's sister.'

"Really," Diane confirmed. "And I saw the way he watched you at Molly's birthday party."

"Watched me?" Christy wasn't sure how she felt about that.

"In the way a woman wants to be watched," Diane said knowingly. "Trust me. He's into you."

Christy grinned. "Into me?"

"Hey, I'm with the times," Diane said, reaching for the light switch.

"Sure, you are. So, what's the deal with Dr. Johnson?" She followed Diane into the back.

"Nothing, really. We're just having dinner."

Before Christy could respond, the sound of sirens shattered the air. Both women looked at each other before running to the windows at the front of the store. An ambulance and a police car flew by as cars and people got out of the way.

"Car accident?" Christy said.

"Maybe. It is the Fourth. Lots of people on the island."

Christy nodded, but she always worried when she saw an emergency vehicle go by and didn't know where Molly was. With her new bike at her disposal, and now with Anya on the island for the week, Molly was never around anymore.

As if reading her mind, Diane put her arm around Christy's shoulders. "She's fine."

Christy let out a long breath. "I know. She's in good hands."

The sight and sound of the ambulance cast a dark shadow over Christy's bright mood. She felt like the air had shifted, and she had no idea why.

"This is the best meal I've had in years," Simon said, and Diane felt her entire body tingle with pride.

"I bet you say that to all the women who cook for you."

"No woman has cooked for me since Tricia passed almost ten years ago." Simon poured himself more wine and held the bottle over Diane's glass. She nodded, and he refilled her glass as well.

"Tell me about her," Diane said, genuinely curious.

"She was the light of my life. She and Elena. Tricia had a heart of gold." He stopped and raised his glass to Diane. "You remind me of her in that way."

"That's sweet of you to say."

"I mean it. The way you've taken Christy and Molly into your life is very telling. Not everyone would do that."

She took a sip of wine. "I can't imagine anyone not stepping in to help those girls. They're really special, and they're all alone."

"Not anymore," he said with a sharp nod. "They have us now."

"They sure do." She smiled at him. "And maybe someone else." She raised an eyebrow, and he looked at her with a question in his eyes.

"Oh?"

"Christy and Jared are on a date tonight."

Simon looked surprised. "Really? Did she ask him out?"

Diane shook her head. "No, he asked her. Why?"

"I can't imagine Jared making the first move. That man is as shy as they come. Except around Molly. She's able to get anyone to open up, if they can get a word in edgewise."

"I know what you mean," Diane said with a laugh. "But seriously, Jared asked Christy to dinner and then fireworks on the beach."

"Hmm. Interesting."

"Why?" Diane sat up. "Is there something I should know about him?"

"Oh, no, not at all. He's top notch. Good upbringing, from what I can tell. Harvard undergrad and grad school, working on his doctorate. Smart and focused. She could hardly find someone better."

"But…?"

Simon put his glass down and propped his elbows on the table, steepling his fingers. "He's a bit of a closed book. Doesn't talk much about his family. I just know what bits I've pulled out of him."

"So? You said he was shy and doesn't talk much."

Simon looked pensive for a moment then nodded. "I guess you're right. Chloe and Avi never stop talking, so I suppose his reservedness just stands out."

Diane wasn't sure what to think but would see what more she could pry out of Christy in the morning.

"Did you hear about the excitement on the island this afternoon?" she asked.

"Excitement? Over what?"

"An overdose. Not what we typically see around here. Some pretty bad stuff apparently."

"Local?"

She shook her head. "No, some young guy on vacation with friends."

"Well, hopefully that's a one-time occurrence. We don't need that kind of thing going on around here."

"I couldn't agree more," Diane said, thinking she and Marge had said the same thing earlier when Marge called to tell her the news.

"What are you studying?" Jared asked before he took a pull of his beer then put down the bottle.

Christy sipped her white zin and looked at the man across the table. The evening was going well. They were making small talk, and she felt at ease. There was no mention of her tears or their conversation from the other night, and she was glad for that. Looking back, she was embarrassed by her heightened emotions and the way she reacted to Chloe's comment. She chalked it up to being worried about Molly and the sudden shift in her own situation, but still, she wished she had handled things differently.

She lowered her glass and realized at that moment that Jared had gotten a haircut. His dark hair still curled around his head, but the curls were a little neater, not so out-of-control, and cut back from his face some. She smiled at the thought that, perhaps, he had done that in preparation for their date.

"English," she answered his question. "I don't really want to teach." She frowned. "I honestly don't know what I want to do. Diane thinks I should become a librarian, but that's even more schooling. Plus, I don't know if I want to do that or if I even have the time or money." She took a breath and sighed. "I know I should have this figured out by now, and I wish I did, but..." She looked away, heat flowing into her cheeks.

"Hey," Jared said in a quiet voice, prompting her to look up at him. "Not everyone has it figured out by the time they're in college or even after. I don't."

She blinked in surprise. "You don't? I thought you were getting your PhD and had your whole life in order."

"Well." He sat back and picked up his beer, holding it in his hand while he spoke, and it occurred to Christy that it was the first time she'd seen him so at ease. She wondered if it was the beer. "I'm getting my PhD, but that doesn't mean I have everything figured out. I think I want to be a professor but am not totally sure. I could go into research for NASA or work in a lab or for a company like SpaceX. Heck, I could become a meteorologist on the evening news." He smiled, and Christy laughed.

"Really? With a PhD?"

"Sure, why not? I'm studying the moon, which influences the tides and weather."

She gave a slight nod and made a noise to indicate her acceptance of this possibility.

"The thing is, I think I'd like to write a book. Working on my dissertation has given me a new appreciation for writing. But working with Molly has made me start wondering about how many kids out there love space like she does, like I always have from the time I was little. It would be really cool to share what I've learned with others, but I can't decide whether that would be on an academic level or just something fun, like writing for kids."

"What about writing textbooks? You know, for elementary schools."

Jared finished his beer. "Hmm, I've never thought about that." He put the bottle on the table. "And that opens up a whole new line of thought."

Christy laughed. "I didn't mean to make things even more difficult for you."

Jared shook his head and looked at his watch. *Is he bored with me?* Christy wondered automatically.

"Want to take a walk on the beach before the fireworks? We've got plenty of time." He motioned for the waitress but stopped and looked at Christy. "Oh! Unless you wanted dessert."

She looked at the remains of her chicken marsala. "No, I'm stuffed. A walk would be perfect."

They paid, and Jared escorted her from the restaurant, his palm on the small of her back. Christy liked the feel of his hand there. When they approached the car, he let go. Christy felt a coolness rush up under her shirt even though the night was hot and humid. She smiled at him as he opened the Jeep's door for her and held her hand to guide her inside. She remembered Fred doing the same type of thing for her mother, but she had never experienced such chivalry in men of her own generation. She had always thought of chivalry as an innate trait, but now she decided that it must be learned.

Neither spoke as they drove to the beach, but it was a comfortable silence. Christy could see what Molly saw in Jared—he was polite, kind, well-mannered, and soft-spoken. He had a gentle confidence that was so unlike most of the guys Christy had known in high school and college. He was a gentleman, so far, and Christy was beginning to understand why Dr. Johnson placed so much trust in him. She found that she was relaxed around him and wondered how she ever could have thought he posed a threat to Molly.

Jared had a season pass to the state park, which surprised Christy—he didn't seem like the beach type— but then she remembered that the Chincoteague Wildlife Refuge was much more than a beach with its trails and recreational activities for birders, photographers, and researchers. She looked at him out of the corner of her eye and decided she could see him as a birdwatcher. The thought made her smile.

Once they were parked in a sandy area where driving was permitted, Jared hastily jumped from the car and was at her door before she had it all the way open. She took his offered hand and let him help her out. He let go of her hand to close the door, and she felt the same loss of heat that she had experienced when he removed his hand from her back at the restaurant. She followed him down to a wooded area and was surprised when he took a trail through the grass.

"Where are we going?"

"Wild Beach," he replied before stopping and turning back to her. "You've never been there?"

She shook her head.

"It's a great place—fewer people, more wildlife, and great trails." He looked down at the long summer skirt that swayed around her legs and the sandals on her feet. "Um, maybe another time?"

Christy shook her head. "If this is the best place to go for a walk, then I'm game."

He took her hand, and she felt the effects of his touch run up her arm and down to her stomach. He turned back, taking her with him.

"We can get there a different way. We'll save the trail walk for later." He stopped and looked at her, pushing his glasses up with his free hand, seemingly nervous once again. "I mean, if you want to go another time."

She smiled, feeling a little shy in the semi-dark of the trees, his hand holding hers. "I'd like that a lot."

Jared wasn't sure when he realized he was holding Christy's hand. It just felt... natural. She made no attempt to let go as they walked down the beach, not even when she bent to take off her shoes. When she stopped suddenly and tugged at his arm, he looked at her, only to find her staring ahead, her eyes wide.

Wild Beach was called that for many reasons. Few people made their way to the end of the eleven-mile strip that was lined with sand dunes and buffered by sand and marsh grasses. The grasses, surrounding marsh, and spindly trees were the perfect habitat for migrating birds—great blue herons, snowy egrets, dunlins, American widgeons, and other birds that loved that type of terrain. To top it all off, there were the ponies.

The wild ponies of Assateague Island had lived on Assateague and Chincoteague islands since the Seventeenth Century. There were several stories about how they arrived there, but the one most accepted by historians and locals alike was that the ponies were shipwrecked after the sinking of a Spanish galleon off Assateague. Today, the Chincoteague Volunteer Fire Company was responsible for the care of the ponies. A pony auction was held every year to help pay for the department's expenses.

Standing about twenty yards ahead of Jared and Christy were three of the ponies, their red and white patchwork coats shining in the evening sun. Though he had read of their history and knew their fame, Jared had never actually seen the ponies in person. The sight of the beautiful creatures standing on the shoreline sent a thrill though him. He felt the same waves of excitement rolling off Christy as she stood, transfixed by the majesty of the scene.

"They're magnificent," she whispered.

Jared felt a lump in his throat as he watched her watching them.

"Magnificent," he repeated at the same whispered level she had used.

Slowly, she turned toward him, and he felt a flutter in his chest. With his free hand, he reached up and gently caressed her face, much the same as she had done to his a few nights back. He felt her catch her breath as his fingers touched her skin. Her hazel eyes held his, sparkling with meaning he didn't dare compute.

The urge to bend down and kiss her was as strong as the ocean's tide, and he felt himself being pulled toward her, though he made no move. He had the sudden awareness that he was the moon and she, the earth, holding him in her gravitational pull, caught between the desire to move toward her and the need to stay in the safety of his orbit.

A loud whinny rang through the air, and she blinked, the moment broken. Jared wasn't sure if he felt regret or relief. He had never allowed himself to get too close to anyone outside of his family. Even the deep love he had for his sisters had its boundaries, and he often wondered how his mother managed to keep the two worlds separate—the one they lived in and the one about which the two of them never spoke.

"Should we head back?" Christy quietly asked, and he thought he detected disappointment in her tone.

He looked at his watch. "Yeah, we should. I didn't realize how long we've been walking. We need to get going if we're going to make it to see the show."

They took one last look at the ponies and turned to go, her hand still in his, and it gave him some comfort despite his misgivings about getting too close.

"Where to next?" she asked.

"It's a surprise."

"Really? We are watching the fireworks, right?"

"Of course. We're just not going to watch them with the thousands of people who are crowding onto the carnival grounds."

He felt her look at him but kept walking. If she asked questions, he wasn't going to answer. He was good at keeping secrets.

Christy took Jared's hand, and he helped her down onto the deck of the boat. She could count on one hand the number of times she'd been on a boat, but she knew that this was nicer than the average fishing boat.

"You said this is Dr. Fieldstone's boat?"

She watched him untie the line and toss it onto the deck like an expert.

"Yeah, he's out of town and said I could borrow it."

She held her bottom lip tightly in her teeth as he walked precariously along the outer ledge of the boat to untie the other line. "Be careful," she said.

Jared stopped and looked at her with concern. "Are you afraid of boats?"

She shook her head, perhaps a little too vigorously. "Um, no. I'm not afraid exactly…"

Jared let go of the line, leaving it tied, and jumped into the boat. He put his hands on her upper arms and looked down at her. "We don't have to do this. I thought it would be nice to be away from the crowds and get a stellar view of the fireworks, but—"

"Stellar?" She asked with a smile. "No pun intended?"

Jared didn't smile. "Christy, seriously. I'm not trying to be funny. If you want to watch them somewhere else, we can."

"No, I'm fine. I'm just not used to being on a boat. And it's going to be dark. And you don't really have any experience—"

"Whoa, stop there. I grew up in the land of ten thousand lakes. I was practically born on a boat."

"Really?"

A dark look passed across his features, but it disappeared quickly and was replaced with a smile. "No, not really. But I did live most of my childhood in Minnesota. We went boating a lot. My father has a boat, and we spent a lot of time at his family's cabin on a lake."

"And you're sure you know how to drive one?"

Jared laughed. "Absolutely. Dr. Fieldstone would not have loaned it to me if he didn't trust my knowledge and ability. I really have been driving boats longer than I've been driving cars."

Christy thought about that, then slowly nodded. "Okay, then," she said with an exhale. "Let's do this."

"Are you sure?"

"Yep, I'm sure. I'm an island girl now. I have to get used to being on a boat. Right?"

"You won't get sick or anything?"

"I don't think so?" She hadn't meant for it to come out as a question and saw the alarm in his eyes. His grip tightened on her arms. Not for the first time, something about him reminded her of Vince, but she quickly pushed the thought away.

"No, I'll be fine. I promise," she said hastily. She gave him as much of a smile as she could. After a moment, he let go and climbed back up to untie the line.

Christy breathed deeply as Jared started the boat and maneuvered it away from the dock. By the time they were out in the middle of the channel, she felt at ease. The slow movement of the boat stirred a breeze that wrapped around her, dispelling the heat and humidity that she had felt on shore. She looked over the side, wondering if she could see any fish swimming by the boat, but the water was murky and moved too swiftly for her to detect anything. She sat back up and leaned her head back. Closing her eyes, she let herself enjoy the peacefulness of the ride. When the boat eased to a stop, she opened her eyes and looked around.

They weren't the only boat out there by far, but there was a hush over the moonlit water, only interrupted by the sound of the anchor that Jared dropped into the water. He joined her on the cushioned bench, and they both looked up at the sky.

"Not much longer," Jared said in a soft voice.

A shiver ran over her. Jared put his arm around her, pulling her close to him. "You can't be cold," he said even as he rubbed his hand up and down the top of her arm.

"No, just..." She tried to think of the right word. "Anticipating, I guess. It's been a while since I've had a night like this." She turned to face him. "Thank you. I needed this."

"You're welcome," he said in a hushed voice, and she felt as though her stomach was filled with the little white birds they saw on their walk. She stared into his eyes and swallowed when she saw them briefly dart to her lips and back up.

She felt him leaning toward her and anticipated his kiss, inclining toward him. Suddenly, there was a loud pop, and a light streaked up into the sky. They both startled and looked to see a burst of color against the black cloak of night.

Neither moved nor spoke for the next forty-five minutes. Christy watched the display without a care in the world. She didn't know if it was the beautiful night or the feeling of his arm holding her close to him that brought on the profound sense of peace.

When the display was over, they sat still while the other boats meandered back toward the shore, and Christy wondered if Jared was as much against the night ending as she was. Finally, he spoke, his voice rich and low.

"I think God intended for our lives to be just like this."

Christy had no idea what he meant, and she was surprised to hear him say such a thing. "God?"

She felt him nod, but they continued looking into the sky. "Yeah. I think when he created the heavens and the earth, he meant for life to be just like this—peaceful and quiet with humans looking toward the heavens in awe."

Christy was quiet for several moments before saying, "You believe in God?"

As if surprised, Jared pulled back and looked at her, his eyes narrowing in disbelief. "You don't?"

"Um, well, I guess I never really thought about it."

"You never thought about whether you believe in God?"

She shook her head, not sure if she felt embarrassed or just confused. "It's not, I mean, he's not something we ever talked about. I mean, Fred was a scientist, after all."

"So?" Jared asked, his face a picture of puzzlement.

"So, aren't most scientists atheists or something?"

Jared shook his head. "Well, there are scientists who are atheists, more now than ever before, I would guess. But throughout the centuries, it was men of the Church who pioneered most of the greatest scientific discoveries ever made."

"Really?" She sat up, completely intrigued. "What Church?"

"The earliest science experiments on record were conducted by Catholic priests and monks. In fact, Buridan, Oresme, and Bacon were the Catholic philosophers who founded modern science. In the very first centuries AD, it was the Catholic monasteries and convents that were bastions of science, ushering in studies of nature, mathematics, engineering, and even space." He smiled and raised and lowered his eyebrows several times. Christy laughed, and Jared continued.

"Copernicus pioneered the idea that the sun was the center of the universe, and Descartes invented the study of geometry. They were both Catholic. Mendel, the father of genetics was also Catholic, and Georges Lemaître, a Catholic priest, formulated the Big Bang Theory."

She watched as he became more animated. He had the same passion in his voice when he talked about God that he had for the moon, and she marveled at his enthusiasm.

"See, it's a modern myth that religion and science are at odds, mostly thanks to Stephen Hawking, but he was wrong. Science can measure quantitative things, but it can't measure truth, beauty, goodness, or other intangible things. Science can only explain so much. Thomas Aquinas, who was brilliant, said that you can't prove that God exists because God isn't a being. He is being itself."

Christy stared at him, narrowing her eyes as she tried to grasp what he was saying. "I'm lost. First, I have no idea who this Thomas guy is, and second, how is someone 'being itself'?"

"Matter is a thing that is in a manner of being. We, humans, are things in a manner of being. Energy is in a manner of being. The universe is in a manner of being."

Christy raised her brow, and Jared seemed to understand that she was falling even farther behind. He waved his hand as if to erase his words from the air.

"Okay, sorry. Science can never eliminate or disprove God because God isn't a thing or a person or a form of energy. He is the culmination of everything, the before and after, the beginning and the end. Hawking spent his life searching for the Theory of Everything, the basic underlying thread that holds everything together. What he never understood or accepted was that the thing that unites and explains everything is God."

He looked at her as though this should make all things clear.

Christy shook her head. "I want to understand. I'm trying to understand…" She was beginning to feel the same way she felt several nights before. Her limited knowledge and understanding were no match for his intellect, which she knew. What surprised her, though, was that he was arguing the case of something which she would have thought was unintellectual.

"Maybe it's too late at night for me to be able to fully understand what you're saying." She didn't want to admit that she was just woefully inadequate when it came to such deep ruminations.

Jared looked at her and grinned, but not in a demeaning way. "It's okay. It's heady stuff. You were brought up in a house where science was God. I was brought up in a house where the God in Heaven was the basis for everything."

"That's just so foreign to me. I mean, my mother used to say things like, 'do the Christian thing,' and sometimes we found a church on Christmas, but that was the extent of it. Fred was staunchly anti-religion."

She thought that the look he gave her might have been one of pity, but he quickly rearranged his expression and eased himself off the bench. "I get it. I went to Harvard, too. Religion wasn't a very popular discussion topic there. Unless you were on the side of Hawking, of course." He turned toward the engine room, or whatever it was called, but then looked back at her. "Don't worry about not understanding it all. Just know that I'm always here to talk. If you have questions about religion or science or how to drive a boat, I'm your man."

He gave her a wide smile before going into the little cabin and starting up the boat. Christy stared out at the dark horizon as they headed back to the shore and thought about all that he had said. Most of it was beyond her understanding, so she decided the only thing she really wanted to dwell on were the words, 'I'm your man.'

"I'm telling you, I thought I was seeing a ghost."

Vince's remark was greeted with nothing but silence. He took the phone from his ear and looked at the screen to be certain he had not lost the connection. After several moments, he heard a voice on the other end.

"And you're positive he isn't there just for the holiday? That either way, you'll have the ability to track down his whereabouts?"

"Absolutely," Vince replied, almost tasting the approval he'd lost after his last indiscretion.

"And you know this how?"

His mouth curled up into a confident grin. "Because I know the gal he was with. And so do you."

Local Authors to Sign Books at SunDial Books

Local authors Kayla Kelly Middleton and Katherine Middleton Kelly will be on hand this Saturday to sign copies of their best-selling books. Middleton will be autographing the cookbook she wrote with her husband, Zach, *Around the World in Eighty Meals*, which is the inspiration for the new Gordon Ramsay cooking competition on Fox Television. Kate Kelly, Middleton's sister-in-law, will be signing her memoir, *Discovering Life on a Barrier Island*. The book details the story of Kate's arrival on Chincoteague, meeting her husband, Coast Guard Commander Aaron Kelly, and becoming a beloved member of our community. Contact SunDial or check out their Facebook page for more information.

The Chincoteague Herald, July 5

Chapter Eight

"So, how was the Fourth?"

Christy knew that Diane was trying to sound casual, but she was not good at being covert.

"It was nice. And yours?" She turned the conversation to her boss as she gave the front window a final swipe with the cleaning cloth.

"Very nice. The fireworks were the best ever. Didn't you think so?"

Christy turned to see Diane smiling at her, one brow raised. She couldn't help but smile back. "Is that your way of asking me if I kept my eyes on the sky and my attention undivided?"

"Well?" Diane asked, moving through the tables and chairs to get closer to Christy. "Did you?"

"As a matter of fact, I did. We both watched the show and then continued gazing at the sky."

Diane frowned. "And? That's it?"

Christy laughed. "Don't look so disappointed. Aren't you supposed to be warning me against moving too fast or telling me to protect my virtue?"

"You can take your time and protect your virtue while still having a little fun."

"Oh?" Christy cocked her head and raised her own brow. "And did you? Have a little fun, I mean?"

Diane placed her hand on her chest and feigned shock. "Why Ms. McLane, are you asking a lady to kiss and tell?"

"Aren't you?" Christy tried to act just as shocked, but she inwardly admitted that she was dying to know the answer. Maybe some tit for tat... "We talked a lot. We held hands. We shared some butterfly-inducing moments staring into each other's eyes. It was a really nice evening. I had fun."

Diane's mouth fell open, and her eyes narrowed. "Seriously? That's all? Not even a goodnight kiss?"

Suddenly wondering if she had done or said something wrong, Christy slowly shook her head from side to side. "I'm uh, um, maybe he just wants to be friends."

"Did he act like he just wanted to be friends?"

"Maybe? I mean, we did hold hands and had those few intimate moments, but he didn't make any moves. And actually..." She bit her bottom lip. "Once, when we almost kissed but were interrupted, I got just a bit of a feeling that he might have been relieved." She tried to shrug it off, but the thought stung just a little. Okay, more than a little.

"Hmm. You know, Simon was very surprised that Jared even asked you out. He said that the young man is extremely shy. Maybe that's all it was."

"I don't know." She tried to smile. "Maybe." She started to turn away but then remembered… "Hey, what about you? How was your evening? Really?"

Diane's eyes lit up, and she beamed with a smile as big as an alligator's mouth—a phrase Christy had once read in a book and now understood just how true it could be.

"Simon is such a gentleman. We had dinner, my sea bass, of course. Then we sat on the deck and talked while finishing the bottle of wine he brought with him, along with a bouquet of flowers."

"Ooh…" Christy cooed.

"We talked and talked, and before we knew it, the fireworks started glittering across the sky. Afterward, he said he needed to head home but that he'd love to take me out this weekend."

"Nice!" Christy could see how excited Diane was and how much she liked Dr. Johnson. "No kiss?"

Diane shook her head. "No kiss, but you know what? It gives me something to look forward to."

Christy nodded. She liked that thought. Maybe she, too, had something to look forward to.

"So, no more apprehensions about Jared?"

Christy thought for a moment and realized she hadn't had any worries about Jared since the night of the full moon.

"You know, Jared has turned out to be much different than I thought. He's a true gentleman, and he's a good listener, and you'll like this part, he's religious."

"I had a hunch," Diane said.

"You did? How?" A movement outside the window caught Christy's eye, and a strange feeling came over her, like she was being watched, but when she looked, she didn't see anyone or anything out of the ordinary. She turned her focus back to Diane.

"I've seen him there a couple times now."

"I'm sorry. Where?"

Diane gave her an odd look. "At church. I said, he's been at the Saturday night Mass a couple times."

"Hmm..." Christy hadn't thought about Jared going to church, though it made sense after their conversation. It made her realize that despite all they'd talked about, there was still very little that she knew about the man.

Christy smiled at the text. A soft light glowed from the phone, the brightness turned down, but otherwise, the room was dark. The windows were open to the breeze that blew in from the Atlantic, but the night air was still heavy with humidity, so only a light sheet covered Christy as she lay, head propped on her pillow, reading the words on the screen.

I've never heard him whistling at work before. And that grin! He can't stop smiling. I think he's got it bad.

Christy thought of the look on Diane's face when she talked about Dr. Johnson, Simon, as she called him. She wondered, why was Diane still single? Why hadn't someone scooped her up before now? She was a heck of a catch. Did everything else in life just get in the way to the point where Diane had accepted that she would always be alone?

The thought made Christy frown. Was that to be her life? Was she to have a date on holidays but spend the rest of her life answering text messages late at night after she collapsed into bed?

She shook her head. No, Molly would eventually grow up and go away to school, then Christy would be on her own. Or would she just be alone? Was there a difference? Jared was a great guy, but he would soon tire of her, of her obligations, of the necessity to put Molly first, of Christy just starting back up at school while Jared planned to be finished by the end of the summer. Not to mention that, at the end of the summer, he would leave and go back to the Midwest. No, Christy couldn't count on anything happening on that front. Even if she admitted that she wasn't intellectually inferior, they were at different points in their lives and on different paths. She would enjoy the few moments they shared over the summer, then they would both move on. It seemed to be how her life went. Which brought her thoughts back to Diane.

Do you think he likes her? I mean, really likes her?

Christy hesitated before sending the message. She felt protective of Diane and wanted to send a warning about not letting Dr. Johnson hurt her, but she decided against it and hit the button. Jared's reply was immediate.

I've no doubt.

Christy watched as the dots blinked, but it was a long beat of time before another text arrived.

He'd give her the moon if she let him.

Christy's stomach did a little flip. Why did she have the feeling that Jared had taken his time to think that through and that, perhaps, he was no longer speaking of Dr. Johnson?

She bit her lips together and pushed the thought away. A fun summer. That was all. She had to remember that. With everything she had going on, she couldn't take the time to mend a broken heart.

It's getting late. Busy day tomorrow. Good night, Jared.

She didn't wait for a reply. She put her phone on the nightstand, case closed, and turned to face the other way.

Jared stared at the screen for several moments before typing a quick good night and putting the phone on the charger for the night. He sighed deeply as he gazed up at the ceiling, one arm behind his head, the other draped across his stomach.

"What's that for?" asked a sleepy voice from the other bed.

"What?" Jared asked.

"That sigh. Something wrong?"

How was someone so young, even half asleep, so intuitive?

"Nah. Go back to sleep, Avi. Sorry to wake you."

Jared heard, rather than saw, his roommate sit up in the dark room. Jared continued to lie in bed looking up at the ceiling and hoped Avi was just getting up to use the bathroom.

"You're going to ask her out again, right?"

Jared considered ignoring the question, pretending he was already asleep or relaying the message that he didn't want to talk about it. He would have succeeded if it had been anybody else, but Avi was like a dog with a bone.

"Maybe," was the only reply Jared was willing to give.

"Why maybe?"

Jared sighed louder, hoping to convey his annoyance. Clearly, he didn't want to discuss this.

"Seriously, man. She's pretty, she's smart—even if she doesn't think she is—and she's got her stuff together. Look what she's doing for Molly. Totally giving up her life and all? Not many people would do that, even for a sibling. She's special."

"Then why don't you ask her out?" Jared asked, not attempting to hide his annoyance. It's not like he didn't know all that already. And his heart already did flips with every little thought he had about her, which happened constantly He wanted to ask her out again. He was tempted to text or call her all the time. Heck, he'd even begun having cravings for coffee and doughnuts and had to curb the desire to get up extra early and drive to Chincoteague every morning just to see her. He wanted to make her life better, easier, happier.

In fact, he wanted to give her the moon.

But what hope was there in starting anything? He wasn't his mother. He couldn't live a lie.

"Come on, Jared. What's your problem? It's so obvious how you feel about her."

How did he feel about her? He felt like… The light of the brightest star in the sky paled in comparison to the twinkle in her eyes. He saw her smile in the crescent moon. With every rising of the sun, he felt the warmth of her hand in his. Yes, he would give her the moon if she let him, and the stars, and the sun, and the entire universe. What he couldn't give her was the truth.

Jared rolled over, his back to Avi. "It's complicated. I can't explain it, but it would never work."

"How do you know if you won't try?"

Jared stared at the blank wall, giving no response, and after a time, he heard Avi lie back down. He thought the conversation was over until Avi added, "Don't hurt her, Jared. Christy wouldn't be the only one nursing a broken heart. Molly loves you, too. Besides, you'd regret losing her for the rest of your life."

Jared silenced his snarl. What did Avi know? He was just a kid. He hadn't even made a move on Chloe yet, and it was just as obvious to everyone how Avi felt about her.

At that, Jared had a sobering thought. Maybe it was just the circumstance they were all in. They were away from home, away from friends and family, working all day, looking for some adventure on their time off, soaking up the salty air and ocean waves. In six weeks, they'd all go their separate ways. Whatever was going on between the four of them would end. Even if Jared stayed through the fall, which he was considering, Molly would be back in school, and Christy would be starting classes. They would lose touch, and he'd have nothing to worry about.

Rather than let the troublesome thoughts weigh him down, Jared decided this was a good thing. A summer fling. That's all this was. He could ask Christy out, enjoy her company, and then let things die down once the summer was over. Then he'd never have to worry about hiding his past from her or starting a future based on a lie.

Vince double-checked the address he'd gotten from Christy's employment papers. This was the house, all right. He assessed the setting.

The house was small, right on the road, with a few trees and close neighbors, but easy to access. Plenty of places to park and sneak up to the house, which was old and probably had old locks, maybe windows that didn't latch or close all the way. He could be in and out real quick. The question was, did he take Christy or the little sister? Which one would he care about the most? Which one would get him talking faster?

Twenty-four years. That's how long his father had sat in prison while that snitch and her kid lived their happy, hidden life. Well, that was all about to change.

The morning sun beat down on Christy's back. She felt the freshly applied sunscreen drip down her skin like spilled milk. Jared tossed a line to Avi while Christy wrestled Molly into her life jacket. Chloe lathered another giant glob of sunscreen on her legs.

"This is so cool," Avi exclaimed as he grabbed the second line, a huge grin rippling across his face. "How did you get Dr. Fieldstone to let you use his boat? I mean, he never even looks at me. I don't think he even knows who I am."

Jared didn't answer as he jumped back in the boat and went into the cabin to take the wheel.

"I think Jared's a little farther up the chain than you are, Avi," Chloe said. "Here, put this on." She pitched the bottle of sunscreen his way, and he caught it, making a face at her as he did so.

"I guess so. I mean, Jared isn't just an intern like us."

"Jared's not an intern at all," Molly interjected, pulling away from Christy as soon as the life jacket was tightened. "He's a PhD student writing about important discoveries on the moon and his hypotheses about them. His paper could have major ramifications on the study of the moon and the way we view gravity here on earth. The metals he's proposing the moon's surface contains could lead to scientific breakthroughs the likes of which we've never even imagined before."

Christy looked at Jared and grinned. His eyes sparkled as he smiled back at her. They both acknowledged Molly's crush on him, and Christy had talked to her sister more than once about the impossibility of Jared returning her affections. The previous night, as Molly excitedly packed her bag for their outing, Molly had assured Christy that she was not going to fight her for Jared's affections. She declared that she knew when she had been beaten; Christy was the only girl Jared had eyes for. Christy had simply rolled her eyes and told Molly to go to bed.

She watched now as Molly leaned over the boat and watched the white foam forming thick bubbles as it gushed out from under them. Christy squelched the urge to grab the child and restrain her, but they were moving very slowly as Jared maneuvered through the channel, so Christy let Molly's curiosity reign for the time being. Motioning to Chloe to keep an eye on her sister, Christy eased into the small cabin and looked through the large window toward the open water.

"Thanks for letting Molly come today. She's really excited."

Jared turned to look at her with crossed brows. "Did you think I'd consider taking the gang out without her? She'd never speak to me again, and I have a lot of research I need her to help me with this coming week."

Christy smiled. "Oh, is that your plan? Give her a fabulous day on the water today, then drown her with work all week?"

Jared laughed. "That's not what I meant, but now that you put it that way…"

The cabin was small, and the air was saturated like a sweat-infused sauna, as was typical of a Mid-Atlantic day. If Christy had squeezed into a space filled with the heaviness of humidity with any other person, she would have felt as though she was suffocating. With Jared, though, it felt as natural as the salt in the air that left its invisible trace on her skin. Realizing that this was exactly how she was beginning to think of Jared, that he was silently and invisibly seeping into her pores and becoming a part of her, she stole a glance at him. As though reading her mind, he slowly turned her way, the amusement gone from his baseball cap-shaded face. She saw his Adam's apple bob as he swallowed, and the cabin suddenly felt terribly small and stifling hot.

The world seemed to fall out from under Christy as she gazed into those blue eyes. Sweat formed at the small of her back, and her stomach spasmed. What was she doing? She wasn't supposed to be feeling like this. She told herself she wouldn't do this, go there, feel this.

"Hey, when are we going to get there?"

Christy and Jared both jumped at the sound of Molly's voice ringing through the small space. Jared blinked, and Christy breathed as though hyperventilating, realizing she had been holding her breath. She turned toward her sister, but Jared answered before she had a chance to process Molly's question.

"It's just up there, a place called Queens Sound. Almost there now."

He had gone back to gazing ahead and didn't turn to look at either Molly or Christy as he spoke.

"Let's get the buckets ready," Christy told her sister, taking her hand and leading her to the back of the boat.

They dug into the canvas bags they'd brought with them, pulling out old metal buckets that Dr. Fieldstone had given Jared for their hunting expedition. Christy jolted as the boat stopped, and the engine went silent. She looked up as Jared walked past her to the back of the boat and picked up an anchor which he tossed into the water. He pulled his shirt over his head. It was the first time Christy had seen him shirtless. He was tanner than she expected.

For someone who worked inside all day, his skin must soak up the sun quickly and easily, and not in the red-as-a-lobster, skin-peeling kind of way she'd expect from someone named Stevenson. Though now that she thought about it, he didn't look Anglo-Saxon at all. There wasn't a trace of Northern or Western European ethnicity in his looks, save for the deep blue eyes. In fact, he looked rather...Italian. With the thick, wavy curls, more of them black in color than brown, and the olive tint of his skin, she wondered how she'd never thought about it before.

"Christy?"

She blinked, noticing the odd way Jared was looking at her and wondered if her own expression had been just as odd.

"I'm sorry?"

"Are you ready to get in?"

Somehow, she had completely missed Chloe and Avi grabbing a bucket and scurrying overboard. Molly stood by Jared, her arms crossed, giving Christy the look of irritation that she so often cast disparagingly at her older sister.

"Oh! Yes. Sorry. I was lost in thought. Must be the heat." She tried to smile, but Jared continued to peer at her, those eyes, adorned with bushy black eyebrows, filled with suspicion. She hurried to her feet and went to the side of the boat. "Okay, Molly, remember, don't go too far from us."

"I know, I know. Sheesh. I'm not a little kid, you know."

"Just humor me." She looked at Jared, and attempting to end all the strange vibes between them, she said, "Last one in is a rotten egg."

"Or a rotten clam," he called before quickly jumping into the water.

"Cheater!" Christy called. She helped Molly over the side then eased herself into the cold water.

Christy squealed when she came up out of the water. She swung her long hair around, and water droplets landed on Jared's face, each tiny splash like a kiss that made his stomach curl into a knot.

"Oh my gosh. I had no idea it would be so cold. It's the middle of July!"

"You'll get used to it," Molly said. "There are thermoreceptors in your skin that signal your brain to the change in temperature. When the cold touches your skin, your sympathetic nervous system immediately releases hormones that cause vasoconstriction in the epidermis. The outer layer of your body begins to reduce in temperature, finding a gradient between your core temperature and the water around you."

"Thanks for the lesson, Squirt."

"You're welcome," Molly said with a smile, completely unaware of her sister's sarcasm. Jared couldn't help but smile.

"Molly," he said. "Do you want some goggles so you can look under the water to find the clams?"

She stuck her head under, presumably with her eyes open, and came up shaking her head. "Nah. My eyes will adjust, and their natural salinity will be unbothered for a suitable amount of time to find enough clams for me to eat. I'll be fine, but thanks." She dove under the water, nothing visible except her feet, kicking just below the surface.

"Should we wear goggles?" Christy asked. "I mean, is it safer that way?"

Jared shook his head. "You don't have to. You can pretty much feel for the clams with your feet and just reach down and pick them up. They're easy to find."

Proving his point, Molly came to the surface as quickly as she had gone under, her hand raised triumphantly in the air clutching several small shells. "I found some!"

"Hand them to me. I'll put them in the bucket," Jared said, taking the shells and shoving them in his pockets. He looked at Christy. "When my pockets are full, I'll put them in the bucket." He gestured to the row of pails he had lined up on the boat's gunwale.

"Are these really safe to eat?" Christy asked. He could tell by her movements that she was feeling for clams with her feet under the water.

"Be careful. The clams can have sharp edges. Gently use your toes to feel around the bottom."

The water came to her clavicle. Every now and then, a wave washed against her face, causing her to spit out a bit of water. Her hair flowed behind her, and she reminded Jared of a mermaid keeping just below the water's surface.

"The clams are perfectly safe to eat. Plus we're going to boil them, so if there is anything harmful, any bacteria or anything, the boiling water will kill it."

She nodded, but her face was serious as she worked her toes in the sandy bottom. Her mouth tightened and loosened, her brow furrowed in concentration, then he saw a small smile begin to work its way across her face. She flipped over and disappeared into the water, her fins—er… feet—flapping for a few seconds before she reappeared with clams in hand.

"I found some!" She placed the shells in Jared's hands, followed by Molly, who was excitedly counting her bounty. A shell fell from the pile he was holding, and Jared laughed.

"Hold on. Let me get these to the boat."

He held his cupped hands out of the water and carefully made his way to the ladder. He used his elbows to maneuver his way up, only losing one clam along the way. Once high enough to hold his hands over a bucket, he released the clams he'd been holding and dug into his pockets for the rest.

"Stay up there," Avi called, making his way through the water. He handed Jared a handful of clams and dug into his own pockets for more.

For the next hour, the group toggled between clamming and swimming. They raced between Dr. Fieldstone's boat and a marker in the water and played a game of Marco Polo, much to Molly's delight. Jared sometimes forgot that she was just a little girl, and he smiled every time she squealed or splashed him like his own sisters would do.

The only thing that bothered him about the day was how quiet Christy had become. She played the games and dug for clams, but he sensed that her heart wasn't in it. He couldn't help but wonder if he'd said or done something to upset her. It was hours before he had a chance to get her alone again.

When Christy went into the house to gather the side items they'd picked up to go with the clams, Jared told the others that he'd help get the food together. Standing in the kitchen, he recalled the only other time he'd been inside the house. The birthday party had been a similar gathering, and he'd felt lost and confused trying to help Christy with the s'mores stuff. This time, he felt lost and confused all over again. His heart and mind were at war, and he didn't know which would win, but he couldn't worry about that now. Something was wrong, and he needed to know what it was.

Christy stood at the counter peeling the plastic from the top of a container of macaroni salad. She had to have heard him come in through the back door, but she gave her full attention to the pasta, a determined look on her face. Once she had it open, she reached for a jar of pickles and began twisting the lid. Her face reddened as she gripped the unyielding jar.

Jared went to her and gently took the jar from her hands. He tapped the lid of the jar on the countertop, rotating it as he did so, then twisted the lid until it popped and placed the jar on the counter. Christy stared at the jar as though in a trance. Jared reached for her, taking her hands in his and turning her to face him. When she finally lifted her eyes to his, he smiled.

"Hey," he said quietly, unsure now that he wanted to ask her what was wrong. All he could think of was lowering his mouth to hers, but then he saw the look in her eyes. Rather than mirroring what he was feeling, her eyes held worry, or was it fear?

"What's wrong? Something's been off all day. Is something bothering you? Are you upset? Did I... Did I do something?"

Christy pressed her lips together until they turned white, and Jared suppressed the urge to fold her into his arms. "What is it?" He asked gently, worry beginning to take hold.

"It's nothing. I'm just..." She looked away, and when she turned back, her eyes were fixed on his neck rather than his face. Finally, she sighed and smiled, looking up at him. The smile didn't reach her eyes. "I had a really good day. It was fun. Thank you. Molly had a ball."

"I'm glad, but..." He blinked and squeezed her hands. "If you had a good day, what's bothering you?"

Christy shrugged. "Nothing. I mean, I guess I'm just off today. Tomorrow is Mom's birthday. Was. Would have been." She looked away; his heart ached.

Jared gave into the feeling he'd had moments earlier and pulled her to him. Her face pressed into his t-shirt, and he felt her shudder, then he felt the unmistakable shaking that accompanies tears.

It's not a lie, she thought as the tears came and her body shook with grief. The following day was her mother's birthday, but that wasn't what was bothering her. The first year after her mother had died, Christy could barely get out of bed on her mother's birthday. The same for Mother's Day, Thanksgiving, Christmas, and every other day that reminded her of her mother, which was pretty much every day. The second year had been easier; and this year, she'd hardly thought about the impending day other than in the wistful, loving way that one fondly remembered loved ones who had passed.

Over the course of the day, however, Christy began to think more and more of her mother. She wanted her so badly, needed her. She had so many questions, so many things she'd never been able to ask her. She wanted her mother's advice about Molly's education, about her own education, about keeping her job at the doughnut shop or finding something that would lead to a career, about whether they should stay on the island or sell and move elsewhere. Mostly, she wanted to talk to her mother about Jared and her growing feelings for him.

Was she making a mistake, hanging around with him, going on dates with him, letting him hold her like this? Should she continue trying to convince herself that this was a summer fling with no meaning, that Jared's leaving at the end of the summer would have no consequences? Should she be more concerned that when Chloe, Avi, and Jared said goodbye in August, Molly's heart would be broken? And could she acknowledge that it was her own heart that would break the most?

"It's okay," Jared whispered. "I'm here. You can cry as long as you want. I'll be here for you."

And that was the problem, wasn't it?

Christy took a deep breath as she pushed herself away from Jared's strong arms. She wiped her eyes with the back of her hands and forced herself to stop crying.

"I'm fine," she said, trying to sound as though she meant it. "I'm really fine. I don't want Molly to see me like this." She gestured toward the macaroni and pickles on the counter. "Can you grab those and take them outside? I'll bring the rest. I just need a minute to get myself together."

Jared looked concerned, perhaps even hurt, but Christy refused to focus on that. "The corn must be done by now. And the clams. Let's go eat while they're hot."

Jared opened his mouth as though to speak, but he simply nodded and went to the counter. He picked up the pasta and pickles and headed toward the door. Before he went outside, he stood in the open doorway and turned back to her. "I meant it, Christy. I'm here if you want to talk. Or cry. Or whatever."

He turned quickly and left, and Christy watched the screen door close behind him. Her knees went weak, and she grabbed the counter for support.

"Mom, if you can hear me," she said quietly. "If Jared is right and there is a Heaven, and if you're there, please tell me what to do. I don't know if I can keep doing all this by myself, but I don't want to get hurt again. I can't say goodbye to someone else I love. I just can't."

"She's going to be sick," Christy said, watching the Whirligig go round and round and Molly's face go from red to purple to white.

"She'll be fine," Jared assured her.

Christy had her doubts, but just when Molly's face was beginning to turn green, the ride came to a stop.

"Can I go again?" she asked the second she stepped off the ride.

"Not now," Christy told her. "Let's take a break from the rides."

They wandered around the fairgrounds, shoulder-to-shoulder with many locals she recognized and even more tourists she did not. They stopped at a baseball toss game with giant, green, plush aliens hanging from above.

"Hey, Jared, I bet you can win this," Molly said.

"Maybe," he admitted, pushing his glasses up.

"Go ahead, Jar," Chloe said. "You can do it. Show us that killer arm."

"Killer arm?" Christy asked.

"Yeah," said Molly. "Didn't you know that Jared was a pitcher in high school?"

As she watched him throw four perfect pitches, Christy couldn't help but wonder how many other ways he could surprise her.

Jared handed Molly an alien, for which she promptly began spouting off possible names as they followed the others through the carnival, playing games and watching the crowd. When Jared reached for Christy's hand, it felt like the most natural thing in the world.

Vince watched the car drive away after dropping the girls off at the house. If the guy had been alone, he could've grabbed him right then, but he had those other two people with him. And that wasn't the plan. He could take the boy and do all kinds of things to him, but that didn't mean he'd talk.

Vince had seen all sorts of guys undergoing interrogations that didn't get anywhere. You could cut off the tips of a man's finger and it didn't mean he'd talk. But forcing that person to watch someone he loved get their fingertips chopped off? Now, that was how you got someone to open up and spill everything they'd ever tried to hide.

Annual Chincoteague Blueberry Festival This Weekend

The Community Center opens its doors at 9 a.m. this Saturday and Sunday to celebrate one of nature's healthiest and most delicious treats—the blueberry! The annual event showcases fresh blueberries, baked goods, ice creams, and other tasty concoctions featuring local blueberries. In addition to edibles, you can find crafts, entertainment, and more. For more information, call the Chincoteague Farm Bureau or check out their website.

Chincoteague Herald July 10

Chapter Nine

Jared texted Christy early in the morning and asked how she was doing. It was a good hour before she answered.

A little sunburnt. LOL! Not too bad. We had a great time. Sorry about my breakdown. Feeling better today.

He typed a reply but paused. How would she take it? Was he being too pushy? Would she be turned off or offended? He closed his eyes and thought about it. He was certain it was the right thing to do. Even if he had no intention of taking things farther between them—and that oath was getting harder by the day—he knew this was right. He hit send and held his breath. He couldn't hold it long enough though. The dots lit up, blinked for a few seconds, and then disappeared. It was another hour before she answered. By then, it was almost too late.

We'd like to take you up on your offer. Are we too late? Where and what time?

Another hour passed. Jared's hands were sweaty, as was every other part of his body, as he stood outside in the blistering heat. The weather was a far cry from the day before with extreme heat and thunderstorms in the forecast, and Jared didn't think even being in the water could help cool him off. Luckily, as soon as Christy and Molly arrived, they would be able to get inside where the air conditioning was on full blast.

When he saw them approaching, it was all he could do to keep his eyes from popping out of his head. Christy was wearing a modest dress, yellow with faint flowers. It flowed around her in a way that made it look like she traveled with her own breeze, though the air was still and heavy. Her hair was neatly braided in one long line down her back, and she had on just a touch of makeup. She couldn't have looked more beautiful.

Molly was wearing a dark blue dress covered with daisies, her hair done in two long braids, one on each side, and she wore a smile on her face, for which he was glad. He wasn't sure Molly was going to be happy about this strange outing, so different from the day before. He knew how he would have felt, did feel, at her age.

The church bell rang as Christy and Molly reached him. "Just in time," he said. "Let's see if we can find seats."

He led the way, stopping in the back and craning his neck for a pew with enough room for the three of them. An usher leaned over and pointed out a pew on the far left, near the front. Jared thanked him and motioned to Christy to go ahead. He followed the two females to the pew and motioned for them to sit. Jared genuflected before sliding in and unfolding the kneeler. As he'd been taught to do as a toddler, he knelt and prayed before taking his seat beside Molly.

He was nervous about how they would react. He wondered if they had ever been inside a church before— the funeral perhaps? Based on the conversation he and Christy had on the Fourth, probably not. He wasn't sure what had given him the idea of inviting them to attend Mass at St. Andrew's that morning, but it had felt right when he awoke with thoughts about Christy's tears over her mother's birthday. He didn't know if being here would help her at all, but he knew that it always helped him to spend time in church, attend Mass, and ask for God's guidance.

Was that what he was doing now? The thought suddenly struck him as the cantor invited everyone to stand for the processional hymn. Was he looking for God to guide his decision about Christy? About his future? Was it a coincidence that they sang, *Christ, Be Our Light?* Was he in need of light in darkness?

Jared forced himself to settle his thoughts as Mass began. Every few minutes, Molly leaned over and whispered a question to him. He might have been irritated, but he could tell that she was fascinated by everything and was eager to know all the answers at once. If only he could provide answers to all the questions one has about religion and eternal life.

Jared found himself glancing at Christy more than he should have and wondered if he needed to go to confession after bringing someone to Mass. He observed that she sat quietly, stood when they stood, knelt when they knelt, and paid close attention to all that was said and done. When Mass was over and the last verse of *How Great Thou Art* had been sung, Jared looked over at Christy, his whole body a jumble of nerves.

"Would you ladies like to go to brunch?"

"I would," Molly said emphatically. "We didn't have time to eat. I'm starving."

Jared smiled and suggested they walk to a café nearby.

Many of the same faces they had seen at Mass smiled at them as they entered.

"It's Christy, right?" said Anne Parker, wife of Paul, the police chief. "From Sugar and Sand?"

Christy smiled. "Yes, hello Mrs. Parker." She gestured toward Molly and Jared. "This is my sister, Molly, and our friend, Jared."

Hands were offered and shaken between Anne, Paul, their daughter, Lizzie, and son, Ben. A small part of Jared poked at his self-consciousness. Friend? Was that what they were? He silently admonished himself. After all, that's all he wanted, right? He dismissed the thought and remembering his manners, spoke to Lizzie.

"Do you go to the high school?"

"I do. I'll be a senior this year."

"And are you in the middle school?" he asked Ben.

"Yeah. Just starting."

"Me, too!" chimed in Molly. "I'll be in sixth grade instead of fifth, but I'll be going to ninth grade math if I can finish my lessons in time, and I will."

Ben opened his mouth and closed it, and Jared decided he needed to have a talk with Molly about just how she should approach the other kids and what she should say, if anything, about her transition and schedule. Christy stepped in and handled the situation beautifully, he thought.

"Molly's a bit precocious," she said to Anne with a smile. "She really keeps me on my toes."

Anne laughed. "I'm sure she does. Your parents must have a hard time keeping up with her."

Jared felt Christy stiffen, but she smiled and said, "They did. Unfortunately, they're not with us anymore, so the parenting falls to me."

Again, he was impressed with how she handled the hardball questions. He wasn't sure how he would have done in her place, but she had been handling these situations for two years. He was sure she'd learned over time what to say and how to say it.

"There's another girl named Molly in my class. She's nice. I'll look for you on the first day of school and introduce you," Ben said as they waited in line for a seat.

"That's so nice of you," Christy said. "Thank you, Ben. Molly..." Christy gave Molly a slight push and hard stare.

"Oh, thanks." Molly gave an apprehensive smile.

The Parkers were seated, and Jared looked around for signs that another table would open soon. He saw a family with empty plates motion for the waitress.

"Hey, Christy!" A voice said from a nearby table. The couple, holding menus in their hands, looked to be in their twenties, the man clean shaven, much shorter than Jared, and the woman a stunning blonde with a deep tan and the looks of someone who worked out a lot.

"Officer Black, hi!" Christy leaned closer to him and said in a low voice, "I won't tell Diane you're here if you return the favor."

The man, Officer Black apparently, threw his head back and laughed. "This is my wife, Taylor. Her aunt runs the place." He looked around and leaned back toward Christy conspiratorially. "But her coffee's not nearly as good as Diane's."

"Hi, there. You must be the Christy who works at the doughnut shop." Taylor held out her hand.

"That's me," she answered, and Jared could tell by her tone that she was surprised Taylor knew who she was.

"Nick keeps me informed about everyone in town, and I've done some work for Diane."

"Taylor's an award-winning landscaper," Nick said with obvious pride, his smile wide and his eyes aglow as he looked at Taylor.

"Stevenson, party of three," the hostess called.

"It was really nice meeting you, Taylor," Christy said.

"Hey, Christy," Taylor called. "We've got a small group of gals who get together every other week for drinks. Would you be interested?"

Jared saw Christy's smile falter as she looked down at Molly. "Um, I'm not…"

"She'd love to join you," Jared said. "Just stop in the shop and let her know when and where."

"Great," Taylor replied. "I'll see you later this week."

When they reached the table, Christy looked at Jared, her jaw set with irritation.

"How dare you speak for me," she said quietly, clearly agitated.

"If you don't want to go, then find an excuse, but don't say no just because of Molly. I'll stay with her if need be, but you have Diane and Marge, and plenty of others, from what I've seen, who would jump through hoops to help you. Learn to accept it."

"This is the best ice cream I've ever tasted," Simon said, licking his purple-tinged lips.

"I told you," Diane said. "It just doesn't get any better than this."

"You know, there's only one thing missing from this blueberry festival."

"Oh? What's that?" Diane scraped the bottom of her cup and savored the last bit of fresh blueberry ice cream.

"Blueberry doughnuts. Now, why do you suppose that is? There must be a doughnut shop on the island."

Diane playfully swatted his arm. "Just when would I have time to bake that many doughnuts, and who's going to work the booth? I wouldn't have been able to keep up at the shop today if you hadn't arrived so early."

"And why is that? You do a huge amount of business. You must be able to hire more help."

"I had more help once upon a time. Then we had that period when everything was closed and nobody wanted to go back to work and now, I don't really want to hire anyone else." She tossed the cup and spoon in the trash and glanced at Simon as they strolled through the community center. He was so handsome and distinguished-looking with his grey hair, green eyes, and wire glasses. She loved looking at him and felt her insides melt every time he smiled.

"I'm ready to be done with being at the shop every morning at six and working well past the two o'clock closing time. I'm tired of mixing batter and frying dough and getting frosting stuck between my fingers. And you know what? I'm just tired."

"Then why not sell? Do you know how quickly someone would snatch that place up? It's prime real estate, right on Main Street, close to the hotels but still part of the charming downtown. You could sell it for a million at least."

Diane sighed. "Believe me, I've thought about it."

"Then what's holding you back?"

"I don't know, to be honest. I always wanted a family to help me run it, a group ready and willing to take it over someday and keep my grandmother's recipes alive.

That just never happened for me, but I don't want to see something I worked so hard at all these years get shut down or worse, go down in flames because the new people don't love it as much as I did."

Simon stopped walking and looked at her. "You can't keep working forever just because you don't want someone else to have it. Have you thought about Christy taking over?"

"Sure, I have. Lots of times, but it's not for her. That's not what she wants, and frankly, she deserves to get what she wants for once. Life has dealt her some serious blows. I'm thinking…"

She started walking again, heading toward an art display.

"What?" Simon asked.

"I'm thinking I want her to get on her feet, to keep working for me until she graduates and has a better idea of what Molly's future holds. Then, once she has her degree and a job with a good, steady income, I'm going to retire. I'm just hanging in there until then."

"Tell me the truth. You were planning on retiring before you met Christy and Molly, weren't you?"

"I was, but when those two walked into my life, I knew the plan had changed."

"Diane! You're not in the kitchen for once."

Diane went to her good friend, Ronnie, and gave her a hug.

"You look wonderful," Ronnie said, casting a glance at Simon and raising her brow in question.

Diane made the introductions and asked Ronnie about her grandchildren. "They're such a joy. Can you believe EJ will be graduating in less than a year?"

"And Todd and the babies? How are they?"

"Wonderful. Todd's going into the sixth grade already. Little Miren is starting pre-K in the fall, and Sarah is crawling. I don't know where the time goes."

"This sunset is amazing," Simon said, marveling at one of Ronnie's paintings.

"Thank you, Simon. It's one of my favorite places on the island."

"This is on the island?"

"It is, but its location is a local secret. My kids love going out on kayaks there."

Simon looked at Diane. "I know a young man who loves to kayak. Maybe you know someone he could take out there?"

Diane smiled. "I don't know. It would cost a hefty price for us to give up the location to an off-islander."

"Maybe we could come up with a fair price," Simon said with a grin.

While Jared went over how to best tackle quadratic equations with Molly, Christy folded laundry, put away clean dishes, and vacuumed. It was nice having him there—she hated doing math—and it felt comfortable to do her chores with him sitting at the table with Molly. She enjoyed listening to bits and pieces of their conversation even if she was still a little irritated with him. She didn't need Jared controlling her social life or telling her how to manage their existence. Still, to be able to have a night out with other women her age... She unconsciously sighed at the thought as she gazed out the window, a NASA t-shirt dangling limply from her hand.

"What's up?" Jared said, suddenly beside her, looking out onto the street.

"Nothing. I was just thinking." She turned toward him. "I should have said thanks."

"For what?" He leaned his head to the side and closed one eye, peering at her with the other as he pushed his glasses up on his nose. The habit had become endearing to her and made her smile.

"For telling Taylor I'd join her and her friends. I actually think it would be fun."

"Christy," he said quietly. "You can't spend your whole life hanging out with Diane and Marge or doing stuff with Molly and her friends." He grinned. "Even if her friends are closer to your age than hers."

"At least she has friends," Christy said, the words out of her mouth before she could stop them.

"Hey," he put his arms around her waist. "You've got plenty of friends. I just think you need some friends you actually have things in common with."

"And what makes you so wise?" Christy asked, keenly aware of the way her body was reacting to his closeness, his hands on her lower back, his warm breath on her cheek.

"I've got sisters. I know how girls are. What's the word women use today?" He frowned. "Tribe? Yeah, you need a tribe."

Christy laughed huskily. "Oh, really? Is that what I need?" What she needed, according to the feelings in her mid-section, had nothing to do with friendship.

Something sparked in Jared's eyes that Christy felt in her own chest. She could barely breathe, and electric pulses ran down her arms, causing the little hairs to stand from her biceps to her wrists. She could literally feel them coming to attention, a brigade of hairs up and down her arm. She could feel everything, every beat of her heart, every movement of air in and out of her body, out of his. She felt his muscles tighten and his hands squeeze her ever so slightly before he dropped his arms to his sides and took a step back.

"Let me know what Taylor says when she stops by." He moved toward the kitchen table and picked up his wallet and keys. "Molly went upstairs. She's finished with this week's math."

"You're leaving?" She felt as though all the air had been sucked from the room, her body still tingling from his touch but her mind reeling with questions.

"Yeah, sorry. I just remembered that I told Avi we'd play tennis this afternoon."

"It's a hundred degrees out there and is getting dark. It's going to storm any minute."

"Yeah, well, I promised." He opened the front door and looked back at her. "I'll text you later."

Then he was gone.

Christy watched him hurry to his car and pull away before she collapsed onto the couch, trying her best to convince herself that she was right. Jared would be leaving in just over a month and had no intention of starting anything, so she had better get rid of any feelings she might have for him other than friendship.

The thought struck her that, perhaps, that had been his objective. If she made friends with other women on the island, she didn't have to rely on him to entertain her. Then, at the end of the summer, he could leave and she'd be just fine with her *tribe*.

A single tear rolled down her cheek and stopped at the corner of her mouth. She licked it away, tasting the salt and bitterness. Friends were one thing, but what if her heart wanted more? And what if Jared was the only person who could fill the emptiness she felt there?

Matching the dark thoughts in her head, a shadow crossed the room and thunder shook the house. Not for the first time that summer, Christy felt something ominous heading her way, and it wasn't the storm brewing outside. The problem was, she had no idea what was coming or how to prepare for it.

"You went to Church?" Diane asked, stopping mid-fill, a scoop of coffee grounds in her hand. She looked at Christy in surprise.

"Yeah, the same one you go to, but you go on Saturdays, right?"

"I do, and I gotta tell you. I really don't want to ruin your weekends, but I was swamped yesterday and could barely keep up. Even though we don't make things to order and the coffee does its own thing, I think I'm going to need another person here on weekends for the rest of the summer."

"What did you do in the past?" Christy asked, measuring out the decaf coffee.

"I had a crew of young people like yourself working here all week, but I'm trying to wind things down, retire, and save some money for myself. I guess I thought I could handle it with just the two of us, and when you started, you already had a weekend job, so I thought, okay, I can handle Saturday and Sunday on my own, but the last couple weeks have nearly killed me."

"I wish you had said something. Of course, I'll work. I'd never leave you with more than you can handle. Isn't that what you've done for me?" Christy would hate to lose those precious days she had with Molly—of course, Molly—but she'd been working on weekends right up until a few weeks ago, so she knew she could make it work.

"I'm sorry, Christy. I really am. It's just that all the other potential employees already have summer jobs, so the pool is limited."

"No, no, it's fine. Molly and I will come in. She can do her schoolwork while I work. No big deal." She thought about the fun she'd had on the boat, despite her sinking mood, and how much she enjoyed the cookout, but Diane had been so good to her. She couldn't say no.

"I'll tell you what," Diane said, perhaps reading her thoughts. "Come in at seven-thirty on Saturdays, help me with the morning rush, and you can go as soon as it slows down. On Sundays, you can come in at eight and do the same thing. I won't keep you until two if I don't have to."

"Keep me as long as you need me. Really, it's fine." Christy turned on the coffee maker and went to check the sugars and creamers. "Can I ask you a question, though?"

"Sure," Diane said with a smile. "What's on your mind?" She began refilling the napkin dispensers.

"Yesterday, Father Darryl—that's his name, isn't it?" Diane nodded.

"Okay, Father Darryl was talking about these two women, sisters, Martha and Mary. He said that Martha, who was doing all the work while her sister sat on her butt, was too worried and anxious and that her sister was making the better choice. I don't get it. Isn't laziness bad? What was Martha doing that was so wrong?"

Diane laughed. "Oh, the age-old question that we Marthas always have to overcome."

"Huh?" Christy had been thinking about the reading and what the priest said all afternoon while she was cleaning house and Molly was sitting at the table. Granted, Molly was doing homework, which was essentially her job, but where was the line drawn between working hard and hardly working, according to this God Jared believed in?

"Martha was a doer. She worked hard trying to maintain a clean house, provide tasty food, and be a good hostess. Those are all important things, necessary things. Jesus wasn't telling her to stop what she was doing or not to tend to the tasks at hand. We all cook and clean and take care of our homes and families. That's not the problem. If you recall, Jesus said to Martha, 'you are anxious and worried about many things.' That's the issue."

Christy stopped what she was doing and looked at Diane. "So, we're not supposed to worry? Just how does that work in the real world?"

"Honestly, it's not easy. But the truth is, we're not supposed to worry. Jesus said, 'Come to me, all who labor and are burdened, and I will give you rest, for my yoke is easy and my burden light'."

"I don't get it," Christy said with a huff.

"God wants us to take our worries and anxieties to him, to leave them at his feet, so that he can carry them for us. Even with all the problems in the world, even with the death he endured, he is still stronger than we are. We might think that he's already overburdened, but he can handle anything, absolutely anything, and that includes whatever is too much for us."

"And how do we do this? How do we just 'hand over' our worries and anxieties?"

"Oh, Christy, it's not easy. It's not in our nature to do that, to ask for help, to let others undo our burdens or share in our anxieties. That's where the second part of the story comes in."

Christy turned her head and looked at Diane with one eye. "Meaning…?"

"Martha's sister, Mary. Now, there's a woman with burdens. Possessed by demons, living a life of sin, then encountering Jesus, who completely transformed her, brought her back to her family, and gave her hope, a new life really. And she thanked him with tears and a jar of perfumed oil poured over his feet, using her hair to dry them, showing him how grateful she was for a new start and the hope of a glorious future. She knew that worry and anxiety only weigh us down and lead to more problems. She knew that we only need to rely on God, to listen to him, to be attentive to his call. When we do those things, everything else falls into place."

Christy thought back to her conversation with Jared. "What about letting others help us with our burdens? Is that bad, too? Not just asking God for help, I mean?"

Diane reached over and took Christy's hands in hers.

"Sweetheart, letting others help is part of God's plan. Maybe, instead of worrying so much about the cooking and the cleaning and becoming angry and resentful, Martha should have just asked her sister to help her before Jesus arrived so that they could both sit at his feet and enjoy his company. That's what we're here for, Christy, to help each other with our loads so that we can spend time enjoying this life and the next."

Diane squeezed Christy's hands and then let go. She smiled and turned toward the kitchen, leaving Christy to ponder all that she heard.

Just before two, after Sugar and Sand had emptied out, the bell signaled the arrival of a new customer. Christy told Diane she would go out and was pleasantly surprised to find Taylor standing by the counter, looking up at the menu. She was wearing work boots with shorts and a t-shirt that were covered with dirt but still somehow looked presentable. A streak of dried mud ran down her arm, and her blonde hair was pulled back in a ponytail. She didn't look at all like the woman from the café who wore a dress, makeup, and jewelry.

"That bacon maple concoction is all Nick talks about. I keep telling him that he's going to have a heart attack at thirty if he doesn't cut back on the doughnuts, Coca-Cola, and all the rest of the junk food he devours."

Christy laughed. "I think it's just awful, but a lot of the men like it, so Nick's not alone. Can I get you something?"

"No, thanks. I don't do sugar or caffeine." She looked at Christy and grinned. "I know. We're complete opposites in just about every way, but what can I say? Love is strange." She shrugged. "Anyway, I came to let you know that the girls are getting together this Friday at my house. We stay away from the restaurants and bars during the summer. We'd love to have you join us."

Diane's words came back to her, *That's what we're here for, Christy, to help each other with our loads so that we can spend time enjoying this life and the next.*

"I need to find someone to stay with Molly, my little sister, but I'd love to come."

"Great." Taylor pulled her phone from her pocket, dislodging a dirty work glove that fell to the floor. She unlocked the phone and handed it to Christy as she bent to retrieve the glove. "Put your name and number in here. I'll send you the time and address. It's my busy season, so it won't be early, maybe close to nine. Will that work?"

Christy thought about Diane's early hours on Saturday and Marge's age and scraped her bottom lip through her teeth. "I'll do my best."

"Hey, if you need someone to watch your sister, just say so. My sister's home for the summer, and she still lives in the big house, so she's right next door if we need her. I can ask if she has any plans for the night, but I'd bet my right arm she doesn't. She's a total book nerd who never goes anywhere."

Christy laughed. "She and Molly sound perfect for each other. But I don't want to bother her."

"What bother? Either she can or she can't, and Mom would do it if Jenny can't. She loves kids."

Christy smiled. Maybe Diane was right back when she told Christy that everyone on the island was family and looked out for each other. "Okay, I'll let you know."

"Sounds good. See you Friday."

Taylor turned to go, but Christy called to her. "Taylor, thanks. I'm really looking forward to it."

"Me, too, Christy. See you later."

Christy watched her go and hoped that the rest of the girls were as friendly as Taylor. A group of friends, a tribe, might be just what she needed. She smiled, already looking forward to Friday.

"I told you, she's just a friend."

The line was silent except for the background noises—the dishwasher running, Rosie noisily lapping water from her bowl. Jared could feel his mother's worry through the phone, could practically see her wringing her hands. He heard a long intake of breath.

"And what have you told her?"

"Nothing, of course. What is there to tell? I don't actually know anything." He was becoming angry, tired of this nonsense. He'd begged his mother for years to be honest with him, to fill in the gaps in his memory, but she wouldn't talk about their past.

His mother paused again before asking, "How close a friend?"

Jared let out an exaggerated sigh. "Mom, she's a friend. What more can I say? All my friends are barely acquaintances, considering I can't tell any of them anything about my past."

She let out an equally exaggerated sigh. "Jared, don't be so dramatic. You can tell her anything that happened within your memory. You've said yourself that you can't recall anything from before we left. You've lived an entire life since then."

"I know," he grudgingly admitted. "It just doesn't feel right, like I'm hiding things that I don't even know I'm hiding. Why won't you just tell me what happened? Isn't it about time?"

"It might never be about time, or the right time. I'm sorry, Jared, I just can't. It would put you in too much danger. Please, just trust that this is for the best."

He wasn't going to change her mind and he knew it. He shook his head and sat down on the pilings that looked over the channel, the facility far behind him, giving him more than enough privacy.

"How do you do it, Mom?" he asked in a quiet, serious tone. "How have you gone all these years without telling Dad? Doesn't he have questions about your past, your family?"

"He used to," she said in a weary voice. "The past they gave us isn't pretty, as you know. According to the history we were given, we have no extended family still living, an abusive husband who might still come after us if he knew where to find us, and just enough education for us to keep living a modest life. Your father used to ask about my parents and where I grew up, but after a while, he understood that it was too painful to talk about, and it was. I'll never be able to forgive myself for the pain this must have caused my parents."

He heard the sadness in her voice and thought she might be crying, but she continued. "I miss them every day, Mom, Dad, Delaney, and John. I would give anything to be able to reach out to them, to talk to them, to help with... I mean, are my parents okay? Are they healthy? Did our disappearance crush them? Do they still wonder where we are, or have they just..." He heard the muffled sobs and sniffles. "Can you imagine what it's like to subscribe to Google alerts for your own parents, holding your breath every time something appears, and crying in relief when it's someone else's obituary? I'm relieved because someone else's parent or child has died. Can you imagine what that does to a person?"

His heart ached for her as he wiped away his own tears. "Mom, I'm sorry. I didn't mean... I'm sorry."

"I know, and I'm sorry, too. I tried my best to give you everything you deserved. I was so proud of you the day you graduated from Harvard. The only sadness I felt was that my parents weren't there to see it, to even know about it. I failed you once and vowed never to do it again, even if it means losing everyone and everything else that mattered. That's what you do for someone you love."

Jared was beginning to understand the lengths to which one would go for someone they loved. He just prayed it didn't come down to having to choose between the woman who gave up her life because she loved him or the woman who might be able to help him find that kind of love in his own heart.

"Oh, Jared, the girls just walked in."

"Hey, Jared!" Emily called.

"Hey smarty-pants, we miss you," came from Missy. Then, "Mom, are you okay?"

"I'm fine. I'm just missing my boy. Jared, I'll talk to you later, honey, okay?"

"Okay, Mom. Tell everyone I said hi. I'm sorry you won't be able to make it down, but I understand."

"I'm sorry, too. It's just too close. Too close to Emily's try-outs, I mean," she said, coding her real excuse for the sake of his sisters.

"I know, I get it. A Harvard graduation was one thing. A vacation on the East Coast is different."

"Yes, it is. But Jared, I'd still like to meet her. Maybe we could work something out?"

"I told you, Mom. Just friends."

He heard her click her tongue before replying. "Fine. If you say so. But Jared, don't let my mistakes become your reasons for not finding happiness. I paid a high price to give you the life you have. Don't pay an even higher price by throwing it away."

He heard what she said, but he also knew what she hadn't said. In their world, secrets equaled love, and that was something he wasn't willing to do. He wouldn't spend his entire life hiding his past from the people he loved, even if it meant never loving anyone.

Merchants Cashing in on Best Summer in Years

Local merchants have seen record numbers of visitors this summer as tourists flock to the island after two unpredictable seasons. "Business is booming," said Jane Richstein of SunDial Books. "We've never seen so many people in the bookstore. They all want books written by local authors and, of course, every child wants *Misty of Chincoteague.*"

Diane Evans is selling doughnuts like hotcakes. "It's been a really busy summer so far," she told us. "I've never had to keep baking right up until lunchtime."

T-shirts, beach towels, and pony souvenirs are flying off the shelves at all the shops on Main Street. With Pony Penning still a week away, local business owners are raking in the cash this year.

Chincoteague Herald, July 18

Chapter Ten

Christy's heart raced when she looked up at Vince's sickening grin.

"How ya doin' Christy?"

"I'm fine. What can I get for you?" She avoided his eyes but still felt his gaze roaming over her. She felt the sensation of thousands of ants crawling across her skin.

"You know, we're having a tough time replacing you. My uncle said I can give you a raise if you come back. How 'bout it?"

"Thanks, but no thanks." She looked around him. "Do you have an order? There's a line of people I need to help."

Vince reached across the counter and wrapped his sweaty hand around her wrist. "Hey, I made you a good offer here. You gonna ignore it?"

"Take your hands off her," said a stern voice from the back of the line.

Christy looked up to see Nick Black making his way toward the counter.

"I said, let her go." His voice was commanding, and his countenance was murderous. "Or I'm going to take you in for harassment and assault."

Vince let go of Christy's arm but not before squeezing hard against the pressure point in her wrist. The nerve shot a pain through her forearm, and she pulled her arm to her chest, rubbing vigorously. The thought occurred to her that she was rubbing away Vince's touch as much as the pain.

"You think about my offer," Vince said before turning to Nick and curling his lips into a snarl. "You have a good day, Officer."

Everyone in the shop watched Vince leave, but Christy felt certain he would be back.

"I'll take over. Go in the back and catch your breath," Diane said, coming up behind her.

"I'll get Nick's, I mean Officer Black's. I know what he wants. It's the least I can do."

"Okay, go ahead," Diane said. "How can I help you?" she asked, smiling at the next person in line.

Christy's hand was still shaking when she handed Nick the bag containing the Pony Pork doughnut. Nick motioned for her to follow him into the kitchen where the sweet aromas from the oven made her feel queasy in light of what had just happened.

"Has he bothered you before?"

"Um, not exactly," she answered, unconsciously rubbing her wrist again.

"What does that mean?"

"He manages Windjammer. I used to work there."

"And?" Nick clearly knew there was more to the situation.

Christy closed her eyes and summoned her courage. "He offered a pay incentive for my willingness to perform extracurricular work activities." She opened her eyes halfway and looked at Nick through her lashes. "I told him no."

"Did he fire you for that?" Nick's face reddened with anger.

Christy quickly shook her head. "I quit. Diane gave me a raise and Dr. Johnson—he's an old friend of my father from Wallops—he said he'd loan me money so I can finish my education, so I gave up my lucrative career in the t-shirt folding business." She tried to smile, but Nick's frown held no amusement.

"You could've filed a complaint, you know. That's not only sexual harassment, but if monetary compensation was offered, it was extortion."

"I know." She wasn't sure she did. "But I just wanted to be rid of him."

"So, why was he here? What was that little show all about?"

"I honestly have no idea. I haven't seen or talked to him since I quit three weeks ago."

Nick's eyes narrowed in thought as he looked around the shop. "Windjammer, huh?"

"Please," Christy grabbed his arm. "Don't go there. Don't do or say anything to him. He... scares me."

"Christy, did he ever touch you before today? In a threatening way?"

Her cheeks blazed as she recalled the evening he propositioned her and how he'd grabbed and twisted her arm until she thought it might break. "He never actually hurt me, but he did grab me. A couple times. The last time, he was pretty rough."

Nick uttered several choice phrases before he bit down on his cheek. "If he ever shows up here again or confronts you anywhere in any way, you let me know. You got that?"

Christy nodded. "But you won't do anything yet, right? I mean, he hasn't really hurt me or threatened me. Not really."

Nick gave her a long, hard stare before shaking his head and letting out a disgusted sigh. "I won't do anything for now, but I meant what I said. Anything, anything at all, you let me know. Understood?"

"Understood."

He turned to go, but Christy said, "Um, could you not tell Taylor about this? Please? I don't want her to think I'm trouble or anything."

Nick grudgingly laughed. "Taylor's the last person you have to worry about. Trouble follows her wherever she goes. Ask her sometime about how she got to be a Saltwater Cowgirl. It's not a pretty story."

She watched Nick walk away and breathed a sigh of relief that Nick, at the very least, had Vince on his radar. She didn't want the police involved, but she was glad to know that he wasn't going to be able to get to her, whatever his game was.

᠉ ᠉ ᠉

"Not a good idea," Simon said after listening to Diane's plan.

"But I'm worried about her. I don't like that he came here and practically accosted her. And right in front of a shop full of people. That's pretty brazen if you ask me."

She took a long drink of her evening decaf coffee while holding her phone to her ear. The sky over the channel was ablaze with wisps of pink and red as the sun set behind her in the west.

"I don't like it either, but I also don't want you getting hurt or making him fly off the handle. This guy sounds like bad news, Diane. I think both of you should just stay away from him. Let the police do their job."

"I plan on staying away from him. I just think someone needs to let him know that he should stay away from Christy."

"Diane, serving him with a no contact order for your shop is not the way to go. It will just get him fired up. He sounds like a cocky SOB, and there's no telling how he'd react to being told he's not allowed to go somewhere. That's serving him up a direct challenge that he might not be able to resist."

"And then he gets arrested for trespassing or violating the order or whatever the charge would be."

"And he's out in what—twenty-four hours? And angry as a hornet. What about this police officer? How often does he stop by the shop?"

"Just about every morning."

"Then ask him to stop in a little more often. See if he could put in an appearance when Christy heads home, just to make sure this guy isn't following her."

Diane nodded. "I could do that. No harm in asking him. Christy's made friends with his wife, so Vince has got three of us to deal with if he's not on his toes."

Simon laughed. "I'm sure just having you to deal with is enough to keep him on his toes. I bet you are one woman who should not be crossed."

"You just remember that, Simon."

"Oh, I will. Believe me, I don't plan on crossing you."

Diane smiled as they said goodnight. She had no intention of letting Simon go.

She'd no sooner disconnected the call when her phone buzzed with a message. She frowned as she punched the buttons to make a call.

"I saw your message. What's up?"

"I just heard a call come over the scanner. Another overdose," Marge said, her voice a mix of concern and anger. "What is going on around here?"

"Oh, my," was all Diane could think to say. "That's just not normal, even amid all the craziness of July."

"I know. I've already texted Kate to let her know. She's going to need to investigate this further. Inquiring minds want to know."

Diane made a noise of disapproval in her throat. "Marge, you have to stop telling that poor woman how to do her job. The paper looks good. The articles are informative and well-written. It has news, entertainment, local sports and events, and witty editorials. Why are you constantly trying to assert authority, of which you have none? You sold the paper. Remember?"

"I know, but she has no experience in this type of thing. I don't know why I let you talk me into retiring and selling."

"Because you need to enjoy what's left of your life, you miserable old know-it-all." She could picture Marge rolling her eyes while trying not to smile. "Besides, doesn't Kate have a degree in Journalism?"

"Yes," Marge answered, drawing out the word.

"And hasn't she already published a best-selling memoir even though she just turned thirty?"

"Yes, but—"

"But nothing. Didn't she work for you as a reporter before you made her the offer?"

"Well, yes, but—"

"Marge, let it go. Turn off the scanner and go to bed."

"What about the overdose? It's the second one this month."

Simon's words came back to her. "Let the police do their job, Marge. That's what we pay them for."

It wasn't until Diane was getting ready for bed that a thought occurred to her. If the police were going to be busy fighting a possible drug problem on the island, how were they going to have time to keep Christy safe? There were only a handful of officers.

"Oh, Simon, I know you're right, but I've got a very bad feeling about all of this," she said aloud.

That night, she prayed for the safety of everyone on the island, but she prayed especially that Christy and Molly would remain out of harm's way.

"How's Christy doing?" Dr. Johnson opened the refrigerator in the staff lunchroom and pulled out a Tupperware container.

"Fine, I guess," Jared mumbled.

Dr. Johnson opened the microwave. Jared felt the man's stare. "You guess?"

Jared shrugged and kept his eyes on his sandwich. "She was fine when I last saw her on Sunday." He felt Dr. Johnson's eyes still on him, but he didn't look up.

"I see."

Jared heard the door to the microwave close, the buttons being pressed, and the oven's motor whirring. He waited to see if more would be said, but the room felt heavy with silence. Several minutes went by, three to be exact. Jared had taken a quick peek and saw the time counting down then heard the beeping and the door open again. Those three minutes felt like hours. He couldn't take the heavy feeling of guilt that hung with the silence.

"I'm sure Christy's busy with work and helping Molly get through her summer schoolwork."

"I'm sure she is. She's probably under a lot of stress these days. That encounter with her ex-boss probably didn't help."

Jared's body went on high alert. He jerked up his head as his heart pounded against his chest. "Encounter?"

"Yes. Luckily that police officer was there to put a stop to it." Without another word, Dr. Johnson left the room, but the heaviness in the air only became more suffocating.

Jared fumbled in his shirt pocket for his phone. It slipped from his hand and he grabbed for it, realizing he was suddenly sweating uncontrollably, but the phone fell to the floor with a clatter.

Jared bent down and retrieved his device from under the table. He looked at his texts, but there was nothing new. Of course, there wouldn't be. Hadn't he told her that he would text later? Didn't he know Christy well enough by now to know that she wasn't going to reach out to him first, especially after the way he ran out on her?

His fingers hovered over the screen. Would she want to hear from him after the way he left? Would she even answer his message? There was only one way to find out.

Hey. Just thought I'd check in. How's your week going? Everything okay with you and Molly?

He held his breath and waited as *Delivered* changed to *Read* and waited some more. He felt the time tick by in his head in much the same way he'd seen it on the microwave clock, only the clock in his head was going in the opposite direction. He continued to wait and wait and wait. When it became obvious that she was not going to answer, he slowly slipped the phone back into his pocket. Maybe she was too busy at work. Maybe she had her hands deep in doughnut batter or covered with frosting. Perhaps she was checking someone out who had a big order.

Jared looked at the half of sandwich that sat uneaten on top of the reusable plastic sandwich bag. He was no longer hungry. He threw away the PB&J and cleaned up his space, shoving the rest of his lunch back into his lunch bag. He knew that Christy was afraid of her former boss, extremely uncomfortable around him to say the least.

Jared was kicking himself for staying inside his own head instead of reaching out to her. He'd told her more than once that he would be there if she needed him, and he had failed her when it counted. Now, all he could do was hope she would forgive him.

By Wednesday, Christy had gotten the message that Jared wasn't going to text as he'd said he would. She'd thought about texting or calling to tell him about Vince, just to talk to someone about it, but she didn't want to make the first move after Jared's hasty departure on Sunday. It had been two days since Vince had shown up at the Sugar and Sand, and she hadn't seen him since. She noticed Nick hanging out in the parking lot on Monday afternoon when she left work, but he wasn't there on Tuesday. Of course, the island police had bigger worries than Vince, according to the grapevine and the Chincoteague Herald.

There were just a few people lingering over doughnuts and iced coffee, which she'd finally convinced Diane to add to the menu, when her phone vibrated in her apron pocket. She pulled it out and looked at the text. She blew a stray strand of hair from her face and thought about the text she'd received.

How's your week going? Everything okay with you and Molly?

Seriously?

That's all she got after the way he ran out on her like a man who'd been burned and needed to flee from the flames? No, thank you. That wasn't the first time she thought he might kiss her only to be left deflated when he'd welcomed some interruption or another.

She didn't have time for his games and had better things to do. Taylor's sister was going to take Molly to the movies, and Christy was going to have a drink with the girls. Maybe multiple drinks. Maybe more drinks than she'd had since her twenty-first birthday bash. Not that she could remember how many drinks she'd had that night, but it had been a lot.

She dropped the phone back into her pocket, fully aware that she'd left him on *Read*. Maybe he'd get *that* message. Christy wasn't going to waste her time on someone who didn't even have the decency to make up a good excuse for wanting to get away from her so fast.

She was glad to be rid of him, truth be told. She didn't have time for a summer fling anyway.

For the rest of the afternoon, her mind conjured all sorts of good reasons for wanting Jared out of her life, but her heart was whispering otherwise. When she arrived at Wallops at three to pick up Molly, Jared was standing outside, the two of them conversing about something that had Molly quite animated, her hands flying with expression as she talked. Christy sat in the car and honked the horn, trying to squelch the feelings bubbling to the surface, the ones that reminded her how she missed him, how she'd checked her phone nonstop for three days, how she missed their late-night chats and his broad smile when she pulled into the lot each afternoon. It had been Linda who had stood with Molly for the past two days, and Christy had worked hard to hide her disappointment from Molly. Now that Jared was there waiting for her, just like he had been ever since she had relieved Marge of pickup duties, she had to force herself to look away.

Molly opened the back door at the same time Christy heard the tap on her window. She had a decision to make. Should she ignore him, showing him that she was angry and didn't want to talk to him? Should she pretend that he hadn't hurt her and feign indifference? Or should she show him how hurt she was that he had completely ghosted her?

Grudgingly, she rolled down the window and looked at him, trying to keep her expression blank, choosing not to let him see any feelings she might have.

"Hey," she said without smiling.

"Hey, I texted you."

"I saw that." She looked away, suddenly feeling like she was going to cry. Why was she acting like a child? Molly handled things more maturely than this.

"Sorry I haven't been in touch. My research is really ramping up. Lots of material to cover before the summer is over."

"Understood," she said. "I'm sorry I've taken up so much of your time." She hated the tone of her voice but couldn't help it. Rather than further embarrass herself or cause a scene, she pushed the button to roll up the window. Jared stuck his arm out as if trying to stop the window's movement, but he pulled it back with a yelp as the glass continued going up.

"Christy," he yelled. "Please."

Though the voice in her head told her to put the car in drive, the voice in her heart matched the one that came from the backseat.

"Christy, you hurt Jared."

Those three little words were more than she could take. She gripped the steering wheel, closed her eyes, and took a deep breath as a tear slid down her cheek. Once she felt some modicum of control, she pushed the button and waited for the window to slide down. She turned to look at Jared.

"I'm sorry I hurt you." Her words were barely more than a whisper, but so were his.

"I'm sorry, too."

"It's been... well, not a bad week, but not a great one. I didn't mean to take it out on you."

He nodded. "I took some things out on you, too. Things that have nothing to do with you, with us." He paused, letting his words sink in. "Do you want to talk about things?" He glanced toward the backseat. "I mean, not now, but..."

She thought about it for a moment. Did she want to explore why he left so suddenly and why it hurt her so much? Not really. That might lead to places she didn't want to go. Did she want to tell him about Vince, how the incident made her feel, how she was now triple checking the door every night and considering getting a very large dog? Yes, she did want to talk to him about that, had wanted that since it happened.

"Yeah, I think I'd like that."

"I can pick you up Friday evening. I'll bring Molly home, save you a trip. We could go to dinner, maybe take that hike to Wild Beach?"

"I actually promised Diane I'd help her do some inventory stuff in the afternoon, then I'm going to Taylor's in the evening. I'm dropping Molly off at the movies to meet Taylor's sister on my way."

"I'm going to see a late movie!" Molly interjected. "Then I'm going to spend the night at Jenny's house. It's going to be so cool!"

"How about Saturday? Molly and I will be at the shop until two, but you could come by after and the three of us could eat dinner together. Maybe you and I could take a walk afterwards." She looked at him hopefully.

Jared smiled. "It's a date." His smile faltered. "I mean, well you know. That sounds good to me."

Christy felt a mix of conflicting emotions wash over her. "Okay. I'll see you Saturday. What time?"

"Four o'clock?"

"Perfect," Christy said. "I'll have time to grab some groceries and shower and change, so I don't smell like fried dough. You can help me make dinner, or you can just keep me company. Do you know how to cook?" She realized they had never had a home-cooked meal other than cookouts. She wasn't a great cook, but she managed to feed herself and Molly. She was sure she could come up with something for the three of them.

"I do know how to cook, to be honest. I'll get the groceries. You relax. How's that sound?"

"Like a slice of Heaven."

Jared laughed. "I'll see you Saturday."

"Okay. See you then." She started to put the window up, but Jared said her name before she pressed the button.

"I'll text you later. I promise."

She nodded. "I'll count on it," she said and enjoyed seeing the red flush that crept into his face and the way he pushed his glasses up onto the bridge of his nose.

つ つ つ

"Please tell me this is your aunt's secret recipe." The perky blonde—Taylor had introduced her as Tori—eyed the two pitchers on the counter.

"Of course! Would I dare serve any margaritas that didn't follow Aunt Ronnie's recipe? They're the best ever." Taylor rolled her eyes as if that would have been akin to grand larceny.

Two more voices rang in the foyer, and Taylor called for them to "Come on in!"

A petite brunette and a drop-dead gorgeous redhead entered the kitchen bearing trays of food.

"This is my best charcuterie yet," the redhead said. She looked at Christy and smiled. "You must be Christy. I'm Holly."

"I've got an amazing assortment of dessert doughnuts." The brunette holding a familiar looking platter stopped abruptly and looked at Christy. "Wait. I picked these up from you earlier today. *You're* Christy?"

She swallowed, wondering if there was a right or wrong response to that question. "I am," she said tentatively.

"Oh. My. Gosh. We are the luckiest group of gals in the world. You have to spill all Diane's secrets. I've tried to replicate her doughnuts for years. I'm Dina, by the way."

Christy laughed. "I'm sworn to secrecy, Dina. Sorry! But next time we get together, let me bring these. I get a discount."

"I knew I was going to like this new girl," Tori said.

The trays were uncovered, and the margaritas were poured. Everyone took a seat at the giant island in the middle of the kitchen and dug into the assorted fruits, charcuterie meats and cheeses, mini dessert doughnuts, and the antipasti that Diane helped Christy put together.

"So, Taylor," Tori said between bites. "What does Nick have to say about the guy we brought in the other day? The overdose. I tried a shot of Narcan, but he was gone before we got to him."

Taylor took a long sip of her margarita. "Nick says it was pretty bad stuff. Second one this month. They're all upset about it."

"Nothing like I've ever seen in my years riding the bus," Tori said.

Taylor looked at Christy. "Tori's an EMT. Dina works at the bank, and Holly's the new manager of the Ropewalk. Have you eaten there? The food is to die for."

Christy thought maybe she and Jared, if things worked out, could go there sometime. "I'll have to try it."

"Do they think this stuff is being made locally?" Dina shifted the conversation back to the overdoses, looking at Taylor for an answer.

Taylor shrugged. "They don't think so, but who knows these days. I just hope it doesn't deter people from coming to the pony swim."

"It won't," Holly said. "I hear the crowd is supposed to be bigger than ever this year."

"Yeah," Taylor agreed. "That's what Nick says. Of course, he'd be okay if people didn't come. He hates working the carnival and walking the grounds all night, but he's always grumpy this time of year. I, for one, love it." She smiled broadly, and Christy suddenly remembered what Nick had said about Taylor attracting trouble. The stories she'd heard finally clicked.

So, she's the one, Christy thought.

Before Christy could ask how it felt to break the glass ceiling over the pony swim and become the first Saltwater Cowgirl, Holly changed the subject.

"So, Christy, you're new to the island. What brought you here? Summer renter or new resident? How do you like it so far?"

"Jeez, Holly," Tori said. "Way to quiz the new person like she's on a game show."

"Hey, I'm just trying to get to know her."

"It's okay," Christy said. She gave them a quick version of her life-story, trying to keep to the bright spots as much as she could, but their faces were all sympathetic by the time she finished.

"Oh, gosh, Christy," Holly said. "I'm so sorry. I shouldn't have bombarded you like that."

"No, it's fine. Molly and I are hanging in there, getting to know everyone, and figuring things out."

"Who's the guy you were with on Sunday? I know every local, and I've never seen him." Taylor popped a strawberry into her mouth and looked at Christy with interest but not in a schoolgirl *who's the boy* kind of way.

"He's a doctoral student at Wallops. My sister, Molly, is helping him do research this summer." When she saw Taylor's mouth drop open, she laughed. "Let me explain a little about Molly." She gave them a brief rundown, and they were all stunned into silence for several moments.

"Your sister sounds amazing," Dina finally said. "I look forward to meeting her."

"You'll meet her later," Taylor said, refilling everyone's pitchers. "She's going to spend the night with Jenny. They're at the movies. I'm sure they'll stop in when they get back."

The evening went on, the conversation flowing easily from one topic to another, and Christy felt younger, more like herself, than she had in the past two years. After Molly popped in to tell them about the movie and say goodnight, Christy relaxed into the sofa cushions and gazed from one to the next. She understood perfectly what Jared had been trying to tell her. She needed this. She needed to be with other people her age. She needed a night without worries. She needed a tribe.

The next thing she knew, the morning sun was falling on her face, and she heard the faint sound of muffled snoring coming from nearby. She opened one eye and found herself stretched out on one end of the sectional sofa. Another body, hidden under a mass of pillows, was on the other side of the couch. She assumed the other women were in the bedrooms she'd seen glimpses of when she'd used the restroom the night before. All the women, none of them married except Taylor, had crashed there rather than driving home. Christy looked at her watch and sat up in a lurch. She dug through the cushions until she found her phone. She texted Diane that she would be there as soon as possible, then texted Molly to tell her to be ready in ten minutes. She rushed to the bathroom, took a quick shower and headed out, leaving Taylor a thank you note on the counter.

It was back to reality.

Diane and Christy worked tirelessly, greeting customers, making coffee, handing out and packing up doughnuts, and cleaning tables as often as possible. It was not a job for two, especially this week, the busiest of the year on the island. Again, Diane asked herself why she did this and why she hadn't hired more help. Thank Heaven for Molly who pitched in without being asked each time they began to be overwhelmed. She refilled coffees, wiped down tables, and emptied the overflowing trash.

At one point, when the tables were full but the line had disappeared, Diane took a moment to sit down while Christy wiped down the counter. Just as Diane sat her bottom down on the stool and blew out a breath of relief, the bell jingled, and Holly Simpson walked in. Before Diane had a chance to go to the register, Holly spotted Christy and smiled.

"Hey, Christy! How's it going?"

Christy smiled and waved. "Exhausting. How about over your way?"

"We've been swamped. Thank goodness the breakfast crunch has ended, and the lunch crunch hasn't quite started."

"Can I get you something?" Christy asked, tossing her dishrag into the bucket under the sink.

"Yes, please. We're almost out of doughnuts already, and we've got the big breakfast buffet tomorrow. There's no way we'll have enough. I was going to call and place an emergency order, but I needed to get some fresh air, so I decided to walk over."

"Hey, Diane, you think we've got time to get an order together for the Ropewalk?"

Holly looked over at Diane and reached out her hand. "Hi, Ms. Evans. I don't know if you remember me. I took over for Hal as the manager of the Ropewalk. We've talked on the phone a couple times."

"Nice to meet you, Holly. Let me think..." Diane considered what she had to do that afternoon and how many doughnuts she could get done before the five-thirty Mass.

"Christy, if you can give me an extra hour or so this afternoon, I think we can get it done."

"No problem." Christy reached for a scratch pad. "Okay, Holly, what do you need?"

Holly rattled off the order and looked around while Christy and Diane perused the list.

"This shouldn't be a problem," Diane said. "I might need to substitute out some lemon for the strawberry filling, but I'll do my best to match the order."

"That would be great. Thanks." Holly paused and looked at Diane. "You know, I've loved this place since I first moved here. I've always thought it has great potential."

"Oh, really?" Diane said. "In what way?"

"Well, the layout is great, but you need more than doughnuts and coffee, especially in the era of healthier eating. I love that you've added iced coffee, but you could offer so much more. You could put in a juice bar with several different flavors, maybe one special flavor that changes every day. You could expand the menu and do fresh baked bagels that could be served as breakfast pastries in the morning but could be made into savory sandwiches at lunchtime. You could also add acai bowls, fresh fruit smoothies instead of the slushy ones you already have, and protein shakes. Those are all really popular these days, and you can't get them anywhere around here. I'd add more electrical outlets in the floor and along the walls so that people could linger, check their laptops, charge their phones. Stuff like that."

Diane didn't know what her expression held— surprise, annoyance, or interest—but Holly stopped talking and blushed. "Sorry. I didn't mean to tell you how to run your place."

"No, I'm intrigued. You have a lot of ideas."

Holly shrugged. "Yeah, well, I majored in marketing and minored in hospitality. You know, restaurants, hotels, conference centers."

"How do you like managing the Ropewalk?"

Holly held open her hands in front of her. "It's okay. I mean, I like the people, and there's always something going on that needs my attention, so I'm kept busy, but I'd like to have my own place someday. Nothing big or fancy, just something fun where people will want to go and relax and enjoy themselves."

Diane smiled. "I know exactly what you mean."

"Well, I'd better get back. Thanks for doing this. I really appreciate it."

"Any time, Holly. I'm always happy to help. And keep those ideas coming. You never know when the perfect place might fall into your lap."

Holly smiled. "I will, Mrs. Evans. See you later, Christy."

"Nice girl," Diane remarked to Christy.

"Yeah, I like her. She was at Taylor's last night. You two have a lot in common."

While they'd been talking several tables had opened up that needed to be cleaned. As Holly left, two more families walked in.

"We'd better get back to work," Diane said, still thinking about Holly and her ideas.

Wild Pony Swim Later This Week

In an already bustling summer, the island is getting even busier as tourists stampede to the hotels and carnival grounds, excited to witness the world-famous Pony Swim. Held every year on the last consecutive Wednesday and Thursday of July, the swim and auction are the biggest events on the island and bring in thousands of eager watchers every summer. Though the exact time of the swim is not known until the day before, approximately 40,000 onlookers are expected to crowd the shoreline early in the morning to get a glimpse of the famous wild ponies. The best views of the swim are from the water but be sure to arrive early to get a good location in the channel. For the first time in history, a woman will lead the Saltwater Cowboys—and Cowgirls—into the water when Taylor Black and her horse, Big Red, begin the charge of ponies. For more information, see the Chincoteague Fireman's Website.

Chincoteague Herald, July 20

Chapter Eleven

Christy was so tired on Saturday evening that she almost fell asleep in church and had to assure Jared that she really didn't mind going with him. In fact, she kind of liked the cadence of the Mass, with its standing and kneeling and processionals.

The priest's reading from the Bible, which she'd learned was called the Gospel, was about how to pray. Jesus taught his disciples the Our Father, a prayer Christy had heard of but never said. She listened carefully as the priest read the prayer and then again when the congregation prayed it together. She liked the words, the idea that God gives us our daily bread and that he forgives our sins. She thought it was especially poignant that the person praying the prayer agrees to forgive others for sinning against them.

She turned and looked at Jared as they drove back to the house in the rain, thinking back over the week and how angry she'd been with him, how hurt she'd been that he ran out and didn't call. Then she thought of Molly's admonishment that she had hurt him. Yet here they sat, on their way back to have dinner and talk. She didn't know what he was going to tell her, and she didn't care. She knew that she had forgiven him, and she felt certain he had done the same.

Jared felt like an expert chef as he seared the fish filets in a garlic, butter, lemon, and olive oil blend. Rain beat on the roof as Christy watched from a barstool that stood by the tiny breakfast bar separating the kitchen from the living room. He had a risotto simmering on the stove and was going to make a sautéed spinach that he promised Molly she would like, much to the little girl's chagrin.

"Where did you learn to do this?" Christy asked, her wide eyes conveying her awe of his culinary skills.

"My mom. She's an amazing cook. She learned from her mom, who was a first generation American." The words tumbled so easily from his mouth that he didn't realize he'd said them at first. His mind raced through the sentences, searching for things he should not have said. He almost sighed audibly when he realized that he hadn't violated any rules. That part of their story was true but also fit the narrative they'd been given.

"Where is your family from?"

That part was a little trickier, and Jared thought through his answer before speaking.

"My great-grandparents were from Venice. They came here right after they married."

He hoped she wasn't going to ask about his grandparents or where his mother grew up. He could spit out the story easily enough. He'd practiced it enough as a kid, but he didn't want to go through all the lies. As far as his great-grandparents were concerned, they may or may not have been from Venice. That he didn't know, and thus, couldn't consider it a lie even it was untrue.

"Has your grandmother ever gone to Italy? Have you? I've always wanted to go there. I mean, who doesn't, right?"

He felt the unease he'd always felt when skirting the details of his past. "She passed away when I was little, just before my dad left. I don't have any memory of my grandparents." One lie and one truth. He could live with that.

Jared removed the fish from the pan and placed it in the prepared baking dish, pouring the reserved sauce over it, adding a topping of breadcrumbs, and sliding it into the oven. "You need a cast iron skillet that can go right from the stovetop to the oven."

"I'll keep that in mind," Christy said with a smile.

"What about you? Tell me about your family, other than your parents, I mean."

He reached for the bottle of red wine he'd picked up that was open and "breathing" on the counter. Christy stood and reached into the cabinet for glasses. She talked while he poured.

"My mom was raised outside of D.C. Her parents were hippies, literally. They went to Woodstock, smoked joints, lived in a van, all that stuff. Then grandma realized she was pregnant, so they got married, bought a house, and morphed into total yuppies. Though I guess there technically weren't yuppies at the time. Suburbanites? Anyway, they had Mom and my Uncle Jim, but he died when I was little. Cancer. Anyway, he never married, so that's it for me. I only had my mom until Fred came along." She took a drink of wine and made a noise that indicated approval. "Italians are supposed to have big families, right? I know you have two sisters. Did your mom come from a big family?"

Jared shook his head. "No, just her. Where's your oregano? I need it for the spinach." While Christy dug through the spice cabinet, he washed the leaves and prepared the same pan he'd used for the fish by adding some fresh olive oil and garlic. He paid close attention to the garlic, not wanting it to burn, but also hoping to avoid talking about his family. Unfortunately, Christy could not be deterred.

"Did your mom have lots of aunts and uncles? Did you grow up close to your cousins? I always wanted a big family, but Fred didn't have any siblings. With my uncle gone, that was impossible. I guess it's true about the population getting smaller because people aren't having enough kids."

"We moved to the Midwest after my mom left my dad, so I was kind of on my own."

"I thought you said your dad left you and your mom."

Jared's hand froze over the pan, clutching the spinach between his fingers. He pressed his eyes shut and tried to remember what he'd told her. Oh well, he supposed he should just go with what he'd been told. He turned off the stove and looked at Christy.

"I don't remember my dad, but he wasn't a good man. Mom and I left in the middle of the night after he beat her up—again. I have no memory of anything before landing in Minnesota. Apparently, we spent some time in a Church-run abuse shelter while the people there found us a way out and got us a place to stay in Ann Arbor, Michigan. I guess I was too young to remember, or I blocked it out. We moved to Minnesota after that." He recited exactly what he'd been told and hated himself for it.

"Oh, Jared." Christy put down her glass and went to him, putting her arms around his waist, placing her head on his chest. "I'm so sorry. I had no idea."

"I don't talk about it much," he said truthfully. He dropped the spinach into the unlit pan and stood there awkwardly for a moment before wrapping his arms around her. He could hear the fish sizzling in the oven, its aroma filling the kitchen, and the low noises from the video game Molly was playing in her bedroom. His heart was racing, He closed his eyes and inhaled the smell of shampoo from Christy's hair. The scent calmed him.

Christy pulled back slightly and looked up at him. "I'm sorry if I brought up hard feelings. I know what it's like to carry pain from your childhood through your whole life."

And she did. He knew that. He knew that she had past hurts and a broken family that found completeness even if only for a short time. She had felt sorrow and pain and had probably wondered where she fit in with the new family her mother and Fred created. He looked into her eyes and found understanding in them. Before he knew what was happening, his lips were on hers. Their arms, already entwined around each other tightened.

Without any thought at all, he lost himself. His hands went up her back and into her hair. The damp strands became entangled in his fingers, and their kisses went from soft and tentative to hungry and searching. He moved his lips from her mouth to her chin and down to her throat. He felt her fingers wrap themselves in his curls, and she let out a soft moan. Her heart beat against him, in perfect time with his own.

"Ew, gross. Is this what you do when you're alone?"

Christy wrenched out from his arms, leaving him weak-kneed. His breathing was labored, and when he looked at her, he saw the heaving of her own chest and shoulders.

"Molly," she gasped. "Um, it's not what you think."

Molly gave her an appraising look. "It's not making out? Then what would you call it? Because what I saw looked like making out."

Christy's mouth fell open. A becoming shade of red flooded her cheeks. "I've let you watch too many chick flicks."

"Whatever. I'm cool with it. Unless you burned dinner. I'm starving."

Christy looked at Jared and grinned. "When's dinner?" she asked innocently.

Jared checked on the fish then tossed the spinach in the pan. "Two minutes," he said. "Stir that risotto, please. Actually, you can turn it off. Set the table, Molly."

He set his mind to the task and tried not to think about how hard it was going to be to walk away from her. No matter what he told himself, he knew that he couldn't resist falling in love with Christy any more than the tides could resist the pull of the moon.

With the shower gone, the evening breeze carried the scents of salt and sand across the beach. Molly ran ahead, holding onto the string of a kite that Jared had brought her. Christy held her flip flops in one hand and Jared's hand in the other.

"She's so in love with you, you know," Christy said, watching her sister dance along the beach under the tail of the kite. "Bringing her presents only cements that."

Jared laughed. "Can I tell you a secret?" He leaned down and whispered in her ear. "I'm half in love with her, too."

No longer worried about anything untoward happening between Jared and her little sister, Christy shook her head and smiled. "It's hard not to be. Look at her. She's so confident in who she is, what she wants, where she's going. I'm more worried about her future and how she's going to handle it than she is."

"She's pretty special," Jared agreed. "But how could she not be? She's got a pretty special sister."

They stopped walking, and Christy looked up at him. She didn't have nearly the confidence that her sister had, and Jared's behavior the previous week had caused her a great amount of inner turmoil. She suddenly thought about the Our Father and how she had forgiven him. She truly had forgiven, but she still needed answers. She figured God was probably okay with that.

"I thought I did something wrong. Why did you run out like that? Why didn't you call or text me?"

Jared inhaled and loudly blew out a long breath. "My family, my past, it's complicated."

"Isn't everyone's?"

He regarded her for a moment, then shook his head. "Not like mine. There are things I can't talk about, things I can't remember. There may be skeletons in my closet I'll never know about."

Christy laughed. "Don't we all wish we had that problem of never knowing? I'm sure most people with skeletons in their closets wish they could close and lock the door on them forever."

Jared stared at the ocean, a faraway look in his eyes. He adjusted his glasses and shook his head. "It's rough not being able to remember things. About my dad, I mean. What if I'm just like him?"

"Jared, I can't imagine—"

"But I don't know. How can I change what I don't know?"

"Have you asked your mom?"

"She won't talk about it."

She reached up and put her arms around his neck.

"Jared." She waited for him to look down at her. "You are the kindest, gentlest, most caring man I've ever met. You go to church. You work and study hard. You've taken on an eleven-year-old as your assistant, for Heaven's sake. You're not abusive, if that's what he was. You'd never hurt anyone. You're not your father. You're Jared Stevenson, and he's a good man."

She saw him wince at her words, but he wrapped his arms around her and pulled her close.

"I hope and pray you're right. Hey," he said, and she felt him stiffen. "Speaking of bad guys. What happened the other day? With that Vince guy?"

Christy heaved a long breath and turned toward the waves. She told Jared everything. When she looked back at him, instead of anger, she saw regret.

"Christy, I'm so sorry. I should have been there. I was such a jerk."

She shook her head. "It's okay. I mean, I really wanted to talk to you about it, but I haven't seen him around lately, so I'm feeling better now."

Jared looked away and lifted his hand to run it through the curls on the top of his head.

"I'm so grateful you're okay, but I feel terrible."

"Jared," she said, rubbing her fingers lightly across his cheek. "It's okay."

He put his arm back around her, pulling her close, and Christy melted into him.

They stood on the beach, leaning on each other, blocking out everyone and everything else. Christy knew she was stepping into unchartered territory, but she couldn't help it. As much as she told herself that this was a meaningless summer fling, her heart knew otherwise. She prayed Jared wouldn't hurt her because she was quite certain that she was one hundred percent falling in love with him.

Sunday evening, after another crazy day at the shop, Christy changed into jean shorts and a teal-colored t-shirt and looked at herself in the mirror. Simon had come by the shop that day, and Christy couldn't help but notice the way Diane looked at him. It occurred to her that her boss had changed in the past month. It was as if she'd gotten younger, her face aglow, and her body more quick and agile than before. Christy stared at her own reflection and wondered if she had changed, too.

She allowed her thoughts to drift to Jared, and she saw the same look come over her that she had seen on Diane's face. Whether she wanted to or not, she had fallen, hook, line, and sinker. This was not at all what she had planned, but it felt right. She wondered, did Jared feel the same way?

She didn't have long to ponder this before the doorbell rang.

"Christy, Jared's here," Molly called.

"Coming," she called back, listening to the sound of his voice as he greeted Marge and promised not to be too late.

"Don't worry about that," Marge said as Christy entered the room. "Molly and I always have a grand time together."

When Jared looked up, Christy's stomach jolted as their eyes met. He felt it, too. Of that, she was certain. What she didn't know was what would happen once he finished his dissertation. Would they say goodbye? Would he leave her with a broken heart? Would he ask her to go with him...? She pushed the thoughts away as quickly as they'd come.

"Ready?" he asked with a smile that reached all the way to the depths of his eyes.

"Yep," she said, her own eyes lost in his.

"Well, don't just stand there ogling each other. Get out of here! Go have fun. Molly and I have a score to settle in Scrabble."

Christy felt her cheeks grow warm, but she thanked Marge and went to Jared, taking his offered hand. Her whole body tingled at his touch.

After he led her to the car and closed the door behind her, he went to the driver's side and slid into the seat.

"Where are we going? You were so mysterious on the phone."

"I can't tell you. Honestly, it's a secret. I've been told that I must take it to my grave."

Christy laughed. "But once we're there, I'll know all about it."

"Ah, yes, but I won't have *told* you about it."

She looked at him, but he stared straight ahead as he drove toward the far side of the island.

"Taylor lives down this way," Christy told him.

"As do some friends and relatives of hers, so I'm told. Diane says they all have this big secret they only share with a small handful of people."

"Diane? Well, now I'm really intrigued. What have you two cooked up?"

"I think it was actually Dr. Johnson's idea, but Diane had to let me in on it because he's as in the dark as you are about the location."

"I'm so confused," Christy moaned.

"Patience is a virtue," Jared said.

She sat back and watched as he turned onto a winding road that took them into the trees. When he came to a stop, she was still none the wiser as to where they were or what they were doing.

Jared went to her door and held out his hand. "Come on."

Wordlessly, she let him lead her down a path to an opening in the woods. She gasped.

Before them was a beautiful cove which encircled water that was so placid it looked like a shiny polished mirror. The trees and low-hanging sun reflected off the surface. Without warning, a large white heron soared just above the water, dipping its feet in for a split second, creating a ripple of concentric circles. Several feet from where she and Jared stood was a small dock where three small boats were tied.

"Are those canoes?"

"Kayaks. I take it you've never been in one?"

She shook her head.

"We'll take the tandem, the one that's made for two. Diane said we could use whichever ones we want."

"Am I dressed okay?" She looked down at her shorts and white canvas shoes.

"Sure, you are, but you might want to take off your socks and shoes. Is it okay if you get a little wet? Because you might."

"I guess so. I mean, I won't fall in, will I?"

"If you fall, I'll rescue you," he said in a husky voice.

She looked up at him and saw her own feelings reflected in his eyes as surely as the sun was reflected on the water.

"Come on," he said, tugging her hand.

He led her to the dock, where she sat and removed her shoes and socks while Jared played with the combination on a large plastic storage box. He opened the box, pulled out two life vests, and handed her one.

"These are just like the one you put on Molly when we were on the boat."

She nodded and pulled the vest over her shirt. After they fastened the straps, Jared helped her into the front of the kayak.

"I'll sit in the back and steer," he said, handing her a paddle. "Just do what I tell you to."

He lowered himself into the boat and pushed away from the pier. He gave her some simple instructions, and within minutes, they were paddling into the open water.

Water dribbled down the paddle and ran along Christy's arms, but it felt good in the lingering heat and humidity of the summer evening.

"I'm told that there's no better place on the island than right here to watch the sunset," Jared told her once they had come to a stop.

They sat in silence and watched the sky. It was as though they had their own private viewing of a National Geographic movie. The water mirrored the sky, creating the same kind of effect Christy imagined the IMAX theater would provide, except this was real. Rather than being inside a movie that surrounded her with its visuals, she was living this masterpiece. She watched in awe as the sky and water were transformed before her eyes.

A swath of red ran across the water and the lower horizon. Upon that lay a layer of orangish-pink, like the color of fresh salmon. That was met by pumpkin orange and then a small strip of yellow. The colors grew brighter before fading into the aquamarine blue of her birthstone and then turning into a bluish grey.

"Wow," she breathed, unwilling to break the peacefulness of the moment. She whispered. "It's like an invisible artist painted that on a giant canvas. I've never seen anything like it."

"That's exactly what happened," Jared said quietly. "An invisible artist painted a magnificent painting on his heavenly canvas."

His voice behind her sent tremors of excitement through her body, instilling in her a longing to touch him. For the first time that evening, Christy wished she wasn't in the kayak.

When they finally paddled back to the dock and Jared helped her out of the boat, she was trembling at his touch. She watched him tie up the kayak before turning to her. He pushed up his glasses then squinted at her.

"Are you okay?" he asked.

Christy swallowed. "Can you…?" She looked away then quickly looked up at him, staring into his bright blue eyes, even more piercing in the twilight. Before she could change her mind, she reached up and gently removed his glasses and said, "Can you kiss me?"

Ever since she'd given in to his kiss the day before, she'd been riddled with anticipation of the next time. The kayak, the quiet night, the sunset, the thought of this God who took the time to create such a masterpiece night after night, all added to her hunger for his touch.

There was no hesitation on Jared's part. His mouth landed on hers within seconds of her request. His arms found her waist, then his hands made their way up her back and into her hair. She tasted him, savored him, and longed for more. Jared eased her down onto the dock, and she let him, pulling him toward her, welcoming the weight of his body on hers. She didn't think she could ever get enough.

Though mere minutes elapsed, it was dark by the time he stopped kissing and gazed down at her, his breath coming in jagged gasps. He felt around the dock for his glasses and put them on, never moving his eyes from hers.

"We need to go," he said quietly.

Disappointment flooded her; her body called out in protest. But she nodded, knowing that this was right. All of it. The kisses, the caresses, the feeling in the pit of her stomach and beyond, and the holding back. Somehow, everything felt just right.

Lunar Cubesat to be Launched from Wallops as Part of
Pony Week

Wallops Island Flight Center is gearing up for the
upcoming launch of a Cubesat, a miniature satellite used
to conduct research. The satellite will be used to study
the moon's crater, the Sea of Tranquility, in an attempt
to determine the metals present in the crater. The 55-lb.
satellite will take three months to reach the moon, and
scientists hope it will yield new information about the
moon composition. "This is a key part of a doctoral
dissertation being worked on here at the lab. We have
high hopes that it will lead to important discoveries
about Earth's natural satellite," said Dr. Simon Johnson,
who is overseeing the project for NASA. The public is
invited to the island to watch the launch. More
information can be found on NASA's website.

The Chincoteague Herald, July 21

Chapter Twelve

Christy slipped the VIP parking pass onto her rearview mirror and locked the door.

"This place is a madhouse," she said to Diane, who exited from the passenger's seat.

"Simon said it would be. These launches are super popular, especially this week."

Christy felt a wave of exhilaration at the realization that all this excitement was for something Jared and Molly had been working on all summer.

"I can't believe we get to be part of this, that Molly has been part of it."

Diane looped her arm through Christy's. "It's really something, isn't it?"

"Have you done this before? Attended a launch?"

They walked arm-in-arm toward the building, sidestepping the throng of people.

"Only from my backyard. This is the first time I've come to a launch in person."

Linda was waiting for them at the entrance and opened the door to usher them inside.

"I'm told I have some very important guests to take to the command center," she said with a gleam in her eye.

"Command center? They have one of those here?" Christy asked in amazement.

Linda chuckled. "Not like the one you see in *Apollo 11*, but yes. Actually, I'll be taking you to the conference room where Dr. Johnson has food set up for the post-launch reception." She looked at Diane. "I've met Christy, so you must be Diane. I'm so happy to meet you." Linda reached out to shake Diane's hand.

"I am. You must be Linda. Simon says he couldn't do his job without you."

Linda waved her hand as her face turned red. "Aw, shucks. That's sweet. I really do love working for him."

They followed Linda down the hall as she pointed out various rooms and their purposes. When they turned a corner, Christy heard a familiar squeal.

"You're here! I thought you'd never get here. Come on!"

They followed Molly into a room where streamers and balloons hung from the ceiling. A cake decorated with a launching rocket sat in the middle of the table surrounded by finger foods of every variety.

"Molly and Chloe decorated the room," Avi said, heading over from the far corner. "They wanted it to be special for Jared."

"It should be," Diane said. "He's been working very hard."

"And here's the man of the hour," Linda said as Jared entered the room.

There was a sheen of sweat on his forehead, and his shirt looked damp. He could have passed it off as a result of the weather, but Christy saw the look in his eye. He was a nervous wreck. When he looked around and met her gaze, she saw an instant shift in his demeanor. He smiled, pushed up his glasses, and went to her, taking her in his arms and pulling her in for a hug. He smelled like sweat and chemicals and ivory soap all at the same time. Christy inhaled his masculinity.

"Thank you," he whispered into her hair. "For being here." He pulled back and smiled at her, the tension in his brow and jaw visibly easing.

"I wouldn't have missed it."

"Are we ready?" They turned to see Dr. Johnson standing in the doorway. He looked at Jared. "There's quite a crowd outside, and someone from the newspaper wants to do an interview."

She felt Jared stiffen, and his arm tightened around her. "Newspaper?"

"I told you this was going to be a big deal," Dr. Johnson said.

Jared shook his head. "No newspapers. No interviews. I can't…"

Dr. Johnson laughed. "You'll be fine. It's normal to be nervous, but they'll ask a few questions, you'll pose for a picture or two, and it will be over. Then you can concentrate on the launch."

Jared shook his head vehemently. "No, no interviews and definitely no pictures." His voice was adamant. "I mean it. I won't go out there if I have to talk to the press or have my photo taken."

The room was silent. Dr. Johnson's mouth hung open. He narrowed his brow.

"Jared, this is standard—"

"I don't care. I cannot have my picture in the paper. I'm not kidding. You can be in the pictures. Or let Molly do it. She did almost as much work as I did."

Christy's gaze went back and forth between the two men. She saw Dr. Johnson's cheek twitch and noticed Jared's set jaw. After what felt like hours, Dr. Johnson nodded and swallowed, not happy but resigned.

"I'll talk to the reporters. Molly," he said, addressing Jared's young protégée. "You're going to be the star of the show today, next to the Cubesat."

Molly looked at Jared, her mouth twisted. "Are you sure, Jared?"

"Very," he said sternly. His body exuded tension, his arm maintaining a firm grip on Christy's waist. His brow was wet with perspiration again, and his eyes unyielding. It was the first time Christy had seen him so close to losing his temper, but she'd seen that look before. Where?

"Let's go," Dr. Johnson said, turning his back on them.

The exuberant mood shifted in what felt like an irreversible turn.

)))

"Three, two, one, blastoff!" The crowd shouted in unison, and Jared watched the large screen as the rocket carrying his Cubesat took off into the atmosphere. His heart clenched in his chest, but it was only partly because he was watching all his hard work being propelled into space.

When he stepped outside, the sulfuric odor assailed his senses and reminded him of the lighter fluid his father used on the barbecue grill. He looked around for Molly and Christy but carefully kept his back turned away from the crowd to avoid being the subject of any photographs. He hadn't done this for any notoriety, but there was a small part of him that felt a wave of sorrow that he had to shun the publicity. He didn't care about being famous or garnering any kind of accolades that his work might spark, but this was just one more reminder that his life was not like the lives of most other men.

Jared stopped and looked up. It suddenly struck him that he had just accomplished something that only a small handful of people would ever do. He became lost in the moment, not noticing the thinning of the crowd and not hearing anything being said. He simply stood with his gaze on the tiny light that was barely visible on the edge of the sky and felt profound awe that this was his project, and that his research might just change the world.

His breath caught in his throat when someone grabbed his hand. He jumped, jolted from his thoughts.

"Sorry, I didn't mean to startle you," Christy said. She looked up. "I get the feeling you're up there, on that rocket ship."

"Yeah," he said with a smile. "I guess I am."

He turned and looked at her. She had dressed up for the occasion in a white sundress with pink and purple flowers. She held out a small box with silver gift wrapping and a blue bow.

"Then, I guess this is appropriate."

"What's this?" he asked.

"Just a small token to commemorate your day." She pushed it toward him. He took it, holding it gingerly in his hand. "Go ahead, open it. Molly helped me pick it out."

He gently took off the gift wrap and opened the little grey box. Inside, he found two silver cufflinks.

"They're the moon. You can see Tranquility." She pointed to the crater on the small disk.

"How did you know?" he asked, his voice cracking. He looked at her in amazement. "How did you know that I like cufflinks?"

Christy smiled. "I didn't. You just seemed like the cufflink type."

"I have a pair. They belonged to my grandfather. It's all I have..." His voice broke off, and he felt a tear in his eye. He didn't know if this sudden bout of emotion was caused by the rocket he'd just sent up, the loss of a man he never met, the thoughtfulness of her gift, or just that she had such keen insight into who he was. He looked back down at the small moons in the box. "I have a bunch of shirts that are made for cufflinks, but that's the only pair I have."

"Well," she said quietly. "These won't be as special or as sentimental as the ones that belonged to your grandfather, but—"

He wrapped his arms around her and kissed her, hard and long. When he let go, he shook his head in disbelief. She was so wrong about the cufflinks but so right for him.

"They're just as special, maybe more. You have no idea what these..." He swallowed. "You have no idea what you mean to me."

He had no idea himself until that very moment.

"I know where he works," Vince said into the phone. He relayed the information about the rocket launch he had attended. "And him and Christy are definitely together. I can go after him or grab her for leverage."

"I want him alive and able to talk. Don't do anything to him. Do you understand?"

"Yeah, yeah. Get to him, find out what he knows. I got it. I got a plan. Whaddabout the girl?"

"She's dispensable."

Vince smiled. "My thoughts exactly."

The next two days flew by at rocket speed. Christy, Diane, Molly, and Marge put in extra hours at the Sugar and Sand. The island was crawling with people like ants on a dropped ice cream cone at a carnival. Christy had never been so tired. Her whole body ached, but both days when they returned home, she did so with a smile.

That week, they spent the afternoons cleaning floors and tables, wiping down counters and windows, and making more doughnuts. They worked until well into the evenings, but when they got to the house each night, dinner was waiting for them, and a handsome, glasses-wearing chef was ready to cater to their every need.

"I could get used to this," Christy said, stifling a yawn, her head on Jared's chest and her eyes heavy. They had a movie on, but Christy was so tired, she was barely following the story. And, of course, there was Jared lying next to her, which did nothing but further impede her concentration.

He leaned forward and kissed the top of her head. She felt a contentment she had never known.

More than once, she'd fallen asleep like that, only to have him awaken her as he carried her to bed. He would tuck her under the covers and kiss her cheek, whispering, "Good night" before locking up the house and heading home. Once, she whispered back, "Don't go," but he kissed her again and turned off the light.

"Go back to sleep," he said. "I'll see you tomorrow."

And she drifted off to sleep with the feeling of his kiss on her cheek.

"Please, please, please can I go? Anya's family has their own boat, and they said I can go with them to the swim and then the carnival. We'll get to see the ponies up close."

"How close?" Christy asked.

"Don't worry," Diane broke into her thoughts. "It's perfectly safe. The ponies are corralled. You can go up to the fence to see them, but you can't get inside."

Christy loved looking at the ponies from afar, but she'd never been closer to one than when she and Jared had spotted them on the beach on the fourth. The ponies had still been at least fifty yards away. She knew Molly didn't have any experience around horses either. Though they grew up in Maryland, a state with a large horse industry and home to the Preakness Stakes, there weren't any horses to be seen in the D.C. suburbs where they had lived. The closest Christy had been to a horse was on her fifth-grade field trip to the Smithsonian when a National Park Policeman had ridden by her school group.

She smiled and recalled bits and pieces about the day. She'd been fascinated by the Natural History Museum and felt quite at home in the Museum of American History, thanks to her history teacher mom. But she had been bored to death in the Air and Space Museum. How ironic, she thought now.

"Earth to Christy," Molly said, as if she knew that her sister's thoughts were in outer space. "Can I please tell Avi yes?"

"All right, all right, you can go. Tell Avi to have his mother call me, okay?"

"Okay! Thank you!" Molly threw her arms around Christy and gave her a loud kiss on the cheek. "You're the best sister ever." She looked at Diane. "I have to go to the bathroom, but I'll be back to help in a minute."

"You look exhausted," Diane said to Christy once Molly was gone. "Go home and take Marge with you. I'll see you in the morning."

"But you have so much more to do."

"Not really. I appreciate you sticking around to help me get a head start on tomorrow's baking, but I can finish making the rest of the batter. Go home. Get a good night's sleep. We're only going to get busier with each day. By the weekend, you'll be begging me to send you home."

Christy let out a long, labored sigh. "Okay, we'll go, but I can stay late tomorrow if you need me to."

"I'm sure I will. I'll need all of you again." She huffed a breath that sent her short bangs flying. "My feet are killing me. Apparently, we've had a record-breaking summer on the island. And man, my old arches can feel it."

Christy laughed. "My young arches can feel it. I don't know how I'm going to dance tonight."

"Oh, you're young and in love. You'll be fine."

Christy shot Diane a look. "In love?"

Diane smiled. "As in love as any young woman I've ever seen. Now go, get some rest before the dance. I'll see you tomorrow."

Christy, walking on clouds, headed toward the back but stopped. "Diane, is there any chance I might be able to see the swim?"

Diane took a long breath and let it out. She frowned. "Well, we won't know until tomorrow what time the swim is, but it's always at slack tide between seven in the morning and one in the afternoon."

"So, no," Christy said. "It's okay. I don't need to. I've just never been here for the swim before. Now that I'm friends with the first-ever Saltwater Cowgirl, I thought it would be cool to watch."

"I'm sorry, Christy. It would be impossible for you to make it there and back in a short amount of time. I'm going to need you before and after."

"I get it. It's okay. There will be other years." She was disappointed, but she had known the answer before she asked. She meant it when she said it was okay. She was just happy that Molly would have a front row seat to the excitement.

"We'll see what we can do, okay? Maybe it won't be as busy as I think it will be."

Christy smiled in appreciation. "Thanks, but don't worry. I'm fine waiting until next year. Maybe by then, I'll have a job where I can take off, and you'll be retired and living it up."

"From your lips to God's ears," Diane said. "Now, go home and get yourself all clean and dressed up. Have fun, but not too much fun. We've got a busy day tomorrow."

The Murray farm looked like a setting in a movie. The barn was lit up inside and out. Music blared from all sides of the big, red structure, while pickup trucks were parked haphazardly all around the yard. The dance was the first of its kind—a night to relax, let loose, and calm the nerves that always built up as the pony swim neared. After a couple years of uncertainty and low numbers of visitors, everyone was excited about this year's carnival, swim, and auction. Taylor told all her friends and fellow riders that she wanted the culminating event to begin with a bang.

Christy's hand was clasped securely in Jared's as they approached the building. When they got to the wide double doors, they saw dozens of people of all ages doing a line dance to a song Christy was only vaguely familiar with. Had Molly not been with Anya, she would have squealed with delight and run onto the floor to join them. Christy didn't have the same inclination.

"I don't have any idea how to dance like that," she said, suddenly feeling very much out of her element.

"You'll be fine. I'll teach you."

She looked at him with an open mouth and blinked several times. "You know how to line dance?"

"I'm a man of many talents," he said with a bow.

"Christy!"

She turned toward the shriek and saw Tori heading in her direction. Her new friend threw her arms around her and then looked at Jared. "This must be the scientist. I've heard a lot about you."

Jared's brow shot up. "Me?"

"Yeah, I ran into Molly on the beach yesterday with her friend. She couldn't stop talking about you and your satellite."

Jared laughed. "I suppose there are worse things I could be known for."

Tori wedged herself between Jared and Christy and put her arms around them both. "Come on. This is my first and only night off all week. I plan on making the most of it."

They made their way around the barn, making introductions and meeting all the under-thirties on the island. After grabbing something to eat and a couple beers, Jared showed off his moves. Christy found that she rather enjoyed kicking up her heels, literally.

Nick arrived around nine, still in uniform, and wasted no time taking his wife into his arms and leading her onto the dance floor. Christy noticed how Taylor glowed as her husband twirled her around the space, her blue dress swinging around her cowgirl boots.

"I want that someday," Christy said.

"Cowgirl boots?" Jared asked.

Christy looked at him and rolled her eyes. "No, silly. I want what they have. Just look at them."

He watched them for a few moments before putting his arms around Christy and tapping her chin so that she gazed up at him. "I don't need to look at them or wish for something I might have. I've already got you. And you've got me."

Her heart melted in her chest as her lips melted into his.

A couple hours, several drinks, and many line dances later, Christy sighed contentedly in Jared's arms as the band played Kane Brown's *Leave You Alone*. When the song ended, Taylor took the stage and thanked everyone for coming.

"Now, it's time to head home, get some sleep, and dream about ponies."

Everyone cheered while Taylor waved her arms up and down to get them to hush the crowd.

"Okay, let's end the evening with a prayer."

Christy looked around, surprised to see everyone bow their heads.

"Dear Lord, thank you for a good year and a good summer crowd. Thank you for old friends and new ones, for blue skies and calm waters, for cowboys and cowgirls and wild ponies. Please keep us all safe tomorrow, those riding, those watching, those visiting, and those working. May the swim and auction be successful, and may your goodness and mercy be with us all. Amen."

As though a signal had been given, the crowd began quietly moving toward the doors. Christy smiled all the way back to the house and felt, for the first time in two years, she had finally found some peace.

Jared tuned into a country station on the radio as he made his way back to Wallops. He wanted to relive every moment of the night, especially the ones when Christy was swaying in his arms.

He didn't know how he had let this happen, when or how he'd let his guard down. He hadn't planned for any of this.

The thought made him chuckle to himself as he looked through the windshield into the dark blue sky where the stars and moon dangled from the heavens.

"You planned this, didn't you?" he said aloud. "I still don't know how I'm supposed to do this. How do I live a lie when my heart is so full of love, it hurts? Show me how, God. Show me how I can love Christy without exposing my past."

"Yeah, I'm sure, it's the right time. The island is packed. The cops are so busy, they probably won't have time to sleep at night. Who'd've thought that this little operation you've got going on here would lead to this?" Vince double checked the lock on the front door, happy that the day was over. He was beat.

"And nobody is suspicious about that 'little operation'?" the voice on the other end of the line asked.

"Nah. I mean, there's been a lotta hype about the two kids who OD'd, but you know, that kinda stuff happens everywhere these days. Besides, they were both outa-towners. They got no reason to link it to us."

"You better be right, Vince, about that and about the other thing. Don't mess this up. You're down to your last chance."

"Don't worry Uncle Frankie. I got this."

He heard the long exhale and felt his blood boil. So, he'd screwed up once or twice and had even landed in the slammer for a short time. The family lawyer got him out, and he had learned his lesson. He wasn't going to leave any witnesses behind this time.

Today is the Day!

After a two-year wait, the ponies will swim across the channel this morning at 8 a.m. Watchers are encouraged to get an early start, whether going by boat or on foot. Parking will be limited outside of the carnival grounds, so plan on wearing your good walking shoes. A shuttle to and from the park will begin at 4 a.m. 150 mares and their foals are expected to make the swim, escorted by the Saltwater Cowboys and Cowgirls, led this year by Taylor Black. The ponies will swim from Assateague Island, across the Assateague Channel, to the east side of Chincoteague Island. The main viewing area is located in Veterans Memorial Park, where a large screen will show a live feed of the swim. Bring your chairs and blankets to better enjoy the viewing. More information is available on the Chincoteague Island website.

The Chincoteague Herald, July 27

Chapter Thirteen

The streets were packed. Christy thought that the 40,000 predicted visitors to the island might have been a conservative number. She jostled shoulders with people as she made her way from her car to the front of the shop. She was grateful for the small lot behind the store, but even that short walk around the building took several minutes. She knocked on the door and watched as Diane hurried to unlock it. Christy shimmied in through the partial opening, then Diane quickly turned the latch behind her. The heady aromas of fresh brewed coffee and recently baked and fried doughnuts flooded her senses.

"It's only six a.m. I can't believe how many people are out there. What time did you get here?"

"The swim is early this year. Everyone wants to be in their spot before eight. I got here at five, so not too long ago."

"We're nowhere near the water. These people won't see the swim at all. They're not heading toward the channel."

"Oh, they know where they're going. They can watch the swim on the big screen at the carnival grounds, and they'll see the ponies as they're paraded through the town on the way to the corral."

"Will we see them going by?" Christy hadn't thought about that possibility.

"I'm afraid not, hon. I'm sorry. They'll come up the southern part of the island and turn into the fairgrounds long before they reach this far."

Disappointed again, Christy reminded herself that she was already resigned to not seeing the ponies swim across the channel, so this shouldn't bother her.

"Makes sense. I forgot where the route was." She looked at the people outside and wondered where Molly was right now and what time they had gotten up to arrive at the boat. Christy and Jared had dropped off Molly at the condo on their way to the dance. Christy was excited for her sister and hoped she had as much fun today as Christy had had the night before. She felt her mouth curl into a wide smile as she recalled the evening and how she felt in Jared's arms while the music played.

"Must have been a good night," Diane said, reading her thoughts.

"How did you know that's what I was thinking about?"

"Because lately, every time I see that smile on your face, I know there's a certain scientist on your mind."

Christy laughed. "Is that how everyone knows him? As 'the scientist'?" She punctuated the phrase with air quotes. "And what about your scientist? Where has he been this week?"

"Busy with all the visitors to the facility. This week is as crazy for them as it is for us."

"I love the excitement, but I have to admit, I can't wait for it to be over so I can catch my breath."

"Well, that won't happen today. Are you ready? As soon as I open the door, we'll have customers."

"Let me put my stuff in the back." An alarm sounded in the kitchen. "And I'll grab those doughnuts."

"Thanks. I'm going to turn on the lights."

Diane wasn't kidding. From the moment the doors were unlocked, people flooded in, ordering coffee, tea, and doughnuts by arm loads. She barely had time to breathe between orders.

"Iced coffee with a Sandy Shore, please," said a familiar voice, and Christy looked up with a smile, her insides warming at the smile she was given in return.

"What are you doing here?" she asked. "Shouldn't you be working?"

Jared shrugged. "Yeah, but I decided to take the day off, just like everyone else within a thousand-mile radius."

She frowned. "Almost everyone."

"Hey, look at it this way. I'll be close by when you ladies close, then we can go get a look at the ponies after everyone else has gone to take their naps."

"I like that idea. I've wanted to get to Assateague all week to see them after they were herded, but I haven't had a chance." She looked at the line behind him. "I'd better get your order. Be right back."

She floated to the coffee machine and thought back to the first time he'd shown up ordering doughnuts for work. Diane said he couldn't keep his eyes off her. She couldn't resist glancing back at him now. He was watching her with a wide grin. She smiled back, feeling a tug in her stomach.

"Are you making an iced coffee?" Diane asked.

"Yeah. Need one?" Christy asked.

"I need three," Diane responded. "Would you mind? I'll get Jared's payment while you get the coffees and his doughnut. I've got six other doughnuts to pack up."

"Got it," Christy said, and she performed her steps in the dance that she and Diane had choreographed in the past few days. They made each other's drinks, doubled their efforts to take orders, using both registers at once, and handed each other doughnuts at a frenzied pace while Marge and Molly—both absent today—had cleared tables and listened for the oven.

"Thought you could use some help," Christy heard Jared say from behind her. "Don't worry about my order. Tell me what I need to do to help Diane with hers. She just got an order for ten coffees and two dozen assorted doughnuts."

Christy hastily showed him where to find wax paper and boxes under the counter and how to figure out which doughnuts were which inside the display case. She grabbed the ticket from Diane and began filling drink orders. Diane continued working the register, telling

Jared what doughnuts she needed while Christy made drinks. By the time eleven-thirty rolled around, the shop was empty, and all three of them were drenched in sweat and spilled coffee with frosting in their hair and chocolate in places on their bodies they couldn't explain.

"This is what you do all day while I sit at a desk? How are you still moving by the end of the day?"

Christy laughed. "Not every day is like this. Believe me."

The bell rang and six very excited people hurried in.

"Christy, it was awesome. I saw all the ponies, and I didn't lose your phone. I took lots of pictures. And we went clamming, just like we did a couple weeks ago, and we saw Taylor on her horse."

"Slow down, Squirt. You're making my head spin."

"She had a ball," Mrs. Kumar said with a smile. "Thank you for letting her go with us."

"Oh, gosh," Christy gushed. "Thank you. This might be the highlight of her summer."

"No, that would be the rocket launch, but this is a very close second," Molly piped up, and Christy felt her cheeks turn red.

"I'm sorry, Mrs. Kumar. She didn't mean it the way it sounded."

Avi and Anya's mother laughed. "Of course, she did, and it's fine." She leaned close to Christy. "I have one just like her, remember?"

Christy smiled. "Thanks. Would you all like some doughnuts? My treat."

"Oh, that's sweet of you, Christy, but it's not necessary. We're on our way to lunch and thought we'd pop in to let you know that we're off the boat and to return your phone."

Molly pulled the phone from her pocket and handed it to Christy. After a slight hesitation, she leaned in and gave her sister a hug. "Thanks again, Christy. This summer has been the best one of my whole life."

Christy held back tears as she said goodbye and watched the Kumars, Molly, and Chloe leave the shop. She noticed Chloe and Avi holding hands and thought, *it's about time.*

A pair of hands wrapped around her waist from behind. She felt Jared's breath as he leaned down and whispered in her ear. "Did you notice Chloe and Avi?"

She smiled and turned in his arms to face him. "I did. It took him long enough to open his eyes."

"Sometimes it takes us guys a while to see what's right in front of us."

She beamed as she looked up at Jared, feeling a warm glow spread through her, but the moment was shattered when the bell jingled. Several loud voices sounded behind her. She turned to see a family with four small children heading toward the counter.

She turned back to Jared. "And now the lunch rush begins."

"Wake up, sleepyhead," Jared whispered into Christy's ear as he gently prodded her side. He watched her slowly come to life, lazily opening her eyes then drawing her mouth into a slow, spreading smile.

"Hey," she said quietly.

"Hey. How was your nap?"

They'd each taken a shower after leaving the Sugar and Sand. Christy had given Jared a plain blue t-shirt to wear with his black running shorts. There wasn't much he could do about his shorts or underwear, but at least he was wearing a clean shirt, though it was a little short on his long, lean body.

After his shower, he'd found Christy half asleep on the couch, so he'd slid in next to her and watched her until he fell asleep, too. He awoke with one leg and his left arm wrapped around her, and he'd never felt so comfortable in his life.

"Do you still want to go see the ponies before we grab something to eat?"

"I do. I just need to tell my body to get moving." She started to get up, but he put pressure on her to stop her from moving.

"In a minute," he said, closing his mouth over hers.

Christy's arm circled around his neck, and she held onto him. Their mouths explored each other for several minutes before he stopped and looked at her with a smile.

"Ponies," he said, reminding himself that they needed to stop and untangle themselves before he did something he'd regret later.

"Ponies," she said breathlessly. Christy blinked her eyes a few times as Jared reached behind them for the glasses he'd laid on the table next to the couch. Christy traced his jawline once before gently pushing him to get up.

"Anywhere in particular you want to eat after we see the ponies?" Jared asked as he stretched, his hands grazing the ceiling.

"I doubt we can get in anywhere," Christy said, sliding on her flip flops.

"I can cook for us again," Jared offered. "We can hang out, watch a movie or a show before you go to bed. Another early morning for you, right?"

"Yeah," she said expelling her breath with the word. "This week has made it infinitely clear to me that I do not want to work in a bakery for the rest of my life. Honestly, I don't know how Diane does it. It's exhausting. Maybe teaching wouldn't be so bad after all."

"I think that's a different kind of exhausting," Jared said, standing and reaching for her hand.

"Agreed. My mother did not have an easy job."

"Nor does my father. Want to ride or walk?" Jared asked her as they headed outside. She locked the door behind them.

"Let's walk. Parking's going to be impossible."

He took her hand as they walked side-by-side to the carnival grounds where the ponies were corralled.

They made their way through the crowds, which were much lighter than they had been earlier. There were about a dozen people standing by the fence, but it seemed that most people had cleared out for dinner or shopping or maybe a nap like they'd just had.

Christy went to a step ladder by the fence. Following the lead of some of other onlookers, she climbed up to look over the top. Jared, tall enough already, stood next to the ladder with his hand protectively on Christy's lower back. He liked the way she oohed and aahed as she pointed out the foals standing beside their mothers.

"They're so beautiful," she breathed.

"The most beautiful site I've ever seen," Jared said quietly, his eyes not on the ponies at all.

Christy turned to meet his gaze, sending a fire forming through his abdomen. He'd spent twenty-four years avoiding close relationships, swearing off love, vowing he'd never have to look someone he cared for in the eye and lie to them. He knew he was going against everything he'd ever promised himself, but he had already fallen faster than a shooting star and knew it was too late to turn back now.

"You're not leaving at the end of the summer?" Christy repeated Jared's words over what could be referred to only loosely as dinner. Instead of going back to the house, they'd grabbed a bite at the carnival—a high-carb, sugar-laden, fried heart attack disguised as a meal.

Jared vigorously chewed a large bite of a fried clam sandwich. He nodded and reached for a napkin to wipe his mouth. "I'm staying through the fall. We won't start getting any information from the Cubesat until October. I want to wait and finish my dissertation after we see what it finds."

With her stomach doing Olympic caliber somersaults, Christy licked the powdered sugar from her fingers but promptly ripped off another spiral of funnel cake. "So, we don't have to say goodbye next month?"

Jared stopped, his hand hovering over the sandwich, and peered at her. "Not unless you're planning on going somewhere I don't know about."

Christy suddenly felt shy, a ridiculous feeling after the passionate kisses they'd shared. A warm flush spread into her cheeks. "I thought…"

She looked away and then back, staring into his blue eyes. "If you're Italian, how come you have blue eyes?" she asked suddenly.

Jared blinked once, then again, puzzlement evident by his tilted head and slightly open, crooked mouth. "Um, Italians have blue eyes. Mostly in the north, but they do have them."

"Is Stevenson your birth name or adopted name?"

Jared opened his mouth to speak but closed it again. A myriad of emotions rolled over his face.

"It's not a hard question," Christy said, unsure why it even mattered except, now that he wasn't leaving her, it suddenly occurred to Christy that she still knew very little about his personal life. Even now, after the late nights and long talks and many kisses, she really didn't know him. Well, she supposed there wasn't much talking going on during the kissing. Still, Diane was right about her feelings. Christy was head over heels in love with this man, but she knew little about him.

"So, are you happy I'm staying through the fall, or were you looking forward to getting rid of me?"

He'd stopped eating and looked serious. Christy had the impression that he was changing the subject. Again. He almost always changed the subject when it came to his family. To be fair, she recognized that she had changed it first, but she had been so afraid to think about the possibility that he might stay, she didn't know how to answer him.

For several weeks now, his leaving was the thing she dreaded the most. But now that he wasn't going anywhere for at least three months, she was too scared to even consider that this relationship—this growing, deepening, evolving connection—might have the chance to become more than she hoped it could be. Did she even dare to begin thinking about a future with him? A permanent future?

"Christy? You okay?"

It was Christy's turn to blink while she pondered her answer. She looked into those beautiful Italian eyes and felt her entire world shift.

"Jared," she said quietly. "Are you happy you're staying?"

He reached across the table and took her hand, still sticky with sugar, still holding the torn piece of funnel cake. "Christy, there isn't any place in the universe I'd rather be, unless you're going somewhere, because I'd follow you to the moon and back."

Jared had completely lost his heart to Christy. He thought about that as they walked, hand-in-hand, into the movie theater. While she used the bathroom, he leaned against a wall and took his phone from his pocket. His thumbs skillfully moved across the screen, and he glanced up every few seconds to make sure she wasn't heading his way.

I get it. Or I'm starting to. You do what you have to do to protect the ones you love. It's not just about physical safety. It's about protecting them from the mental and emotional ghosts of your past. It's about protecting them from the knowledge that evil may lurk right around the corner and that your lives can be taken and changed in an instant.

He paused, looking toward the ladies' room, then continued.

Your suspicions were right when you asked if she was someone special. She is. Her name is Christy, and she's the most special person I've ever met. When my work is done, I'll bring her home. You will love her as much as I do.

Jared felt Christy before he saw her. He looked up and smiled, realizing that he was the tide and she was his moon, influencing his every thought and move by the gravitational pull she had on him. He put his phone away and pushed up his glasses. He'd finish his text later.

"All set?" he asked.

"Yep. Is it totally cheesy that I'm super excited about this? I've wanted to see this movie ever since I first stepped foot on this island."

Jared chuckled. "Can I be honest?"

"With me? Always."

His heart skipped a beat as he thought about her words and what he had been in the middle of telling his mother. He would be honest with her as best he could.

"I've wanted to see this since July Fourth when we saw the ponies on the beach." It was the night he began to fall for her, and he would forever associate the wild ponies with his desire to kiss her with wild abandon.

As if reading his mind, Christy leaned up and kissed him gently on his lips.

"I'm glad we're seeing it together."

As he led her into the theater, he thought, *I want to do everything together, you and me, forever.*

They took their seats, nestled among the many families. Jared put his arm around Christy, pulling her to him. He didn't care that they were the only people their age in the theater. He just wanted to be with Christy, wherever that was, whatever they were doing. When the movie started, the title, *Misty of Chincoteague*, flashed on the screen, and he found himself clapping along with the dozens of families and young kids around them.

Christy had told him that she'd never seen the 1962 classic based on the best-selling book that put this little island on the map. He loved watching her reactions to the story and smiled at her as she laughed and cried her way through the motion picture. When it was over and he'd asked her if she had liked it, he already knew the answer she would give.

"I loved it. I loved everything about it. I loved the story and the characters and everything."

Christy never stopped talking about the movie the entire walk back to her house. She delighted in the quest of the brother and sister to buy the Chincoteague ponies, Phantom and her foal, Misty. And Jared delighted in Christy's innocence and childlike enthusiasm.

When they reached the house, they slowly walked, hands intertwined, up to the front door where they shared a long, tender kiss and then said goodnight. Jared made sure Christy got safely inside, not that he worried about her safety on the island. He just liked the idea that he was her protector, the one who would do whatever was necessary to take care of her. He didn't know what would happen come October, but he knew that he wanted to spend the rest of his life protecting her the same way his mother had spent the past twenty-four years protecting him.

Christy closed the door and sighed. Their kisses stirred feelings she'd never felt with anyone else. They weren't just physical. Her mind and her heart were as alive as her body was. And now, there was good reason for her to let herself feel this way.

Jared was staying through the fall.

Was it too much to hope that he might stay forever? They'd been spending a lot of time together, not just the two of them, but all three of them. Molly loved Jared as much as Christy did, and Christy knew that Molly saw him as the brother they never had. Christy, on the other hand, did not feel at all sisterly toward the man though she felt that the three of them were on their way to becoming a family. Weren't they? That's what it felt like.

Which made her wonder about his family. Why did she always feel like he was holding out on her when it came to his family? He loved them. That was apparent in the affectionate way he talked about them in those few times he allowed himself to open up about his home life. He loved and looked up to the father who adopted him, but there was a darkness about his birth father that went beyond the abuse Jared didn't remember but thought might have taken place. Was that why he was reluctant to tell her more? Did it make him sad? It certainly made him anxious. She felt it every time the topic came up. Maybe, now that Jared was sticking around, she could get him to share more.

Christy locked the door, kicked her flip flops to the side, and made her way toward the bathroom to get ready for bed. As she reached for the light, a hand snaked its way around her head and over her mouth. She started to fight, but the cold, hard metal of a gun against her jaw stopped her.

"Hey, there, Christy. You and me got some unfinished business to tend to."

She felt sick as the carnival food and movie popcorn whirled in her stomach, but she knew that the feeling wasn't caused by the sugar or the oil-drenched food. It was caused by the familiar New Jersey accented voice that whispered in her ear.

Coastal Storm Predicted, Damage Could Be Severe

The National Weather Service has issued a coastal storm warning for the Mid-Atlantic area which could have devastating effects on Assateague and Chincoteague. The warning has been issued for late Thursday into Friday. Primary threats associated with this system are heavy rainfall, tropical storm-force winds and powerful gusts, isolated tornadoes, and hazardous marine conditions. Storm surges may exceed twenty feet in height. The risk of severe flooding is high. All residents and visitors are warned to take precautions or evacuate.

The Chincoteague Herald, July 28

Chapter Fourteen

Christy's first thought was, *Where's Molly.*

Thankfully, Molly was spending another night with Anya and attending the pony auction for most of the next day.

Christy's second thought was, *I'm going to die.*

"Don't scream or try to fight me. This ain't my first experience with a gun."

Christy didn't know if he wanted any kind of response, but she was too frightened to even shake her head. Her mind raced with thoughts, none of them good.

Was Vince going to do whatever he intended to do here or take her somewhere else? She was always told, don't let an attacker take you somewhere else. Did she have a choice? Would Molly return home to find Christy lying in a pool of blood? Who would take care of Molly? Would she be left alone? Why didn't Christy have a will? Would she ever get to tell Jared how she felt about him?

"Now, I'm gonna take this gun away, and you better not fight me. Don't try to run or anything. I guarantee my bullet is faster than your legs."

He took the gun away from her cheek and lowered his hand from her mouth but didn't loosen his grip on her. She felt the hand with the gun slide down her backside, feeling his way along her shirt and jean shorts, and bile rose into her throat. His hand stopped and slid her phone from her back pocket. She heard the phone drop onto the floor, and he gave her a squeeze before poking the gun in her back.

"Where's your sister?"

Christy's mouth was dry, and she tried to get enough saliva to answer, but her tongue felt like it was licking paper. She tried to form words to no avail.

Vince tightened his grip on her jaw causing Christy to wince in pain. "I axed you a question."

She tried again. This time, the words came out in a faint whisper. "She's spending the night with a friend."

He swore, then said, "Just as well. I'd have to deal with yous both."

His accent was thicker than she'd ever heard it, and she wondered if he'd morphed into an alter ego, perhaps the person he was before he was exiled to the island.

"You expectin' anyone here tonight?"

She shook her head.

"Your boyfriend coming back?"

"Not my boyfriend," she gasped.

"You sure about that?"

Had he been spying on them? She knew he was a creep. Now she had a pretty good idea that he might be a kidnapper or murderer, but what other sick games did he play?

"Just a friend."

"Friends don't kiss like I saw you two doin'. Just sayin'."

"He's Molly's..." Molly's what? Boss? Camp director? "Molly's friend."

He grunted. "Strange relationship you three have then. He'd come for you, though, right? If he thought something was wrong?"

What was this about? Why did he keep asking about Jared? He was talking about Jared, right? He had to be, but what could he want with him?

"I don't understand."

He yanked her around to face him with such force, she thought he might break her neck. She let out a cry of pain, and he slapped her hard in the face. Her head jerked to the side. She tasted blood and saw stars floating across the dark room. Tears filled her eyes, her breath caught in her throat.

"Don't play games with me. I don't play well with others."

He held onto her upper arm with an iron grip and looked around the dark room.

"I gotta bag here somewhere."

She wondered if she could distract him, but he held her arm like a vice. Her face was burning in pain. He yanked her again and dragged her across the room, knocking over a lamp and moving a chair out of place. He kicked a bag out of the corner as he pushed her face-down onto the couch.

"I ain't taking any chances," he said as he pulled out a nylon rope and began wrapping it around her hands which he'd twisted behind her back. The rope cut into her wrists and her shoulders hurt as her arms were pulled together.

After he finished tying her hands together, he yanked her up by the hair. She screamed in pain, and he hit her again, this time just below her temple. He wore a large ring that caught her eye, ripping open her eyelid. Blood began running into her eye.

"We're gonna go outside now, slowly and calmly." He poked the gun hard into her side. "Don't do anything to call attention to us. I got a car parked down the street. We're gonna walk like there ain't nothin' going on."

He took a black sweatshirt from the bag and pulled it over her head. It hid her tied hands and covered most of her head and face. The putrid smell of body odor attached to the shirt almost made her gag, but she held her breath and tried not to think about his shirt on her body, touching her face.

They made it to his car without notice. Most of her neighbors were either out for the night, already tucked in bed, or on the couch watching TV. He opened the back door and shoved her hard. Without the use of her hands, she went down on the seat face-first, hitting her head hard on the drink console between the back seats. She saw stars for the third time that night and wondered if the consecutive blows would cause a concussion or if one hit was enough. He shoved her legs in so that she was half sitting on the floor, half lying on the backseat, then he closed the door which pushed against her rear and made her position even more uncomfortable.

They drove for several minutes before he stopped and turned off the engine. That meant they were still on the island. Thank goodness. She had visions of waking up in New Jersey, hours from home, with no way to escape.

But now that they arrived at wherever he was taking her, what was he going to do with her? There was no good answer.

The phone rang and rang, but nobody answered. Diane looked at the clock—six forty-eight. They opened in ten minutes, and there was still so much to do. Christy had never been late, at least not without calling and never without a good reason.

Diane knew that Molly had spent the night with Avi's family, so she wasn't going to Wallops today. Neither Christy nor Marge would have run into an issue with getting her anywhere. Maybe Molly got sick, or Christy, and both were home but up all night and too tired to answer the phone. Maybe Jared had stayed over, and Christy had left the phone in the other room without thinking. No, Diane didn't think they were there yet, but who knows? How well did she know either of them? Maybe they ran off together. Maybe she went home with him and was running late getting back to the island.

She shook her head. Christy was too responsible for any of that. She would have called.

Diane looked at the clock again. Six fifty-five.

She called Marge, unsure of what else to do.

"What do you want this early?"

"Good morning to you, too."

"It's barely morning."

"You've been awake for hours, and you know it."

"So?"

"Knock it off. I don't have time for this. Do you know where Christy is? Was there a change in plans? Did Molly come home last night?"

"How would I know where Christy is or if Molly came home?"

"Don't play innocent with me. Did Christy go home last night?"

Marge hesitated for just a moment before answering. "Jared dropped her off just after ten-thirty. They shared a nice, innocent goodbye kiss, for a change, then he left like a good boy, and she went inside. She must have been worn out because she never even turned on the lights. That's the last I saw of her."

"And this morning?"

She heard Marge push back the kitchen chair and waited.

"Car's still there. No sign of life that I can see. Want me to walk over and check?"

Diane took a deep breath. "Um…" She thought about the responsible young woman she'd gotten to know. "Yes, go check. Stay on the line."

She glanced at the door and didn't see anyone waiting to get in, so she left it locked. Maybe most of the people on the island would sleep in a little this morning.

"I've got to get my shoes on and a robe. Hold on. I'll be back."

The seconds felt like hours as Diane waited for Marge to return. She pictured the woman as she walked from her house to Christy's, down the gravel driveway, across the street, up the weed-infused gravel drive, up the two front steps. Marge mumbled complaints the entire way. Then Diane heard the knock and Marge's calls for Christy.

"She's not answering."

"Can you see anything inside?"

"No, curtains are closed. Hmph," Marge intoned.

"What?"

"I don't ever remember seeing the curtains closed since they've lived here. Hold on." Diane waited and then heard Marge say. "The door's unlocked."

"That can't be right. Christy's a city girl. She'd never leave the door unlocked."

"Diane," Marge's voice had gone up an octave. The hair stood on the back of Diane's neck. "Something's not right here. There's a lamp on the floor, and—"

"Marge, get out! Get out now!"

A knocking on the front door of the shop caused Diane to jump. She let out a scream and dropped the phone. When she turned toward the door, she'd never been so happy to see a customer in her life.

She rushed to the door and undid the bolt. Before Nick could say good morning, she sputtered, "It's Christy. Something's happened to her. You have to get to her house now."

Someone was knocking on the door. No, they were banging. Hard.

"Jared! Avi! Open up!"

Both men scrambled out of bed and rushed to the door. When Avi, who had reached it first, pulled open the door, Dr. Johnson stood on the other side, red-faced and puffing short gasps of air. He looked past the men into the room.

"Jared, is Christy here?"

The momentary embarrassment at being asked such a question quickly turned into concern. "What do you mean, is she here? Of course, not. Why? What's happened? Is Molly okay?"

"Molly's fine as far as I know. Christy's missing. She didn't go to work this morning, didn't call, and it looks like there was a scuffle of some sort in the house. I hate to ask, but did you two have a fight? A little rough, uh, se—"

"No! Neither. What are you saying?"

"She's missing. There was a fallen lamp, some overturned furniture, curtains drawn. That's all I know. The police are on their way there now."

Jared's heart pounded like a bass drum. "I don't understand. I took her home last night, watched her go inside, made sure she was okay. She was fine."

As he talked, he moved around the room, throwing on shorts and a shirt, shoving his feet into a pair of Sperry topsiders, grabbing his phone and wallet. He paused and looked at his phone. Nothing. Not even an answer to his late-night text,

Made it back to the center. Text you tomorrow. Good night.

He'd fallen asleep almost as soon as he'd hit send. Why didn't he wait for a response? He might have known something was wrong when she didn't answer.

"Jared? You coming?"

He tucked the phone into his front pocket and followed Dr. Johnson, his mind asking questions to which he had no answers.

Inside his supervisor's car, he leaned his head back and closed his eyes.

Dear God, please let her be okay. Please don't let anything happen to her. Please let her be okay. I love her, God, please protect her. Please let her be okay.

He repeated the prayer over and over in his mind as they made the long, painful, thirty-minute drive over the causeway and onto the island.

Christy opened her eyes, thought she did anyway, but it was pitch black. Was it morning or still night? Her entire head and face ached. Pins and needles ran up and down her arms and her wrists throbbed. She was still lying face-down, but she was on what felt like a bed. His bed? The thought made her nauseous and she fought the urge to throw up.

The last thing she remembered was Vince roughly pulling her from the car. They had been under a house that was up on stilts. He'd pushed her up the wooden staircase, but she kept falling, unable to find her balance with a throbbing head and without the use of her hands. After she fell for the third time, Vince uttered a string of curses. She saw him raise the hand with the gun, squeezed her eyes shut as he swung his hand closer, and felt the blow that sent her spiraling into blackness.

He must have knocked her out and carried her inside. Her head hurt worse than it had the night before, the worst pain she'd ever felt. She lifted her face from the bed and felt her hair matted to her face. As she blinked, trying to bring the room into focus, she realized that her left eye was plastered shut with a sticky paste. What was it? Before she could begin thinking of possibilities, she detected the smell of blood. Maybe she had been shot.

No, she was pretty sure she'd just been cold-cocked. She had a flicker of memory—Vince hitting her in the face, blood spurting. With the memory, she suddenly felt the same stickiness on her cheek and her nose. Her whole face was caked with blood. She closed her eyes, eye, and put her head back down.

The bed reeked, or was it the sweatshirt that still covered her upper body? The combination of pain and the smell of sweat and blood sent her stomach into turmoil. She forced herself to shimmy to the side of the bed where she wretched, adding to the already heavy scents in the room.

The door swung open, revealing Vince in the doorway. The words he called her were crass and unsurprising. He had a mouth on him; she'd heard him utter words and phrases the previous night that would make a sailor blush. He grabbed her by the arm and pulled her from the bed, careful to avoid her vomit. He shoved her into the attached bathroom and told her to use it. She looked at him helplessly.

With a sick smile, he pulled down her shorts and underwear, pushed her onto the commode and waited for her to relieve herself. When she had finished, feeling utterly humiliated, he pulled her to her feet, yanked up her clothes and dragged her down the hall into a dimly lit kitchen. The blinds were drawn, and the sun that filtered in gave the room an eerie glow.

"Now, you're gonna call your boyfriend and get him over here." He held out a phone, not the iPhone she'd seen him use at the Windjammer. This was a model she'd never seen. She stared at it for a moment before raising her eyes to his.

"I don't have a boyfriend."

The hit was swift and hard and made her whole body jerk.

"Give me Giovanni's number. Now."

Maybe it was the many blows she'd sustained, or maybe his accent had grown thicker, but she thought he said Giovanni. She was afraid to question him, afraid of another blow, or worse, so she just stared at him, her mouth open.

"Did you hear me?" He shouted in her face. "Give me his number!"

"I, I don't know a Giovanni. I—"

Another hit, this time to her stomach. She jerked forward, heaving again, but nothing came up. Her head reeled in pain.

"Don't give me that. You..." He shook his head and spat out another string of profanities. "Look, I don't want to keep hurting you. Just do what I say. Give. Me. His. Number."

"Please," she begged through tears. "I'm not lying. I don't know anyone by that name. I swear."

He eyed her for a long time before putting the phone down on the counter and running has hand over his bald head. He rubbed his nose with the palm of his hand, and she saw it. A glimpse of something she'd seen only for a split second a few times before. There was nothing about them that was remotely similar, nothing that anybody could pinpoint, nothing that would say they were related. But in that instant, she recalled that first night she and Jared talked on the beach and how, for just a nanosecond of time, Jared had reminded her of Vince.

It wasn't the only time some move he made or the expression on his face seemed familiar. Vince and Jared were related.

"You can't be here," Nick told Diane. "If you're right, if this is a crime scene, you can't go inside."

"Is she here? Did you find her?"

Nick shook his head. "No signs of anyone in the house, but her phone was lying on the floor outside the bathroom."

"She would never leave without her phone. She would never be out of touch with Molly. She let Molly borrow her phone yesterday to take pictures, and she drilled it into Molly's head that if anything went wrong, she was to call the shop immediately."

Nick arched his brow and tilted his head. "Like what? Was Christy worried that something was going to happen? Did she think someone was going to try to hurt her or her sister?"

Diane shook her head, feeling exasperated. "No, no, nothing like that. I just mean that she worries about Molly all the time. She's relentless about Molly being able to reach her. She'd never leave her phone anywhere."

"Were they running from something? Someone? Was there a reason she was so worried?"

Diane was becoming more frustrated. "No! They're orphans. They only have each other. Christy is just very protective of Molly."

Nick glanced back inside the house. "Where's Molly now?"

"She stayed the night with a friend. Not locals. Their son is an intern at Wallops. Molly and his sister have become friends. His family has rented a condo on the island several times this summer."

"Have you talked to Molly or this kid's family this morning?"

Before she could answer, she heard sirens heading their way. She turned as Paul's cruiser raced down the street. It came to a stop in front of the house.

"What's going on?"

Nick briefly filled him in. "I was just asking if Diane has talked to the sister."

Both men turned to Diane. She shook her head. "No, I don't know how to reach them. Molly doesn't have a phone."

"I know how to reach them," Marge said. "They're staying at Sunset Bay. Last name's Kumar." Marge looked at Diane. "Reporter, remember? I know stuff."

Diane resisted the urge to roll her eyes. "Do you want me to call and check on her?"

Nick spoke up before Paul answered. "Paul, you should know something." He cast a quick glance toward Diane then focused on Paul. "In addition to signs of a struggle, there's blood on the floor and wall."

Diane gasped.

Paul muttered a curse. "I'll call Sunset Bay. Nick, call the station. See if you can get someone from the state to come do a crime scene analysis. ASAP." He looked at

Diane. "After I call, I need you to come to the station with me. Tell me everything you know about these girls and anyone they've associated with." He stopped and rubbed his chin with his thumb and index finger. "She has a boyfriend, right? What's his name? Where can we find him?"

Before Diane could answer, Simon pulled up to the curb. He and Jared got out of the car. Diane pointed at Jared. "He's right there."

Jared put his head down on the table in the small room that he supposed served multiple purposes— meeting room, lunchroom, and today, interrogation room.

Without giving him any information, Officer Parker had told Jared that he needed to accompany him to the station, either willingly or under duress. Being in the back of the police car had brought back memories long buried. His mother crying beside him in the backseat of a squad car, flashing lights, yelling men in police uniforms and tactical gear, a man being led from a building in handcuffs, his cold eyes finding them through the shaded back window. That was the last night he and his mother were Maria and Giovanni. Everything changed after that—their names, their address, their backgrounds, their entire lives.

By the time Jared and Officer Parker arrived at the police department, Jared's shirt was soaked with sweat, and his body was tense with the trauma of a barrage of memories mixed with worry about Christy and anger that he was being detained and unable to help in the search.

The sound of the door opening alerted Jared. He sat up as Paul walked into the room.

"Okay, Jared. I have some questions for you."

"Am I a suspect?"

"In what?" Paul gave him a blank stare.

"In whatever happened to Christy. Do I need an attorney?"

"I don't know, Jared. Do you?"

Jared pushed his glasses up and stared back at Paul. He tried to look tough and told himself not to be intimidated. He'd done nothing wrong.

"I'd like to make a phone call."

"You can do that in a minute."

"Aren't I entitled to a phone call?"

"You're not under arrest, Jared. I'd just like to ask you a few questions."

"Is someone looking for Christy? What about her ex-boss? Is someone looking for him?"

"Yes, we have a BOLO issued for him as a person of interest. Now, I need to know what time you dropped off Ms. McLane at her house."

Jared sighed and answered Paul's questions. He couldn't tell if he was also a person of interest, or if they were just trying to establish a timeline. He was frustrated and irritated, hence his answers became more defensive as they went on. Finally, he'd had enough.

"Look, Officer Parker, I'm going to be straight with you."

"I'd appreciate that, Jared."

"I did not hurt Christy. I did not and would not ever cause her harm. I'm going to tell you something I haven't even told her yet. I love her. I love her more than anything. I would protect her with my life. I appreciate you trying to get answers, and I get that I'm among the prime suspects, but I would never, ever do anything to her. Not ever. I love her."

The last three words were said just above a whisper. Jared had a true understanding, more than he had the previous night, more than ever before, just why his mother did all the things she did over the past twenty-four years. You do whatever you can to protect the ones you love.

Through the throbbing pain, blood-soaked eye, putrid rag in her mouth, and the ringing in her head, Christy's mind recalled all her conversations with Jared. He had no memory of his biological father. He had no memory of his early childhood. He avoided talking about his grandparents and other relatives outside of his immediate family.

Though it physically hurt to think, she had enough wherewithal to hold onto one solid, sacred thought—she must protect Jared. Even if it meant dying for him, she would protect him. She had to. She loved him.

She could see Vince pacing outside on the back landing, smoking a cigarette and talking to himself while ominous clouds gathered in the sky above him. He was agitated. His plan was not going the way he intended. How could she use this to her advantage?

Vince tossed the butt over the railing and returned to the kitchen. The smell of cigarette smoke mingled with the smell of blood, vomit, and body odor. Christy swallowed hard, not wanting to throw up while the rag was in place. The tautness of the gag he'd tied around her added to the pounding in her head. Every little sound, smell, or movement caused her increased pain. She had to concentrate, had to maintain some control.

"Okay, here's how this is going to go," Vince told her. "I'm gonna ask some questions, you're gonna nod or shake your head. If you cooperate, I'll untie the gag. Capiche?"

She nodded, trying her best to block out the pain that the small movement caused.

"You don't know anyone named Giovanni. Is that right?"

She nodded, keeping her eyes focused on his to convey her sincerity.

"But you do have a boyfriend, right?"

She wasn't sure how to answer that. Was Jared her boyfriend? She decided that, in her best interest, she should give the closest answer she could to the truth. She nodded once.

"And he's tall, curly black hair, blue eyes, right?"

Again, she nodded once.

Vince walked over to the counter and pulled a jagged knife from the block by the stove. He held it up and slid his finger across the blade. Terror filled her and she felt sick once again.

"Okay, I need to ask you some questions that you're gonna answer without the gag. If you scream, I cut off a finger. If you do anything I don't like, I cut off another one. Got it?"

She nodded and he yanked the gag from her mouth. Instinctively, she took several large breaths, her head hammering with each inhale and exhale.

"Now, this guy, what's his name?"

He clearly didn't know, or he wouldn't have had such a tirade earlier. It obviously hadn't occurred to him that Jared didn't go by Giovanni. Did Jared even know that was his name?

"Water, please," she gasped.

He gave her a disgusted look but took a glass from the counter, filled it from the tap, and held it to her lips. She drank greedily, spilling more of the refreshing liquid down the front of her than she was able to swallow, but it felt so good in her parched mouth. He took it away, and she licked her cracked lips.

"Thank you," she whispered, truly grateful that he had shown her this one tiny courtesy, even if it was to extract information from her.

"Name," he demanded, tapping the knife's blade on his palm.

Waiting for the drink had given her time to think. She answered, "Jonathan."

He nodded. "Makes sense," he said. "Okay, where does he live?"

"Somewhere out west. I don't know."

He hit her across the temple again but not as hard as the other hits had been.

"Where does he live now?"

"Off island. Wattsville, maybe?" She made a face of uncertainty, trying to look believable as she delivered the false information. "I've never been to his house. He always comes here."

He eyed her with suspicion but let the answer pass.

"Is his mother here? In Whats-it-ville?"

She shook her head but stopped when the pain hit. She closed her open eye for a moment to make the pain stop, then opened it and looked at Vince. "I don't think so. I've never met her. He doesn't talk about her. They may be estranged."

Was this Jared's father? The one who abused them? The one they ran from? No, he was much too young. Still, the mere thought that this man might have been capable of producing such a gentle, caring, intellectual person made her nauseous all over again. Whatever the relation, she couldn't let him find his way to Jared or his mother.

Vince leaned down close to her face, his stale breath assaulting her senses as much as all the other smells in the room.

"I think it's time to get loverboy over here so that he can answer these questions for us. Don't you think? Wouldn't you like to know who he really is? The truth might surprise you." He stood back up and looked at her. "Now, I need you to make a call." He picked up his phone and held it up. "What's his number?"

"I honestly don't know. He put it in my phone, and I've never looked at it. I don't even know the area code."

She braced herself for another hit, but he just looked at her curiously before apparently deciding that this was probably the truth.

"Then we'll try the next best option. Who would know how to find him? Your boss lady?"

Christy started to say no but stopped herself. If Vince didn't know about the connection between Diane, Simon, and Jared, then that was good. On the other hand, if she could get a message to Diane...

"She could find him."

Vince stared at her for a long time, and she saw him calculating how to handle this. Thunder rumbled in the distance; a far-off flash of light illuminated the darkened room. Christy felt like she was in a horror movie.

Vince spoke in a cold, calculated voice. "Let's give her a call."

Update—Nor'easter's Threat Heightened

The National Weather Service has updated its coastal storm warning for the Mid-Atlantic area, which will have devastating effects on Assateague and Chincoteague. The warning has been updated to Thursday around noon and into the early hours of Friday morning. Primary threats associated with this system are heavy rainfall, tropical storm-force winds with powerful gusts, isolated tornadoes, and hazardous marine conditions. Storm surges may exceed twenty feet in height. Flooding has begun in outlying areas. All residents and visitors are warned to take precautions or evacuate.

The Chincoteague Herald, July 28

Chapter Fifteen

"The store's locked. Lights are off. Not a soul anywhere," Nick told Paul over the phone.

"Not surprised. I'm sure he's got her."

"What about the boyfriend?"

"Funny thing. I think he may be involved, but I'm not sure if it's willingly or unknowingly."

"Come again?"

"I've done some digging," Paul said. "This guy, Vince, is trouble. A record a mile long and get this. He's part of the DeCarolis family. I'm guessing you're familiar with that name."

Nick felt like he'd been kicked in the gut. He hadn't heard that name in years, but it was an infamous name in the town where he'd grown up. "What did you say the boyfriend's name is?"

"Jared Stevenson."

Nick shook his head. "Not a name I ever heard in Jersey."

"Yeah, well what if his name isn't really Jared Stevenson? What if his name was changed when he was four?"

"When would that have been?"

"1998—the same year the DeCarolis family was taken down by the wife of one of the family leaders. According to the papers, the wife and kid disappeared, and I can't find any trace of either of them anywhere."

Nick didn't like where this was going. "Paul, you gotta let this go. You can't keep digging. You could be setting this guy up to be in real danger."

"That's what I'm afraid of, Nick. If the DeCarolis family has moved its operation, or any part of it, to Chincoteague, the whole island's in danger."

Nick swallowed and took another look through the glass window.

"Permission to break in?"

"Be my guest."

Diane wrung her hands and paced the floor in the locked shop while Simon tried to make calls and find out what was going on with Jared. Diane knew that he felt responsible for Jared and the interns even though they were all legal adults.

She felt that it was best to stay at the shop where Christy would be able to contact her most easily if she was able to. She didn't know what to think about Jared. He had stars in his eyes every time Christy was near. She couldn't imagine him hurting her, and neither could Simon. Vince DeCarolis, on the other hand...

"They're holding him as a possible suspect. He hasn't been arrested." Simon told her after hanging up the phone. "I'm going to get in touch with my attorney."

"This is ridiculous. They should be out there looking for Christy."

The shop's phone rang, but Diane made no move to answer, frozen with fear.

"Are you going to get that?"

"I'm… What if…?"

"Diane, answer the phone." Simon's voice was gentle but firm.

Diane looked at Simon for a split second before racing behind the counter and answering the landline.

"Sugar and Sand, this is Diane."

"Diane." The raspy voice was barely audible, but Diane recognized it at once. Her heart leapt in her chest.

"Christy," she breathed turning to look at Simon who was already up and heading toward her. She hastily turned on the speaker and lay the phone on the counter. "Where are you?"

"I need to find Jonathan." Her voice was ragged and barely audible.

"Jonathan?"

"The man I've been seeing. I need to know how to find him. His mother is in danger. He needs to come."

"His mother?" She looked at Simon, but he shook his head and gave a slight shrug.

"Yes, she's here. She was hurt. I came here to help her. She needs him."

"Christy, where are you?"

There was a muffled noise on the other end and then a moment of silence before Christy answered.

"Tell Jonathan to call this number. Are you ready?"

Diane grabbed a napkin, and Simon handed her a pen from his pocket. She wrote down the number.

"I got it."

"Diane." Christy's voice was so weak. Diane could hardly hear her "Please, hurry."

"Christy—"

Before Diane could ask anything else, the line went dead.

"What do you think?" she asked Simon.

"I think we need to call the police. Now."

Paul sat down across the table from Jared and opened a file folder. Jared couldn't see what it contained.

"Jared, according to my information, you graduated from Harvard. That's quite an accomplishment."

Jared didn't respond. He kept his hands folded in front of him on the table and waited for Paul to continue.

"You were raised in Minnesota, mother is Jessica, father is…?" He looked up at Jared and raised one brow.

"Devon Stevenson."

Paul nodded. "Your stepfather is Devon Stevenson. What's your real father's name? That seems to be missing from the record."

Jared had no idea what 'record' he was talking about. He unfolded his hands and sat back, looking at Paul.

"I don't know," he said, telling the truth. "I was only four when we left. He was abusive. That's all I remember."

"Left where?"

Jared shrugged. "Again, I was four."

Paul sat and looked at Jared for a long time before nodding. "You see, Jared, there are some discrepancies in your file. I can't find any information about you or your mother before 1998. Neither of you has any social media, so essentially, you have no past and, by today's standards, no present."

"Yet, here I am," Jared said, not at all sure where his calm came from. Nervous and shy by nature, he suddenly felt like a different person, the person he'd been trained to be since that night in the squad car.

"Jared, this kind of missing information sends up all kinds of red flags. I need you to be honest with me. Is there someone out there who might want to hurt you or someone you care about? Someone like Vince DeCarolis?"

For the first time that morning, Jared felt a shift in the universe. He'd been wracking his brain, trying to figure out who would want to hurt Christy, why someone would take her, other than her creepy former boss. Suddenly, Jared wondered if he'd been asking the wrong questions, focusing on the wrong possibilities. Could it be? Was there a chance? Was Christy's disappearance tied to his unknown past? Was Vince connected to his past?

"Does the name Giovanni DeCarolis mean anything to you?"

Jared's mind began to whirl. Images, voices, scenes from the past began to assail him, running though his mind like a broken movie reel in an old-time movie house.

"Officer Parker, I really need to make that call. Now. I can't, won't answer anything until after I use the phone."

After a long, hard stare, Paul stood and handed Jared a phone. "You have five minutes," he said before leaving the room.

Jared assumed that this small room in this small department on this small island was not rigged with microphones and recording devices, but he couldn't be sure. He dialed the number and waited for an answer.

"Mom, I'm in trouble. You need to make that call we always talked about. The time is now."

"She what?" Paul said into the phone, his voice laden with incredulity. "Where is she? What else did she say?"

Diane gripped Simon's hand in her own. "She called Jared 'Jonathan' and said that she was with his mother who was hurt. She said for Jared to call this number she gave me. That's all. The line went dead after she gave me the number."

Paul swore before asking, "And she didn't say where she was? Could you hear anything? Voices, sounds, anything that might tell us where to find her?"

"Nothing. I'm sorry."

"You're still at the doughnut place?"

"Yes. Should I go somewhere else?"

"No, stay there. She may call back, and she knows she can reach you there."

"What about Jared?"

"I guess he has another phone call to make."

Diane didn't know what that meant, but Paul had already disconnected the call. She looked at Simon as thunder boomed outside the shop.

"I guess we just wait," he said.

Diane nodded. "And pray."

"Why hasn't he called yet? What's taking so long?"

Christy shook her head. "I don't know. Maybe Diane had to make some calls or go looking for him."

Vince shook his head. "I don't like this. Something don't feel right. You told me he might be estranged from his mother, but you insisted he'd come if you said she needed him. What gives? Was that some kind of trick?"

His face was red. He reached across the table and picked up the knife. "If you're playing some kinda game with me—"

"I'm not," she assured him and hoped he couldn't see through her lie. "Even if they're not on speaking

terms, he's a good guy. He'd help. I know he would."
She wondered if her words were more for him or for
her. Jared would obey, right? He would come find her,
wouldn't he?

"What do you know about his mother?"

"Nothing. I don't know anything. He has sisters and
a stepfather, all out west. Montana, Wyoming? I'm not
sure." One thing she did know, if this guy was as
dangerous as Jared's father, she wasn't going to give him
any leads on finding Jared's mother.

Vince played with the knife, shifting it back and
forth in his hands. "You better hope he calls soon. Real
soon."

Paul sat back down across the table. "Jared, what do
you know about Vince DeCarolis?"

"Nothing. Christy used to work for a guy named
Vince. I'm assuming that's him. He manages the
Windjammer. He threatened her, said she had to sleep
with him to keep her job. She quit. That's all I know."

"Jared, Diane heard from Christy a little while ago."

Jared swallowed. He splayed his hands on the table
and pushed down, letting the hardness of the table give
him some strength and stability. "Where is she? Is she
okay? Can I see her?"

"Jared, listen," Paul commanded. "She called Diane
and said—"

The door to the room flew open, and a man in a dark suit rushed into the room.

"What the h—"

"I told him he couldn't come in here," a woman said from behind the man. Jared thought she was the receptionist. He didn't recognize the man.

"Chief Paul Parker?"

Paul stood, matching the man's height. "Yes. Who are you?"

"Jack O'Neil, Witness Protection. I need you to stop questioning this man."

Paul's mouth fell open. Jared thought his own expression probably matched Paul's.

"Witness Protection? What's going on here?"

"I'm afraid I'm not at liberty to answer that." The man looked at Jared. "Mr. Stevenson, we have to leave. Now. Arrangements are being made to get you and your mother to a safe location."

"No," Jared said, standing up. "I'm not going anywhere, not without Christy."

"I'm sorry, Sir, but you don't have a choice. We believe you're in grave danger. You need to come with me."

"I'm not leaving," Jared insisted with confidence and bravado he'd never felt before. "Christy's the one in danger. I'm not going anywhere until we know she's safe."

Jack looked at Paul. The police chief raised his hands. "Quid pro quo?"

Jack narrowed his eyes. "Meaning what?"

"You let Jared stay and help us, I'll tell you where you can find Vince DeCarolis."

"And the storehouse of narcotics he's been selling here on the island."

They all looked toward the doorway, where Nick Black stood with a bulky bag in his hand. He walked to the table and put down the bag, unzipping it to reveal several plastic bags of white powder.

"This was hidden in the back of the store. My bet is, there's a whole lot more where this came from. I need a warrant to search his house. If my gut's right, you'll find this and Christy."

"I need to make a call," Jack said before hastily departing from the room.

Vince was jumpy, and his nerves only made Christy's more heightened. He paced the room, kept looking out the windows, and wouldn't stop playing with that damned knife. Thunder rolled and lightning flashed across the sky. Whether it was real or the effect of a concussion, Christy felt the house swaying in the wind. Everything hurt, her head most of all, and the thunder and lightning made it worse.

"Can you please untie me? My arms are numb. You've beaten me too badly for me to try anything. My head's killing me, and I can't see out of my left eye."

Vince gave her a once over and sighed. "I'll untie your hands, but I ain't letting you loose."

He left the room and came back with another set of ropes. He bent down and tied her ankles to the chair before using the knife to cut her wrists loose.

As soon as the air hit the open wounds on her wrists, pain shot through her, but it felt so good to be able to move her arms that she hardly felt it after the initial pain. Tears sprang to her eyes as she moved her arms and rotated her wrists, which were starting to bleed.

A noise outside startled both Vince and Christy. He stood abruptly, grabbed the rag off the table and secured it back in her mouth, then paused and looked at her now-freed hands. He huffed.

"Don't move," He commanded before heading to the front of the house.

Christy looked around the kitchen. What was in reach?

She didn't see anything she could get to without drawing attention. She'd have to find a way to get to that knife.

Nick was the official lead on the team that surrounded the house, but he deferred to the state hostage negotiator to take charge. Doors and windows opened in the neighboring houses. Police personnel motioned for the people to stay back. Positioned on the roof of a nearby house was Nick's best friend, Zach Middleton, a former Army sniper and part-time member of the police department. They'd needed his assistance twice, once when his sister was being held by her ex-husband and once when Zach's own stepson had been kidnapped. Nick hoped they didn't need him now.

"Mr. DeCarolis," Wayne said into the bullhorn, his voice almost drowned out by the howling wind. "This is Anthony Wayne with the state police. I'm advising you to open the door and release Ms. McLane."

There was no movement inside the house, no lights on, no music or television playing. Anthony looked at Nick. "You sure about this?"

Nick shrugged. "Not really, but you got any better guesses?"

"Mr. DeCarolis," Wayne was back on the bullhorn. "We'd like to talk to you. Can you call the number on the sign?"

An officer struggled against the wind to hold up a placard with a number written on it.

They waited, but there was no movement, no peering through the blinds, and no ring of the phone.

"Mr. DeCarolis, if we don't get an answer from you within the next sixty seconds, armed police are going to enter the house. Again, I advise that you release Ms. McLane."

A watch was set to a countdown. Beginning at thirty seconds, Wayne called out warnings in ten second increments until he reached the final ten seconds.

"DeCarolis, we're coming in in nine, eight, seven…"

Nick took a deep breath and reached for the door handle. What he wouldn't give to be patrolling the fairgrounds at that moment.

When Wayne reached one, Nick pushed open the unlocked door, and a loud crack exploded around them.

The house shook with the force of the thunder. From out of nowhere, rain began to fall. The anticipated storm had reached the island.

"There's a firestorm out there, and I don't mean the weather."

"What's going on?" Christy asked.

"Nothin' for you to worry about. Somethin' at a house down the street." He was sweating profusely and kept looking outside. "Why hasn't he called?"

Vince rounded on Christy and held the knife to her throat. "Why hasn't he called?" he screamed, and she felt the sharp edges of the knife scrape her skin.

Just then, the phone rang. He pulled back and grabbed the phone, setting it on the table and putting the call on speaker.

"Talk," he said.

"Is this Vince?"

"Who's this?"

"This is Paul Parker with the Chincoteague Police. Who's this?"

"How'd you get this number?" He eyed Christy and held up the knife in front of her eyes.

"Do you have Christy? I'm told she called from this number."

Vince spat a string of vulgarities. "Where's Jonathan?"

"Is Christy there?"

The wind rattled the doors and windows, the house grew darker as thunder rolled, and lightning illuminated the windows around the closed blinds.

"Son of a... Look here, I wanna talk to Jonathan. If I don't hear from him, whatever happens is on you."

Vince ended the call and reared back before delivering a blow that sent the chair crashing to the ground. Christy's head and left shoulder exploded in pain.

"Now look what you've done."

Sweat ran down his face and dripped to the floor. He was unraveling. Christy knew her time on the island, on this earth, was drawing to a close. She felt her strength draining away. Everything hurt so badly. She closed her eyes and let the blackness overtake her.

"I've got to go," Jared told Jack, who blocked his way to the door.

"You can't go anywhere. The DEA is on its way along with the Organized Crime Unit. We don't know the level of threat to you or your mother, but we've advised her to pull up stakes."

"And what? Become someone else? Force her and my father to change careers? Make my sisters give up everything they've worked for and achieved? Leave their grandparents without any explanation, forwarding address, or knowledge of whether they're dead or alive? And what about me? Throw away my degrees? Forget that I'm a Harvard grad? Leave Christy and Molly behind?"

Jack clenched his jaw as Jared plowed forward. "No, no, and no. I'm not doing it. I'm not going through that again. Do you have any idea what it's like? For your whole life to be a lie? To not even know your grandparents, to not even be able to talk about them? To pretend your life, your background, even your name is something they're not?" He ran his hand down his face and pushed back his glasses. "Do you know what it's like to watch your mother look over her shoulder for your entire life? Second guess everything she wants to say before it even comes out of her mouth? I'm done! I won't do this anymore."

"Jared, listen to me." Jack laid his hand on Jared's arm. Jared flung it away.

"No, you listen to me. I've spent twenty-four years wondering who I am, where I came from, and who my family is. If my mother wants to keep running, she can, but I won't do it any longer."

An officer stuck his head into the room. "I was told to let you all know that she's not there. They're not there."

Jared felt his heart crack inside his chest and wondered if people died from a heart that had been torn open by fear and grief. He sunk back down into the chair.

Jack's phone buzzed. He answered, keeping his eyes on Jared.

"Yeah, he's here." He held the phone out to Jared who, after a moment, reluctantly took it.

"Jared, you're okay. Praise God in Heaven. Did Jack tell you the plan? He's got someone on the way here. We'll meet up in—"

"Mom, I'm not going."

The line went silent. Jared waited as patiently as he could, considering the past several hours had been nothing but waiting.

"Jared," her voice cracked. "You have to. They'll find you."

"Evidently, they already found me, so what's the use? Why should I have to give up my life, *again*, just to wait for them to find me *again*? I'm done, Mom. I can't do it. I can't change everything, leave everyone, and disappear. I can't and I won't."

"It's because of her," his mother said quietly.

Jared hesitated. "Yes. And no. It's because of me. This isn't what I want. It's not who I am."

"Do you even know who you are, Jared? I mean, who you really are?"

"Mom, does the name Giovanni DeCarolis ring a bell?"

"I don't get it," Nick said to Trooper Wayne. "It's like nobody's lived here in ages."

The scents of mold and mildew hung in the air. Dust had settled on every surface, and mouse tracks littered the counters, sink, and stove. There were no clothes, no dishes, no basic toiletries, no household items.

"I know this is the place. It's on his paperwork at the store. I verified it with the landlord. This is where DeCarolis is supposed to live."

"My guess is he's squatting somewhere. Using this as a legal place of residence but living and keeping the bulk of his product somewhere else, some place he can't be connected with."

Nick picked up the phone and called the department. "Hey, Black here. I need a list of every empty building or house on the island."

"Do you know how long that's going to take?" Stacey answered. "How am I going to get that kind of information?"

"I don't know. Call a real estate agent. Ask Paul, he'll know. Just get a list and get it fast. Christy McLane's life depends on it."

Zach Middleton walked into the house as Nick was hanging up the phone.

"Call my sister. Tell her to send an email blast to every subscriber on the island." Zach gave Nick detailed instructions. "Almost the entire island subscribes to the paper. News will travel fast, answers will pour in. You know how this place works. Everyone will jump in to help."

Another loud crack of thunder boomed overhead. A loud popping sound ripped through the air, and all the lights on the island went out.

Breaking News—Chincoteague Police Need Your Help

State and local police are on the lookout for Vince DeCarolis, manager of Windjammer Surf Shop. DeCarolis has known ties to the New Jersey Mafia and may be behind the recent narcotics problem on the island. He's bald, approximately 5'11" with multiple tattoos on his arms and chest. Consider him armed and dangerous. Police are seeking any information on his whereabouts now or in the past twenty-four hours. They are interested in any houses or buildings he's been seen in or around in recent months. Police are also in need of the addresses of any empty spaces—buildings, houses, or other structures—on the island. Call the Chincoteague Police Department with your tips or information.

The Chincoteague Herald, July 29

Chapter Sixteen

Against Jack's protests, Jared left the police department on his own. The police had nothing to hold him on. He was an adult able to make his own decisions about his personal protection.

He did his best to shield his face from the pelting rain as he ran down the sidewalk, sloshing through at least an inch of water. Seawater pushed in from the eastern side of the town and flowed into the street. When Jared reached the doughnut shop, he pounded on the door until Simon opened it and let him in. Inside the shop, it was eerily dark and quiet.

"Any word?" Jared asked breathlessly, water dripping onto the floor surrounding him.

"Nothing," Diane said, rushing toward him. "What's going on? Do you know anything?"

He nodded. "I know enough. That guy, Vince, he's…" What was he? Family? An associate of Jared's father? A hired hand? "He's somehow involved with my family." He looked at Simon. "My real family. Don't ask me about them. I don't know any more than you do. My mother's kept me in the dark my entire life. All I do know is that he's dangerous and he's after me, not Christy. I've got to find her before…" He let the rest of the sentence trail off, not sure what Vince might do to Christy if Jared didn't show up.

"Where's the number she gave you? I've got to call him. It might be her only chance."

Diane looked to Simon for guidance. They both looked tired and older than they were. Neither said a word, but Diane handed him the napkin with a trembling hand.

Jared pulled his phone from his pocket and looked for a source of light. Simon held his phone over the napkin, flashlight enabled, and Jared dialed the number.

"It's me, Giovanni. I want to talk to Christy."

"Well, well, well. If it ain't my long-lost cousin. Where you been all these years?"

"I want to talk to Christy. I need to hear her voice."

Vince looked at the body at his feet. There was no movement. He wasn't sure she was breathing at all. He looked at the knife on the table and cursed himself for being so careless, but then he shrugged. He hadn't planned on keeping her alive anyway.

"Little Christy can't come to the phone right now. She's incapacitated."

"You listen to me, if you've hurt a single bone in her body, I will make you pay with my own hands."

Vince nudged her leg with his foot. No response. He looked at the swollen cheek, the disjointed nose the blood-covered eye. His gaze went to the shoulder that seemed bent at an awkward angle. He smiled.

"Don't worry. I didn't hurt a *single* bone in her body."

"Where is she?"

"Well, now. I can't tell you that. What I can tell you is, if you share some information with me, I can share some information with you. It's a sort of trade. You tell me how to find your mother, and I'll tell you where to find your girlfriend."

He heard the long intake and release of breath and wondered who his cousin would choose. He knew it wasn't a fair choice. Your mother or your girl? How could a man choose? He had to sweeten the pot.

"I tell you what. If you tell me where your mother is, I'll tell you exactly where Christy is, but I wouldn't wait much longer. She's lost a lot of blood. Honestly, I'm not sure she's breathing."

He heard the guttural noise his cousin made and waited while Jared called him a string of names and made threats that Vince found laughable. He'd seen the guy— tall and athletic but pathetically intellectual. The wuss wouldn't know how to use any muscle he had.

"Do we have a deal?"

"Where is she?" Jared said through gritted teeth.

"Where's Maria? Come on, you give, I give."

Vince only had to wait a few seconds before Jared rattled off an address.

"Very good, cuz. Now, I'll call you back once I've got confirmation that you're telling me the truth."

Vince disconnected and looked back down at the woman on the floor. For good measure, and to prevent her from trying anything, he kicked her hard in the midsection. When she did nothing more but emit a soft groan, he kicked her again, much harder, and she cried out without ever gaining consciousness.

This won't do. He'd made a promise to his uncle. He had to keep that promise, or he'd never get all the way back into the family. He looked at the knife lying on the table. He had no choice, really, and it was a shame. She was such a young, pretty girl. Well, what did they say? Everyone was young and pretty in Heaven?

Vince picked up the knife, squeezed his eyes shut, and plunged it into her side. He opened one eye to be sure that he'd done it right. The knife was standing up, protruding from her right side. Lightning flashed, illuminating what he could see of the silver blade. He pulled the knife out, stared for a moment at the red blood, thick and dark in some places, shiny and wet in others. He dropped the knife to the floor.

There's your payback, Giovanni, he thought.

Giovanni was just a kid when his mother had turned on the family, sending both Giovanni's and Vince's fathers to prison, along with most of their male relatives. Vince had been a kid at the time as well. Now his cousin could suffer the same fate the rest of them had—he'd have to continue living after losing everyone he loved.

Vince grabbed his keys and headed for the door. He'd spent the night loading the product in the trunk of his car, which was registered to a dead person in the state of Maryland and couldn't be traced to him. He was clearing out while he could.

Christy felt the blood oozing from her side, the throbbing in her head, the searing pain in her shoulder. She felt all of it, but somehow, she felt okay. She felt better than okay. She hadn't led Vince to Jared or led Jared to Vince. She had done her best to protect him, to show him how much she loved him even if she would never be able to tell him.

Scenes from her childhood flashed through her mind—her dad's smile, her first bike, her best friend in elementary school, going to the zoo with her mom and Fred, Molly's birth, her senior prom, the first time she saw Jared, and his loving face as he gazed into her eyes on the dance floor. She let herself drift away to a faraway place. She was floating. Everything was black, but she could see tiny lights everywhere. They were stars! She could see stars. She reached out and touched one, causing it to grow bigger in her hand. It grew until it was the moon. She was walking, floating, touching the surface and bouncing back up, gliding across the Sea of Tranquility.

Then she saw him. Not Jared. Not Vince. Him. The man Jared was teaching her about, the one who taught his followers that prayer. He was holding her, raising her, lifting her up, her arms outstretched to feel his love. Then she remembered what he said, and she knew what she had to do.

With the last breath she could push through her body she whispered, "I forgive you."

"We caught a break." Officer Matt Singleton ran into Paul's office. "We got a ping on the cell phone. You're not gonna believe this, but it's on the same street as the house they raided."

"Let me see that."

Paul looked at the information Matt provided. "Is this house on the list we're compiling?"

"It sure is. I've already sent the address to Nick."

Paul picked up his phone and keys and took the paper from Matt.

"I'm heading over there. Let me know if you find out anything else."

Jared saw the police cars heading down Main Street, water propelling out from under their tires. He took one look at Diane and Simon and bolted from the dark shop.

As he ran, he thought back to the night he had chased Christy down the beach. That was easy compared to this. Each step took all his muscle strength to pull his feet from the rising water. Wind and rain battered him as he tried to pinpoint where the cars were heading.

He knew he could never keep up on foot, but he also knew that it gave him an advantage. He ran through yards, hopped fences, and sloshed across the terrain, always keeping the sounds of sirens or the flashing of red and blue lights on his radar. The wind was both a foe and a friend, depending upon his direction. When he finally reached the street where the cars had come to a stop, a strong gust hurled him face-first into a yard across from what looked to be an abandoned house with six police cars pointing in various directions in the street and yard.

Jared pushed his way through officers, the rain his ally in fighting their grip on his arms as he moved toward the house. Before he reached the stairs, he was stopped by three men—Paul, Nick, and another man he recognized from the department.

"You can't go in there," Paul said. "It's a crime scene, and Vince may be armed and dangerous."

"I don't care." He struggled against them, but between the three of them, their hold was too tight. "Please, I need to get inside."

A loud voice behind him made him stop and turn to look at an officer in state police raingear holding a bullhorn.

"Mr. DeCarolis, we know you're in there. Send out Ms. McLane and come out with your hands up."

Jared turned back toward the house and held his breath. There was no movement, as far as he could see, from inside.

"Mr. DeCarolis—"

The man stopped and everyone stared, some with guns pointed, as the front door opened. Someone in a black hoodie stepped out and then collapsed onto the landing. The figure began to push itself up, a large, serrated knife in one hand, and Jared could feel the anticipation of the men around him, guns ready.

"Drop the weapon," several voices called out. "Drop it now!"

The hand, hidden inside the voluminous shirt sleeve, released the knife. The weapon fell through the railing, landing with the blade penetrating the rain-soaked ground.

The door to the house stood open, but no other figures appeared. A voice from around the back could be heard calling out through the wind and rain.

"There's no car. Repeat, no car."

Jared didn't understand what that meant. Something above him caught his eye. He looked up and saw a police officer in the doorway, his gun aimed at the unmoving body that had dropped the knife and then crumpled back onto the wooden landing. The officer shouted down to them.

"All clear in the house."

With his gun drawn, the officer turned the body over. Even through the rain and at a distance of a good twenty feet, Jared could see the man's reaction. He winced, shook his head, and looked down at the group standing in the yard. Jared watched as the man gently pulled the hoodie away enough for him to reach inside to check for a pulse. A loose strand of blonde hair fell from the hoodie as the officer started CPR, and Jared heard a loud, inhuman cry. As his knees buckled, he came to the realization that the crying was his own.

Diane sat in the waiting room, where the electricity had been restored, clutching Simon's hand. She hadn't been able to stop crying since she got the call from Nick. At the sound of her name, she looked up to see Molly running in her direction.

"Diane, where's Christy? Where's my sister?"

Diane looked at Simon and tried to hold back her tears. This poor child had gone through so much already. How could she face more tragedy?

The Kumar family stood nearby along with Chloe, who had joined them at some point. It seemed to Diane that nobody knew what to say.

The double doors opened, and a doctor walked into the room, looking around anxiously. "Family of Christine McLane?"

Diane and Molly looked at each other, then they both stood and faced him.

"That's us. We're her family," Diane said.

She felt Simon stand and take her hand. Her other arm was draped protectively around Molly.

Dear God, she prayed, *please don't let this child go through another loss.*

"Mrs. McLane. Your daughter has sustained multiple, serious injuries. She has a concussion, a deep cut above her eye, a bruised cheekbone, and a dislocated shoulder. It's a miracle that none of her bones were broken. We don't know what kind of damage she may have suffered to her frontal cortex or temporal lobe. It's possible she might have problems with speech, comprehension, or some academic processing." He took a long breath as he looked down at the iPad in his hand. Diane felt as though he was giving them time to process this information before he gave them the bad news. When he looked back up, his expression was strained. "She has a cut on her throat, but it's not deep. The cut over her eye should have been stitched, but it was too late for that. We've patched it up the best we could." He took a deep breath and looked at Diane. "She was stabbed in the spleen, and we've repaired what we were able to. We did stop the internal bleeding, but she needs to remain in our care for several days to be monitored and recover."

Diane nodded.

"I want to see my sister," Molly insisted. "I need to know she's okay."

"She's in recovery," the doctor said. "I'll come get you all when she's awake."

They watched the doctor walk back through the doors. Molly started crying, and Diane sat back down and cradled the child, smoothing down her brown hair, telling her it would be okay. Diane looked up when the outside doors slid open.

She almost didn't recognize Jared when he walked in. His shoes were sopping wet, leaving large, muddy footprints in his path. He wore a navy, Chincoteague Police Department sweatshirt and grey sweatpants that only went to his shins. His curly hair hung limply around his hollow face. He looked like he was going to pass out at any minute.

Simon went to him and led him to a chair. "Are you okay? What happened?"

Jared looked at Molly and then at Diane and Simon. He swallowed as tears filled his eyes. Diane wanted to reach out and cradle him, too.

"How is she? Is she…?"

"She's okay," Diane said. "She's going to be okay. Then the big, soft-spoken man put his head in his hands and cried like a baby.

It took a long time for Jared to find the strength and the words to say all that he had to say. He started from the very beginning.

"My father, my real father, was the DeCarolis family hitman." Diane recoiled in shock, which was not surprising to him. "It's estimated that they killed at least a dozen people in the early to mid 90s. My mother turned him in."

"Sweet Mother of Mercy," Diane said.

"I didn't know until just a little while ago. All I knew was, when I was four, we were put in the back of a police car and taken to a police station. From there, we were taken through the back door to an unmarked car and put in a hotel. We were given new names, new backgrounds, new lives." He closed his eyes and shook his head. "I never understood what happened. In one night, I lost my father, my grandparents, my cousins, my friends, my house, my toys, everything. We had to start all over. Mom had to learn a new career, and I grew up knowing nothing about my former life. I begged and pleaded, I threatened to run away. I gave my mother hell, but she never broke. As I got older, I understood that she had done it for me, to get me out of there, to prevent me from being indoctrinated, but it didn't make it easier." He looked at Diane and winced. "I was not a very understanding son."

"It wasn't your fault," she said in a soothing voice.

"I know, but I didn't treat her fairly. She was trying to protect me from our past, from the members of the family like my cousin, Vince."

The name left such a strong distaste in his mouth, he wanted to spit out the filthy feeling it evoked in him.

"We moved to Minnesota. I went to school, Mom went to work, and we did the best we could. Then Mom met my father and eventually had Emily and Missy. Mom never told them anything. She stuck to the story like it had been her story her entire life—only child, parents and grandparents deceased. She reads obits every day, waiting to see the names of her loved ones."

Diane took his hand and squeezed it but didn't say anything more. It felt comforting, both Diane's gesture and the chance to finally talk about everything.

"I had a hard time making friends. At first, I was afraid I'd say something wrong, let out a secret I wasn't supposed to share. I lost myself in books, in my studies, in my fascination with other worlds. As I grew older, I felt like I was living a lie. I didn't understand how my mother did it. How did she sleep beside a man every night, profess her love for him, have his children, yet never tell him the truth about anything? I didn't get it. Until today."

He looked away, heavy tears welling in his eyes again. He turned back to Diane.

"She did it because she loves me and would do anything to protect me. She gave up her entire life to protect me because that's how much she loves me."

His pain was visceral. He felt his breath coming in short, fast waves. He'd heard what happened to Christy, how she might have died. He had continued to think she might die up until Diane told him she was going to be okay. He would have done anything to stop it, to stop Vince from taking her, hurting her.

"How did he find you?" Simon asked.

Jared shrugged. "No clue. Apparently, Vince was on the outs after a botched job got him sent to prison for a while. He was working his way back into their good graces by starting a drug operation here on the island. The Windjammer was a front for the operation. If it was successful, he'd be able to say that he was contributing to the family, making up for past mistakes."

"Where's Vince now?" Diane asked, and Jared noticed the way her eyes darted around the room as though she expected the man to materialize before them.

"On his way to jail. They caught him with a roadblock at the end of the causeway." Jared snorted. "Not the smartest one in the family for starting up an operation in a location with only one way out."

"Where is your mother now?" Molly asked, and Jared looked at her and blinked. He had forgotten she was there. Would she be traumatized by his story, by what his past did to her sister?

"She's safe. They moved her and her family somewhere new."

It was Simon who asked the question that Jared had no answer to. "So, what happens to you now?"

Jared looked up at him and sighed. "That's the million-dollar question. And one I'm not going to be able to answer until Christy is better."

Though the truth was, he knew his choice had already been made because he was still here.

There wasn't any part of Christy's body that wasn't in excruciating pain. She had no rational thoughts, only pain. She slipped in and out of consciousness, unable to open her eyes or move her mouth. Everything hurt, including her brain. She just wanted to sleep…

Once the anesthesia had completely worn off and medication made the pain bearable but didn't inhibit thought, she became aware of several things. Her first thought was that Vince had mummified her, maybe even buried her alive. She started to panic. Her face was covered with cloth, her arm felt pinned to her side, and there was a heavy feeling in her mid-section, like something was sitting on top of her. She couldn't move, couldn't fully open her eyes or mouth. It hurt to breathe. Her heart raced. She had to get away.

It took several attempts, but she found the strength and ability to open her eye. Only one because the other was bandaged shut. Wherever she was now, it was dark and smelled like antiseptic. Where had he taken her? What had he done to her?

She heard light breathing nearby and stiffened. He was there.

Her heart beat even faster, and that's when she heard the other sounds. There was a beeping noise that was getting faster and louder. Were they in a truck? Was it backing up? Where was he taking her? Could she get away? She felt like she was hyperventilating.

She felt a sudden movement and heard her name, felt the squeeze of her hand. She pressed her eyes tightly and let the tears flow.

"Christy, it's okay. You're safe. I'm here."

He was here. Not Vince. Jared. He was here.

The lights went on amid a flurry of activity.

"She's awake," she heard Jared say.

"Her heart's racing," said another voice. "Christy? Christy, can you hear me? Are you able to speak?"

Water. She tried to say the word, but she couldn't get the thought to reach her mouth. She felt her lips moving, concentrated, then in a mere whistle of a sound said, "Water."

There was a ripple of joy across the room that even Christy could feel. What did that mean?

"No problem, Christy. We've got water."

She felt a straw being pushed through her lips, but she didn't have the strength to suck. She felt a tear trickle down her cheek and tried to turn, to push the straw away.

"It's okay, Christy." The unfamiliar woman's voice was soothing. "We'll try something else. Ice, Meg, please go get me some ice."

Christy heard the door swing open and footsteps leaving the room. All her senses were heightened.

"How do you feel, Christy? Other than thirsty. Are you in any pain?"

She tried to shake her head. She had aches and some distant throbbing, but she didn't feel any real pain.

"Can you talk to me?" the woman asked. "Can you tell me if you're in pain?"

"No pain," she whispered.

"Here, Morgan," another voice said, and within seconds Christy felt a cold, wet ice cube being pressed to her lips. It was the most wonderful thing she'd ever felt.

"You're a real fighter, Christy," said the woman she assumed was Morgan. "You went through some pretty bad stuff, but you're going to be okay. Everyone on the island has been praying for you. I'm told that Father Darryl offered a Mass for you on Sunday."

Sunday? What day is it now? she wondered.

"We're all pulling for you." Morgan took the ice away. Christy wanted to beg her to put it back. "Here, I think you can handle this," Morgan said.

The ice returned, but it wasn't Morgan's soft finger holding it to her lips. Christy opened one eye to see Jared's face hovering over hers.

"I'll let Dr. French know she's awake."

Christy heard the nurses leave and the door close.

"Hey there," Jared said in a hushed voice. There were tears in his eyes. "You have no idea how happy I am to see you awake."

There was so much she wanted to ask, so much she needed to know. She heard the thoughts in her head but getting them to her lips took such effort.

"Vince?" she finally whispered.

"He's gone. In jail. Hopefully for a very long time."

"I tried…" she licked her ice-wet lips and blinked. "Tried to warn you."

"I know. You did a good job."

"He knew…. knew you… Giovanni…"

"I know. It's okay."

"Tried…to…save…you."

She saw a tear run down his cheek and heard him sucking in small breaths of air. His voice caught as he whispered back. "I tried to save you, too."

Longtime Shop Owner Retires

There will be changes on Main Street in the New Year.
Diane Evans, owner of Sugar and Sand Doughnuts has
retired after satisfying our community's sugar needs for
the past thirty years. Diane, who moved to Chincoteague
in 1972, has no plans to relocate. "This is my home and
will always be home. I'm anxious to sit back, relax, and
see what the next chapter will be for me and for Sugar
and Sand."

Holly Simpson, who has lived on the island for five
years, is delighted to become the new owner of the
business. "I have so many ideas and plans for the space,
but I promise everyone that two things will not change.
As long as I'm in charge, Diane's doughnuts will always
be on the menu, and we will always have fresh-brewed
coffee."

The Chincoteague Herald, January 1

Chapter Seventeen

In the end, it was Christy's sleepy, pain-slurred words to Jared that led to their decision. It had become their mantra, the mantra of the entire family.

"I tried to save you."

Even with Vince in jail, there were still members of the DeCarolis family, including Vince's Uncle Frankie, who were operating the family business. Everyone knew that Jared, Christy, and even Molly would never be safe as long as they family business was still in operation. They were given round-the-clock protection while Christy recovered, but that wouldn't last forever. Though it pained them, and broke Diane's heart, they knew their time on the island was coming to an end.

Luckily for them, the IRS caught up with Uncle Frankie, and the family business fell apart.

Eighteen Months after the Business was Shut Down
Chincoteague Island, Virginia

Jared looked out the window at the channel that flowed into the vast Atlantic Ocean. The full moon shone on the water. When he was a little boy, he was afraid of the water, but he never knew why. He still didn't know. It was his stepfather who first coaxed him into a boat, who took him fishing, who taught him to water ski. Devon Stevenson was the only father Jared had ever known, and Jared was happy to keep it that way. The little he now knew about his real father was more than enough. The rest could stay buried.

"Can't sleep?" Christy's arms went around his waist.

"Just wanted to look at the moon," he replied. "You should go back to bed. You need your rest."

"I'm fine. I'm just making sure you're okay."

He gently turned to face her, laying his hands on the swell of her round belly. "I'm not the one who has nightmares. I just wanted to look for the Sea."

Christy looked around him and gazed upward into the sky. "It's still there. It's not going anywhere." She looked back at him, holding his gaze in hers. "And neither am I."

He leaned down and buried his face in her hair, taking in the scent of the shampoo she'd been using since they first met. She was everything to him. It still pained him that he'd almost lost her, that losing her would have been because of him.

She pulled back, looked up at him, and gently pushed his glasses up onto the bridge of his nose. He had started wearing contacts, but she preferred his glasses. Like that first night on the beach, she reached up and caressed his cheek.

"I'm here. I'm alive. You're alive. Everything is okay." She'd become good at reading his mind.

He lovingly touched the scar to the right of her left eye. "Why is it that you're always the one reassuring me even after what you went through?"

"What we went through."

She was right. After he had learned the details of what happened, he imagined every hit, every punch, every kick as though it had happened to him. He felt her pain in the hospital room, in rehab, at physical therapy. When her body ached, his body ached. When she cried, he cried. She pushed herself to get stronger while he pushed himself to finish his doctoral studies.

They'd come so close to losing everything, but they had gained each other. They cheered each other on, pushed each other to see things through, and supported each other through nightmares, doctor's appointments, meetings with federal agencies, dissertation rewrites, and college final exams. On the day they professed their vows—standing before the altar at St. Anderw's, with Father Darryl presiding and Diane, Simon, Molly, and all their friends and family in attendance—they'd promised to stand by each other in sickness and health, for richer or poorer, in good times and in bad. They were easy promises to make since they'd faced all those situations, and worse. They were more than ready for whatever life handed them.

"You really should get some sleep," Christy told him. "You have a big day tomorrow."

"Do you think they'll remember me?"

"Who could forget those big blue eyes?" she asked.

Jared smiled. "I wonder if one of them will have the same eyes."

"I'd be willing to bet on it."

"It's a miracle that Nonna and Nonno are still alive after all these years."

"I think they were waiting for you to come home."

"I have cousins I've never known, a whole family I never thought I'd meet." Though they'd known this day was coming for a few weeks, Jared felt unprepared. He was nervous but also hopeful. He was a child awakening on Christmas morning with both the anticipation that he would get what he wanted and the dread that he might only get coal.

"What if they're angry with us? What if they don't want anything to do with us?"

"Jared, sweetheart, we've talked about this. You've talked to them. Everything is going to be okay. Everything is already okay. You, me, Molly, your mom, we're all alive and well and doing just fine. No matter what happens from here on out, we're all going to be okay."

He knew she was right. Molly was excelling in school and already looking into colleges. She was delighted to have two new sisters who were thrilled to welcome Molly and Christy into the family. His mother was safe, and his stepfather finally knew who the real Jessica—

Maria—was and loved her even more for all she had done to protect her family. Christy was planning to return to school to earn a Master's in Nursing after the baby arrived and Jared recently signed a contract with MacMillan to write a science book for middle school students. He would work closely with Wallops as a writer and researcher. Everything was perfect, and Jared thanked God every day that Christy was there with him.

In the hospital, after she was fully awake and able to talk, she shared her dream with him, the one she'd had when she was certain she was dying. She thought that maybe she had died for a short time. His heart constricted when he recalled the officer administering CPR. He didn't know what happened between the time she was stabbed and the time she managed to crawl out of the house onto the porch. What he did know was that she was willing to give up her life to save his.

"Ooh," Christy exclaimed.

"What?" Jared asked as worry took hold of him.

Christy smiled and moved his hand to a spot on her lower belly. After a moment, he felt it, a little thump against his palm. He looked at his wife with a sense of wonder and awe. "Is that...?"

She smiled and nodded. "Little Sally is going to be quite the soccer player."

Jared shook his head. "Little Neil is going to take even bigger steps on the moon than his namesake did."

"Either one works for me," Christy said.

"Me, too," Jared said honestly. "Do you have any idea how much I love you?" he asked Christy, her face glowing in the moonlight.

"As much as I love you," she said. "Enough to lay down our lives for each other."

They both knew it was true, for it's what he would do for her in a heartbeat, what she did for him on that stormy summer day, and there is no greater love than to lay down one's life for his friends.

The End... For Now.

Acknowledgements

When I published the first book in my Chincoteague Island Trilogy in 2016, I had no idea it would become such a big fan favorite or that it would lead me down so many wonderful roads. I had just returned from my first trip to the Holy Land, and so much of *Island of Miracles* was born from the friendships I made and things I experienced on that trip. I knew there was something special about it, and apparently, so did you, my readers.

Here we are, six years later, and I felt myself unresistingly pulled back to that little island off the Eastern coast of Virginia. While I wanted the beloved characters of the first three books to still be on the island, I knew that this trilogy needed to stand on its own. Officer Nick Black inserted himself into this book like my dear, sweet, Nick White inserted himself into our lives, so his prominence in this book is not surprising to me. I fell in love with his character much the same as I did with the thirteen-year-old boy who became part of our family.

Throughout my writing of the Chincoteague books and all my books, I've had constant love and support from so many people. Always in my corner cheering me on and lending a hand to read, bounce ideas, or attend my events are my wonderful friends, Anne and Cheryl. I love you both so much. Thank you for always jumping in when I need you. I wouldn't be able to turn out a book worth reading without my parents, Richard and Judy, my

Aunt Debbie, or my beautiful friend, Jeanne. Thank you for your support and your help in getting my books ready to hit the shelves. Thank you, Pat Woods, graphic designer, for always making time to do my covers (and redo my covers and redo them again). Your artistic talent is brilliant. I feel so blessed to be able to work with you. Thank you, Cayley Ross, my new editor, a bright young woman who is going to take the publishing world by storm!

I never would have had the courage or the time to write any book were it not for my wonderful, loving husband, Ken. Thank you for always being there for me, for reading my books and helping me make them better, and for understanding when I'm lost in a book and don't emerge from my office for days at a time. Thank you to my wonderful girls, Rebecca, Katie Ann, and Morgan, who inspire me every day. I love you all.

About the Author

Amy began writing as a child and never stopped. She wrote articles for magazines and newspapers before writing children's books and adult fiction. A graduate of the University of Maryland with a Master of Library and Information Science, Amy worked as a librarian for fifteen years and, in 2010, began writing full time.

Amy Schisler writes inspirational women's fiction for people of all ages. She has published two children's books and numerous novels, including the award-winning Picture Me, Whispering Vines, and the Chincoteague Island Trilogy. Amy enjoys a busy life on the Eastern Shore of Maryland.

The recipient of numerous national literary awards, including the Illumination Award, LYRA Award, Independent Publisher Book Award, International Digital Award, and the Golden Quill Award as well as honors from the Catholic Press Association and the Eric Hoffer Book Award, Amy's writing has been hailed "a verbal masterpiece of art" (author, Alexa Jacobs) and "Everything you want in a book" (Amazon reviewer). Amy's books are available internationally, wherever books are sold, in print and eBook formats.

Follow Amy at:
http://amyschislerauthor.com
http://facebook.com/amyschislerauthor
https://twitter.com/AmySchislerAuth
https://www.goodreads.com/amyschisler

Book Club Discussion Questions

1. Christy sacrificed her education and life as she knew it to take care of Molly. What do you think that did to her mentally and emotionally? How has she handled the situation, and do you think she's done a good job?

2. Jared's mother keeps their past secret from everyone, including him. Before you got to the end, did you have an inkling as to what the secret was? Do you think she should have told Jared or her husband the truth about their past?

3. Diane moved to the island and opened her doughnut shop, fulfilling her dream to share her grandmother's recipes with the world. Is there a family recipe you love baking for others? What makes it so special?

4. Molly's educational needs aren't being met, but the decision to move her up a grade is a difficult one faced by parents of prodigies. What do you think you would do if you were in Christy's position? What are the pros and cons of being moved up in school, and how do you think a parent or guardian should handle this decision?

5. Do you see a future for Diane and Simon? Is it ever too late to find love? What kind of obstacles might stand in the way?

6. Life is full of unexpected twists and turns that influence us as individuals. What advice would you give Christy or Jared that might help them navigate the murky waters they go through?

7. Jared hopes to discover something amazing on the moon, perhaps even lithium, a limited but valuable resource on Earth. What valuable things do you think scientists might discover on the moon or beyond? Would you be interested in space travel yourself?

8. By the end, several sacrifices were made for the benefit of others. What were they? Which was the greatest sacrifice? What would you be willing to give up in order to save the life of someone you love?

9. How do you think Christy grew as a person from the beginning to the end of the novel? Who or what helped her to evolve into the person she became and how?

10. How did the newspaper articles at the beginning of each chapter fit into the storyline? What clues did they give you about what was to come in the narrative?